KISMET

SOUNDS OF THE CITY
BOOK ONE

Reina Bell

REINA BELL

Kismet by Reina Bell

Published by Reina Bell

www.authorreinabell.com

Copyright © 2022 Reina Bell

ISBN: 979-8-9854184-5-3

Cover & Interior Design & Formatting by Stacey Blake, Champagne Book Design

Editing by Caroline Acebo

Proofreading by Liz Gilbeau

To my husband, here's to a lifetime of NFL games and Broadway shows. You are my kismet now and forever.

"Do you think the universe fights for souls to be together? Some things are too strange and strong to be coincidences."
—Emery Allen

FROM THE AUTHOR

If explicit use of F-bombs and steamy jocks with hearts of gold are not your thing, then this book probably won't be either.

This adult contemporary romance novel is recommended for readers aged 18 and older due to mature content.

KISMET PLAYLIST

"Good Girl" – Carrie Underwood
"Stone Cold" – Demi Lovato
"IDGAF" – Dua Lipa
"abcedfu" – GAYLE
"Apologize" – Timbaland ft. OneRepublic
"Go Crazy" – Leslie Odom Jr.
"Into You" – Ariana Grande
"Give Your Heart a Break" – Glee Cast
"Shallow" – Lady Gaga and Bradley Cooper
"Endless Love" – Lionel Richie and Diana Ross
"I Can't Make You Love Me" – Bonnie Raitt
"Am I Wrong" – Camila Cabello
"Genie in a Bottle" – Christina Aguilera
"All In" – Lifehouse
"Smells Like Teen Spirit" – Malia J
"Paper Rings" – Taylor Swift
"All of Me" – John Legend
"Perfect" – Camila Cabello and Nicholas Galitzine
"Silent Night" – Idina Menzel
"Dream Girl" – Idina Menzel
"Brave" – Idina Menzel
"Whatta Man/Seven Nation Army" – Nicholas Galitzine &
Cinderella Original Motion Picture Cast
"All I Want Is You" – U2

KISMET

1

SAWYER

The jab to my ribs caught me off guard. I glanced down as the enchanting brunette from last night's rehearsal dinner linked her arm through mine. She'd been introduced as the girlfriend of Boston College's golden boy, starting quarterback Hunter Sterling, which translated meant: you can look, but don't touch.

The petite beauty with brilliant green eyes capable of bringing a quintessential playboy such as myself to his knees wasn't the bridesmaid I'd been paired with, but who the fuck was I to question fate?

Tucking her against me like a football I had no intention of fumbling, I inhaled whatever coconut product she'd applied to that sexy body of hers as beads of sweat formed beneath my tux. I slipped a finger behind the strangulating collar and gave it a tug.

Love the destination wedding idea. Hate that I'm expected to wear a penguin suit when it's heat index level: hell.

Hades during a heat wave had nothing on Puerto Rico. That had to be the reason why I was finding it a chore to simply . . . fucking . . . breathe.

The tiniest bit of movement to my left piqued my curiosity again.

She raised her chin; the emerald weapons of mass

1

destruction were puffy and glistened with fresh tears as they bounced back and forth between my own eyes, which had no right drinking her in like they were. Even in four-inch heels, she barely topped out at five seven—without the stilts, she'd be at least a foot shorter than me.

With a matter-of-fact voice, she said, "Sorry to disappoint you, Sawyer Jackson, but you're stuck with me for the duration of this wedding and reception."

Her dark tone was in stark contrast to the flawless, uplifting vocals that'd earned her one standing ovation after another at the karaoke bar last night.

I was anything but disappointed. She'd clearly misread my reaction: awestruck by her allure.

Well, damn.

A woman had never left me speechless before.

Searching for a way out of the mindfuck I'd found myself in, I turned my gaze to the couple standing in front of us, arm in arm.

"Shouldn't you . . ." I managed to whisper.

Less than twenty-four hours ago, we'd rehearsed for this very moment. Except Kennedy had walked down the aisle with her boyfriend—who was projected to be the number-one overall pick in this year's NFL draft—and I had been partnered with the voluptuous blonde bridesmaid who now dangled off said QB's arm.

Before Kennedy could explain the impromptu swap, the band kicked off, and my job as a groomsman beckoned.

Throughout the ceremony, I should have been focused on the couple at the altar—one of my best friends was marrying the love of his life, the sappy fuck—yet I hadn't been able to tear my eyes away from a certain damsel who'd appeared to be in distress.

Yeah, her smile was a facade, all right. And for some reason

I couldn't quite figure out, I needed to know who or what had made the woman with the voice of a goddamn angel cry.

Why do you even care?

It wasn't that I was a total ass—I swear—but I also wasn't one to dwell on the emotional sensitivities of women. Unless it was my mother or sister, of course.

As a twenty-five-year-old professional football player, I was more than content to live the cliché life of a rich-as-fuck bachelor, or as the media liked to call it, being a lady-killer, a manwhore, or a real catch—depending on the day and what gossip site indulged your guilty pleasure.

My gaze lay briefly on my former partner, and I tried to recall her name.

Melanie? Maybe it was Melody or Melissa.

Anyhoo, her collagen-injected smirk was as artificial as her tits. The same tits she'd kept shoving in my face from the moment we'd first met yesterday until she'd disappeared a few hours after I'd turned her down.

I'd considered taking those bags of silicone to bed tonight. But in the light of a new day, it wasn't me she was eye-fucking, it was the douchenozzle standing in front of me.

It didn't take an FBI profiler to figure out who'd wronged Kennedy.

Hunter Sterling was a tool.

Case closed.

At least the chicks I hooked up with knew where we stood, and unlike Hunter, I'd never allowed anyone to consider herself my girlfriend. I didn't date anyone long enough to warrant the "what are we?" talk.

The mere thought of such a categorically balls-shriveling chat gave me the willies.

After the bride and groom's destiny was sealed with a kiss, we were shuffled from the hotel terrace overlooking the ocean to the best air-conditioned ballroom that Condado, Puerto Rico, had to offer. Kennedy sat silently beside me at the bridal party table, and I'd noticed she was on her third glass of wine—which seemed peculiar, considering I hadn't seen her ingest as much as a drop of alcohol last night.

Like an elite stalker in the making, I'd watched her that closely.

After downing the last sip, she set her empty glass off to the side and turned in her seat, locking her eyes on mine. "You play football too, right?"

Not only could Kennedy sing like she'd been born with a microphone in her hand, but her speaking voice was equally as melodic.

She was straight-up mesmerizing.

I rested an elbow on the table and leaned closer. "How much do you know about football?" I aimed for personal and engaging, and hoped I didn't come across as condescending.

She arched a perfect eyebrow. "Enough—it's consumed my life for the past two years."

My dick twitched behind my zipper.

Gorgeous, emotional, and feisty—a dangerous trio. Check yourself, man.

Answering her original question in a way that wouldn't piss her off took effort. Chicks usually gushed over my successful career, but if I'd learned anything about Kennedy Quinn in the short time I'd known her, it was that she was unlike any chick I'd met before.

"I'm a tight end for the Miami Mavericks."

I wanted to add: "Third overall draft pick four years ago, Offensive Rookie of the Year, First-Team All-Pro, Pro Bowler, and I've led the league in receiving yards for a tight end ever since." But I didn't think she'd be impressed if I did.

Her soft mouth transformed from a straight line to a partial upward curve.

Progress.

"How do you know Seth and Abby?" I asked, shifting focus to the newly hitched couple who'd gathered us all here.

Before answering, she reached for the wine that had miraculously appeared. As her full lips latched on to her glass, I experienced a vision of all the debauched things I wanted those lips to do.

I blinked and looked at my uneaten churrasco.

Get ahold of yourself, man.

"Abby and I have been friends since kindergarten." Kennedy's throaty voice brought my gaze back to hers. "How about you? Have you and Seth been friends since the days you wore Spider-Man underwear?"

Is that a hint of playfulness?

Normally, I would have fired back with something along the lines of: "Who's to say I'm not still wearing Spider-Man underwear? Wanna find out?" But my slick self had apparently taken a sabbatical.

"I met Seth freshman year at Clemson—we bonded over being the only two freshman recruits to make the starting roster. I transferred away my sophomore year, but we'll be brothers for life."

It was no surprise she didn't ask why or to what school I'd transferred. If she assumed my relocation to The Ohio State University had been a calculated football move, she'd have been correct.

Kennedy nodded, then took another seductive draw from her glass. My zipper showed no mercy for my hardening cock.

You need professional help.

I grabbed my water goblet and chugged until all that remained was a pile of ice. Wiping my mouth on the back of my hand like an uncivilized Neanderthal, I blurted out, "Isn't Sterling your boyfriend?"

Her cheeks turned pink, and I immediately regretted being so selfish. Anyone with even a touch of common sense could see this was a delicate matter and not something she'd want to discuss with a practical stranger—and definitely not a stranger with a dick. But when she licked her lips in a nervous gesture, I couldn't help but groan on the inside and forgive my own transgression.

Slapping on the best goddamn poker face I'd ever seen, she replied, "Hunter *was* my boyfriend, until I walked in on him with his stupid fucking face between Melody's stupid fucking legs."

Melody.

Boom!

I was right—it was an *M* name.

Wait. Whoa. What?

There was too much to process, and the word "fucking" rolling off Kennedy's pout was *fucking* with my brain.

See, much more natural coming from me.

But it was too late. Dirty thoughts involving Kennedy and fucking showed up like a landlord on the day rent is due.

I coughed, or more accurately, I choked on my own saliva.

"Sorry," she grumbled. "I shouldn't be so crass."

"When? Where?" I wanted to add: "Why?" Because in a million years, I'd never come up with a reason for that mutant to cheat on her.

Kennedy released a heavy sigh, sat back in her chair, and smoothed her napkin over her lap. "Last night. At the bar." I thought that was all I'd get, but she continued, "When everyone was getting ready to leave, I couldn't find Hunter. I figured he'd gone to the restroom, so I decided to do the same. You can imagine my surprise when I walked in the ladies' room and found . . ."

She made motions with her hands as though there were no words to describe the horror she'd faced. Still trying to figure out the severity of Sterling's brain damage, I sat there without reaction.

Her face pinched into a tiny scowl. "Is this when you go all bro code on me and take his side?"

It was hard not to laugh, or at least crack a smile—fuck all, was she adorable.

Shaking my head, I wiped the evidence of amusement off my face. "Hell no, he's not my bro. He's an asshole."

And that's when Kennedy Quinn smiled so goddamn bright, I thought the Rapture was imminent.

"I think we just became best friends, Sawyer Jackson."

2

SAWYER

Had Sterling already been claimed by CTE?

He fucked over Kennedy for what? Implants? Acrylic nails? Or was it the hair extensions that had made his tongue go rogue?

Kennedy had dazzled a room of hundreds with her voice and presence alone, and he'd given that all up for a sloppy bathroom quickie in the back of a somewhat seedy bar?

Disclaimer: Any sexcapades in somewhat seedy bar bathrooms I'd partaken in had never resulted in infidelity—not that I knew of at least.

Kennedy pushed her chair back, got to her feet, and offered me her dainty hand. I accepted it without hesitation. The air between us crackled with electricity. If she felt it too, she didn't let on.

"Game time, Tight End. We've got a Cupid Shuffle to make our bitch."

Well, this was a pleasant surprise—for a number of reasons I hadn't figured out yet.

I chuckled. "Are you back to being crass?"

Kennedy blushed, and her subsequent giggle had me rubbing my sternum.

Goddamn, she was lethal.

"Hold up. These suckers gotta go." She kicked off her heels

and then proceeded to pad barefoot to the dance floor. She looked over her shoulder and flashed me that heart-stopping smile.

Is this how Jorah Mormont felt? If she smiled at me like that again, I'd consider taking on a fleet of wights if necessary.

Kennedy Quinn was the most beautiful creature I'd ever seen.

Just like poor Jorah, my Khaleesi had gifted me a FastPass to the friend zone. She'd specifically called me her *best friend*— if I'm not mistaken.

I never am.

Reluctantly, I admitted to myself this was probably for the best. She'd just broken up with her boyfriend, and while I normally didn't mind being someone's rebound lay—those ladies could be mighty enthusiastic and typically cursed the notion of a safe word—I didn't want to be Kennedy's.

We reached the dance floor just as "Cupid Shuffle" began. Dammit, I wasn't drunk enough for this shit.

The music and laughter that encapsulated us were deafening and distracting, but my sense of sight was exclusively for Kennedy. With her at my side, we were in our own little world—a world where she moved with fluidity and rhythm, and I looked like a decrepit kangaroo on crack.

A really bad batch of crack.

Kennedy hopped along to the asinine song with the carefree nature of a five-year-old on a sugar high. "Dude! You should be able to move better than this!"

Strands of silky hair came loose from the fancy knots that decorated her head, and I wondered what it would be like to tuck them behind her ears.

Way too intimate, bro.

"You know"—she bumped me with her hip and then

threw me a wink—"for an athlete . . . you're kinda stiff and really suck."

You have no idea how stiff, pretty girl.

When my living hell came to an end, I tried to leave the dance floor, only to be hauled backward by Kennedy's arms twined around my waist.

She was quite strong for a pipsqueak.

I turned in her embrace, and our bodies brushed up against each other. Her head fell back, and she looked up at me through long, thick lashes. Her pink lips parted.

My heart raced like Secretariat at the Belmont Stakes. Maybe dancing wasn't good for my well-being.

It was definitely that and not the beauty in my arms.

"Sawyer . . . will you please dance with me?"

All I could do was stare at her like a fool.

She frowned. "I don't mean all night. Just a few songs. I promise to cut you loose in time for you to pick up chicks."

Je-sus she's intoxicating.

And what's this "pick up chicks" bullshit?

I shook my head, feeling like one hell of a confused motherfucker. "Yes, but after I have a few shots in my system—because what we just did was fucking embarrassing. Shots first, and then you can use my body in any way you see fit."

I waggled my eyebrows waiting for her reaction.

Kennedy laughed again—and that was the exact moment I learned that sound had a direct line to the unexplored, beating organ living behind my ribcage.

It was going to be a long-ass night hanging with my new friend.

Kennedy reached the bar first. I stood behind her and shoved my hands into my pockets so I wouldn't be tempted to do something I'd regret.

Like grope her? Or is it her hair you're so fascinated with?

As she leaned over the bar on her tiptoes to peruse the liquor selection, the bartender ogled her. I knew exactly why he was so transfixed on the vicinity south of her face. The strapless peach-colored garment hugged her every curve just right. She couldn't have worn a more flattering dress if she'd tried. Abby had good taste.

The bartender rested his elbows on the bar. "What can I do for you tonight, babe?"

What kind of fucking question was that?

In a breath, I was at Kennedy's side. "What are you thinking? What's going to make me dance like Bruno Mars?"

The bartender backed up, and his lewd expression vanished.

Mission accomplished.

Kennedy's chin turned upward, and she looked me in the eye, completely oblivious that she'd be total spank material for the sleazy fucker tonight.

One shoulder hitched to her ear. "Kamikazes?"

"Sounds good, Quinn."

I ordered us two shots each, and when I turned back to her, contemplation spun in her eyes.

"You do realize that's my *last name*, right? You didn't forget my name already, did you? Because I could find that rather insulting, considering I just taught you how to dance."

This girl.

I stepped into her so close that her tits pressed against me, and I could have sworn this time she felt the magnetism between us too. Her face flushed, and my voice dropped an octave. "You do realize I'm a guy and guys call their *friends* by their last names, *right*?"

She laughed.

Hard.

11

Call me lame, but I liked being the one responsible for that sound coming out of her.

Your balls have officially left the building.

When our shots arrived, we raised the first set in the air.

"What are we toasting to?" I asked.

Kennedy tapped her chin with her index finger and looked up, giving the impression this question required a significant amount of deliberation. Then she smiled and bopped me on the nose with that same finger.

Game over.

I wanted to throw her over my shoulder and announce to the room that I'd claimed her as my own.

"Friendship!"

Fuck my life.

"Friendship it is, Quinn."

We clinked our glasses, and Kennedy slung her shot back while pinching her nose.

She did a full-body shimmy, and more tendrils were freed from her once-elegant hairstyle. "Eff me, that burns!"

I set my empty shot glass down on the bar. "What's with plugging your nose?"

"It doesn't taste as bad this way."

Without pause, she sucked down her second shot—again pinching her nose, again breaking out into a frantic dance while she complained about how badly the "gasoline-tasting shit" burned going down.

Even her shot ritual had me bewitched.

Sawyer Jackson should be immune to such things.

Preach.

Kennedy reached for my second shot, and my hand intercepted hers. "Hey, Tiger. Slow your roll. You've already had more than three glasses of wine and two shots, and I haven't seen you eat anything yet."

She looked up at me with a blank expression. Fuck—did I hurt her feelings?

Then she burst out laughing. The kind of laugh reserved for watching episodes of *South Park* and cat videos on YouTube. Not that I'd know anything about the latter.

"You? Sawyer Jackson, the NFL's notorious heartbreaker, is telling *me* to slow down? Say it ain't so."

She pressed the back of her hand against my forehead, and as much as I craved contact with her skin, all I could muster was a half-assed smirk as my gaze fell to the one remaining shot.

Though her tone was playful, her words stung. Coming from anyone else, I would have been in smug agreement, but coming from Kennedy, I was forced to acknowledge a different kind of feeling. One that fucked with my head.

Embarrassment?

Guilt?

Regret?

Nah, couldn't be.

I spun my empty shot glass on the bar. "So, you *do* know who I am." I sounded a little colder than I'd intended.

She seemed unfazed. "Yes. But don't worry, no judgment." She ducked her head, forced our eyes to meet, and lowered her voice. "I'll even help you pick out a chick or two tonight if you want."

My head snapped up so fast it startled her.

"What do you mean by that?" The bite was gone from my words. I'd do anything to have her go back to looking at me like she had been ten minutes ago.

"Since you don't have a wingman tonight, you'll have a wingwoman! Me! Ta-da!" Kennedy threw her hands up in the air, at the same time sending my remaining shot glass skidding across the bar.

"Good Lord. Sorry—I'll order more. Bartender!" She raised her hand like she was in kindergarten.

Maybe the spillage and reordering of the shots would distract her enough that she'd forget all about the uncomfortable conversation we'd just stumbled into. Reminiscing about my playboy reputation didn't even make the long list of things I was willing to discuss with Kennedy tonight.

Her eyes gleamed with a naughtiness I could only hope I'd get to see behind closed doors one day.

"You've helped me tonight, so now it's my turn to help you," she purred.

Fuck me.

Thankfully, Kennedy's charming persuasion had the bartender filling four more shot glasses. I lifted one to my lips, eyeing her over the top as I prepared myself for whatever nonsense was about to come out of that pretty little mouth.

"I *insist* on helping you with the selection process. I know most of the chicks here, I can help you figure out which ones won't turn into stalkers when you're done and refuse to give them your number."

The liquor couldn't get down my throat fast enough.

Then I grabbed another and slammed that one back too.

Kennedy's hands were on her hips, and the mock scowl from earlier had returned. "Whoa, Tight End. Who needs to stop, collaborate, and listen now?"

Christ.

"Did you just make a Vanilla Ice reference, Quinn?"

"I sure did. Glad you're paying attention. We've got work to do."

I rolled my eyes. "You really think I'm going to let you help me pick up chicks?"

"So, we *are* looking for more than one?" she asked, cocking an eyebrow.

"Huh?"

"Plural, Sawyer." She snapped her fingers in front of my face. "You said *chicks* with an *s*, as in more. Than. One."

My tongue felt too big for my mouth. "Wait. No. I mean, yes. No. Yes."

Fuck, she had me flustered.

Kennedy giggled.

That did not help.

"Well, which is it, Sawyer?"

"Yes, I said *chicks* as in plural—but that's not what I meant. I only need one. Wait, I don't need any. Not tonight." I inhaled like I'd just been waterboarded. "What I'm *trying* to say is that I don't need your help because I'm not picking anyone up tonight."

Jesus Christ, the English language was hard.

Feigning innocence, she asked, "Why not?"

My chin dropped. "Because you, Kennedy Quinn, are some serious women repellant."

She threw her head back and laughed, and I imagined what it'd be like to run my tongue up her creamy, exposed neck all the way to her ear, where I could pause and have a nibble.

Then she brought her head back to center. One look at her sweet face and I seriously doubted the future of our friendship.

"Are you saying I'm a cockblocker of epic proportions, darlin'?"

"Does alcohol always bring out the Southern belle in you?" I drawled right back as I stared into her heated gaze.

But before I could take our harmless flirting to the next level, we were interrupted by the douchenozzle—I mean, Hunter Sterling.

"Hey, doll. Can we talk?" Hunter spoke to Kennedy, but he glowered over her head at me, suspicion and disapproval written all over his punchable face.

Doll?

Kennedy barely glanced at him, but I noticed the way she drew her shoulders back defensively. "I have nothing to say to you."

Hunter coughed into his hand and shifted his feet. "I really need to talk to you, Kennedy." But it was clear, based on her expression, that Kennedy was fresh out of fucks to give.

I straightened. If it became necessary to intervene, I wanted to be at eye level with the prick.

Hunter's eyes narrowed. "What's going on?" His tone did a one-eighty as he looked between Kennedy and me. "You know who he is." It wasn't a question. "He just wants to get in your pants."

Before I could respond, Kennedy's face turned a scary shade of crimson, and her eyes went wide. She spun away from the bar to face him. "You. Don't. Get. To. Ask. Me. That." She poked him in the chest with her finger, accentuating nearly every word with a strike. "It's. None. Of. Your. Mother. Fucking. Business. Asshole. Got me?"

She held her arms out wide like she was the Night King taking on Jon Snow and his band of misfit wildlings.

I reached over, rescuing the freshly poured shots in her path and setting them aside.

Hunter stood with his mouth gaping, rendered speechless.

So I wasn't the only one she had that effect on.

"What the fuck, Hunter? I found you with your face in someone else's—" She flailed her arms around, searching for the word she wanted to use.

I bit my tongue; it was too tempting to fill in the blank for her.

"Va-jay-jay!" she finally squeaked.

The look on Hunter's ashen face wasn't just embarrassment, it was downright mortification.

"I can't believe the words coming out of your mouth right now," he growled at her.

Without further thought, I gripped Kennedy's hips, prepared to shield her behind me. The intimate contact with her made me woozy.

The bartender continued serving drinks as he watched the drama unfold out of his peripheral vision, probably realizing that Hunter was one aggressive remark away from meeting my fist. The tension in my body was reaching an unavoidable peak, but Kennedy continued standing up for herself, and fuck if I wasn't proud of her.

"I am *so sorry* that you find my choice of words offensive, but you can save the concern—it's no longer any of your business what is coming out of or *coming in* my mouth."

I pulled my lips into my teeth.

Drunk Kennedy was badass.

Her rich, brown locks brushed against my chest, and then she was looking back and up at me through a veil of the sexiest lashes.

"Sawyer."

I tilted my chin down so I could meet her eyes. "Quinn."

My fingers involuntarily squeezed her hips, and I felt the sigh as it swept through her body. A confusing rush of awe, desire, and need drop-kicked my ass right there.

Kennedy grabbed a shot off the bar, and I didn't try to stop her. This time, she didn't plug her nose.

That's my girl.

Wait. What?

I slid my hand down her arm until our fingers interlaced, and then I led her back to the dance floor—neither of us looking back.

3

KENNEDY

After Sawyer and I danced like no one was watching—when in fact, *everyone* was watching—I returned to the bar for more shots, switching over to Jäger bombs.

Probably not the wisest decision I'd made in my twenty-one years on Earth, but hey, I was nursing a broken heart.

Resigned to the reality that my boyfriend—let me rephrase, the man I was supposed to *marry and make babies with*—had cheated on me with none other than the plastic princess of my sorority, I was on an unscripted journey to rid myself of all memories related to Hunter Sterling.

And if liquor was the means, then Sawyer Jackson was my chaser.

The hunk of hard flesh hadn't left my side since I'd informed him that he was the lucky man who by default was obligated to hang with this hot mess—for part of the night, at least.

Abby, feeling terrible that her dreams of happily ever after were coming true while mine had been squashed in a trashy bar restroom, thought Sawyer would be a fun distraction.

She hadn't been wrong.

And while he'd been kind and understanding about the last-minute swap from blonde and busty to brunette and hey-they're-a-handful, I hadn't expected him to be my breakup buddy for the night.

Yet, here we were.

"I can't do it. I'm gonna puke," I mumbled into Sawyer's side. His body shook with laughter, and my stomach churned. "You're not helping."

He tightened his one-armed side hug around me. "Come on, Quinn, give the people what they want."

I smiled to myself when he called me by my last name. It was cute—sweet, even. He'd been doing it all night; not once had he called me Kennedy, and I kinda liked it. There was a sense of rightness about it all, but I shook it off.

It's the booze giving you the faux feels, sister.

Sawyer towered over me, especially after I'd ditched the torture devices Abby made us wear. All six-foot-whatever of him was solid muscle, and my wayward, drunk self had relied on his rugged frame for stability too many times for me not to have fantasized about what he looked like in the buff.

I needed to remain impervious to his charm and model good looks because tomorrow I was headed back to Boston to finish my senior year at Berklee College of Music, earning my bachelor of music in performance, and Sawyer would be back in Miami enjoying his off-season. Although the man was infamous for his one-night stands that had women all across the football scene waiting in line with damp panties for their chance, I wasn't a one-night-stand kinda girl.

But those eyes—sweet mother of dragons, did he have the bluest eyes I'd ever seen. They were like two perfectly cut sapphires that shimmered under constant stage lighting.

But this was Sawyer Jackson.

And I had no business being all up in his player grill like I was.

But fuck did it feel good.

And fuck did it feel good to say *fuck*.

Like, *fuck you, Hunter.*

Or how about, *who gives a fuck what Hunter thinks?*

It was a thing of beauty really. Except I couldn't think about the act of fucking Hunter because then I'd probably end up crying and that would be *no bueno*.

The guy was a cheater, yes. But did I say he sucked in bed? No. No, I did not.

The two things were unrelated—or were they?

Did Hunter think that *I* sucked in bed?

Did I?

Fuckity fuck.

Focus, drunk girl.

For the past half hour, Abby and company had insisted that I sing with the wedding band. She even played the but-it's-my-wedding card.

I glanced up to see Sawyer's dreamy gaze studying me—again.

Sometimes he smiled, but sometimes he just stared at me like I freaked him out or made him a little angry.

You did call him a bad dancer.

And you did insinuate that he's a manslut.

But how fabulous would it be to run my fingers through his messy dark hair and kiss that unfettered cockiness right off his face?

Dial it back, sex-kitten wannabe.

Since we'd started tearing up the dance floor like a drunk version of Danny and Sandy at the Rydell High school dance, he'd been handed three phone numbers, had a few beers sent his way, and was asked to sign a ridiculous number of boobs.

Seriously? Who asks someone to sign their boobs? Hookers—that's who.

"Okay, let's think. What can I sing that's easy?"

"Ariana Grande?" he offered, and I swatted his arm.

"*Easy*, Sawyer. Ariana Grande is far from easy."

I pressed my fingers to my temples, closed my eyes, and scrolled through the catalog in my brain for songs that I knew like the back of my hand. Songs I could probably pull off on my death bed if necessary.

The way your liver is cursing you in German, that may be your reality.

My lungs deflated on an exhale, and I said a prayer to the Jägermeister gods to be kind. "All right, let's do the damn thing."

"You've got this, Quinn," Sawyer said with a wink.

I slipped out of his platonic squeeze and started toward the stage. I made it three strides when I turned back around. "Maybe this is a good time for us to part ways. As your self-proclaimed wingwoman, I suggest you try to find one of those autograph-deprived boobies. Time's a-tickin', Tight End." I tapped at my empty wrist.

"Watch is on the other wrist, Quinn."

Then his grin disappeared, and I couldn't decipher what came across his face next.

He raised his glass, motioning toward the band. "Go do your thing."

What the heck does that mean? Is he going to watch me, or is he going to round up the boobs?

Sawyer raised a loud eyebrow at me. "Now, Quinn," he ordered, and I felt a stirring between my legs. Then he lifted his chin at me and winked, and that stirring turned into a throb.

I once read somewhere, probably in a gossip magazine, this was his signature flirt move.

Lord, have mercy on my darkening soul.

This man was the epitome of a bad idea. He was the wolf Little Red's grandma warned her about. He was a walking, talking, dressed-in-a-tux sin waiting to happen.

But that didn't make him any less attractive or make my panties any more secure.

Carefully taking backward steps, I made my way to the band without severing our stare. "If I puke, it's your fault." I brought two fingers to my eyes and then pointed them back at him.

"Save it for later, and I'll even hold your hair back while you do."

My wrist pressed to my forehead, and I fake swooned. "What did I ever do to deserve you, Sawyer Jackson?"

His palms came up, and his shoulders went to his ears. "Hey, what are friends for?"

———

A few hours later, I was lying spread-eagle on Sawyer's hotel room bed.

I wore one of his T-shirts, and my hair was piled in a messy knot on top of my head. A few long bangs clung to my heated, damp face.

"I'm gonna be sick again," I announced.

Remarkably, my feet carried me to the toilet, where I dry heaved until the spasms eventually subsided. The room spun around me as I sat back on my heels and steadied myself.

Sawyer appeared in the doorway and leaned against the frame with his arms crossed. "Sounds like that was the last of it, Chuckles. How about we get your drunk ass in the shower now?"

"Chuckles?"

"Yeah, because you upchuck like a fucking boss."

If humiliation and gratitude created a love child, my name would have been on that birth certificate.

Sawyer wasn't convinced that Hunter would stay away from our once-shared hotel room, even though he had last night; Sawyer also didn't think I should be alone since I was "impressively shit-faced," as he put it.

I'd made it through six songs at the reception, nailing them like it was a freakin' Broadway audition. To celebrate, I did shots like a Boston College frat boy on St. Patty's Day.

Sawyer's concern for my poor life choices and shady sleeping arrangements had been touching, especially considering it was crystal clear that I was anything but bangable in my condition.

"Are you suggesting I stink?" I pushed off the bathtub to get back on my feet. I peeled the nasty hair from my face and tried to tuck it back in the elastic.

"Not a suggestion—it's a stone-cold fact, Chuckles," he replied with a crooked grin.

"Duly noted, friend."

Sawyer disappeared only to return a minute later with another of his T-shirts. "Here's a clean one. I think you got puke on that one."

I looked down; he was right.

You're a classy girl, Kennedy.

"Do you want a pair of boxers? I think I have some Spider-Man ones if you're interested."

I met his mischievous gaze.

Damn those eyes.

I was pretty sure the Devil's eyes were also blue; I'd have to keep that in mind.

"Ha. Ha. I think I'm good. But thank you for being willing to share your superhero panties with me." Keeping my eyes glued to the floor, I bit my inner cheek.

"Quinn."

I looked up. "Sawyer."

"Never call a man's boxers 'panties' ever again. That's basically verbal castration."

My hands went to my knees, keeping me upright while I coughed out a hoarse laugh.

Sawyer's hand rubbed my back, and my thighs quivered.

They were quivering because I was dehydrated, drunk, and on the verge of needing intravenous fluids.

Yeah. That's right.

Still caressing my back, Sawyer said, "Don't laugh too hard. You've got nothing left to hurl. Next it'll be your kidney coming up, and I'll be tempted to sell it on the black market."

My butchered laugh turned into a groan, and Sawyer offered me another wet washcloth; it was the fourth one he'd given me so far. Our eyes connected briefly as I wiped off my mouth, and that's when his fingers traced my temple before tucking my bangs behind my ear. My thighs outright clenched together this time.

Traitorous body. Whose side are you on anyway?

Time stood still for a moment, then Sawyer cleared his throat. "I'll let you shower."

He exited the bathroom, and I released the breath I'd been holding.

After I'd showered, brushed my teeth, and put on vomit-free clothes, I stepped out of the bathroom to find Sawyer lying on the bed—his hands behind his head on the pillow, his long legs outstretched, crossed at the ankles.

He still wore his tux from the wedding, minus his jacket and bowtie. He didn't notice me at first, and I took the innocuous moment to study him. Eyes glued to the ceiling, he appeared to be deep in thought. I could see the outline of his strong jaw and chiseled features in the low lighting, and I wanted to touch his perfect skin that had been bronzed by the Florida sun.

Of course, I knew all about Sawyer Jackson. What self-respecting NFL fan didn't? Not only was he the best tight end in the league, but I also couldn't stand in line at the grocery store without seeing him on the cover of some magazine, usually with a model at his side.

Not wanting him to catch me leering, I cleared the tickle in the back of my throat. Sawyer's head rolled across the pillow, and he smiled at me without otherwise moving from his relaxed position. His smile faded as I stepped closer and into the glow of the bedside lamp, and then in one quick movement, he swung his legs over the side of the bed farthest from me, giving me his back.

Shuffling through his open suitcase, he asked, "Feel better?"

"Much," I answered. The shift in energy left me feeling awkward. "I can go to my room now."

He strode past me with his arms full of clothing. "Don't be ridiculous, Quinn. I'm going to shower—make yourself comfortable. I'm starving, and you need to eat, so order us a bunch of shit from room service."

My heart jumped around in my chest, and my stomach did a backflip.

He didn't want me to leave.

"On it! I shall order us *a bunch of shit* right now!" I sounded like a cheerleader who'd consumed a few too many wine coolers, and he laughed, low and easy.

"Don't forget water. See if they have some kind of sports drink—something with electrolytes, but no caffeine. If you order anything with sauce or condiments—ask for it on the side. I'll take the mahi-mahi if they have it—no starch."

Unable to hide the humor in my voice, I asked, "Is this how you speak to your maid, Master Jackson?"

Sawyer dropped his head to the side. "Really, woman?"

"Your personal shopper, perhaps?"

All he did was lift his eyebrows.

"Assistant?" I pressed.

"Quinn."

"Sawyer."

"I don't have any of those things. I even do my own laundry, which means I'll be the one washing the shirt you puked all over."

Well, okay then.

Late the following morning, I woke to Sawyer's chainsaw snores coming from clear across the other side of the bed. The bed was massive—the kind of specialty bed made for giant athletes like Sawyer Jackson—but still, the guy had gone to extreme lengths to keep a safe distance between us, even resorting to arranging pillows down the center.

I wasn't sure if it had been a chivalrous gesture or if I should have been offended.

After eating an obscene amount of food—and most importantly, drinking our electrolytes—we'd mutually agreed that two mature, albeit still drunk, adults could sleep in the same bed and keep their hands to themselves.

That's when Sawyer had gone to work on building the Great Wall of Abstinence.

Then we'd bantered until the sun came up, and my cheeks were now stiff from hours of laughter.

"Sweet baby Jesus," I groaned and rolled over, reaching for the water and Tylenol I'd had the forethought to set out last night.

I grabbed a pillow and tossed it at my bedmate, who was passed out facedown. "Sawyer Jackson, time to get up. Desperate housewives of Miami await you, friend."

The snoring stopped, and the pillow came flying back at me.

"Do you always make this much noise in the morning?"

"Wouldn't you like to find out?" I teased.

Innuendos—they'd been a big part of our drunk dialogue. Hence, the pillow wall.

And the deep ache between my legs that never quite went away.

"This is why I never let girls stay the night," he deadpanned.

I gasped for dramatic effect, and his head popped up on the other side. His hair all bedhead sexy, he lifted his chin and winked at me. "Kidding, Quinn. We're friends, you can stay the night anytime."

My eyes took a trip around my head and then landed on Sawyer's naked back. The sheet had slipped to his waist—putting all his ripped muscle glory on full display.

The sly grin etching the corner of his mouth told me he'd caught me checking him out. His expression turned thoughtful. "If I recall, I put my digits in your phone last night—that's a first for me."

If I rolled my eyes any harder, they were going to get stuck. "I'm not sure that's something you want to brag about."

Sawyer flipped over, threading his fingers together and resting them behind his head. "So? Are you going to call me? Or is this when you sneak out while I'm in the shower and I never hear from you again?"

My head fell back, and I had an instant case of the giggles. When they finally abated, I asked, "You really want me to call you?"

He was joking, right?

He was Sawyer Jackson. He obviously had all the friends and hookups he could ever need, and who was I? I was just the musically inclined, jaded ex-girlfriend of a talented jock who hoped he'd get his chance to be as successful as Sawyer someday.

"Or you could text, whichever you prefer," he answered. "I keep email to business connections only, and I don't communicate on social media—but we could always send owls back and forth if you're into that kind of thing."

For real?

I decided to play along. "Your limited run as my groomsman, hype man, and babysitter has officially come to an end." I raised my arms above my head and did a barely gracefully pirouette as I danced my way to the bathroom, pausing at the door to drop into a curtsy. "You are off the hook, friend. Your women repellent and epic cockblock will be out of your hotel room just as soon as she puts her dress back on."

Not waiting for his reply, I retreated to the bathroom.

I had just closed the door when Sawyer's voice boomed, "Did you just call my cock *epic*?"

Settled in the hard chair at the terminal, I pulled out my phone. I had a plethora of messages to go through—all of which I'd been avoiding since Friday night. Now was as good a time as any to face them.

Going in order from easy to why-do-I-have-to-do-this, I'd saved Hunter's reply for last.

All the alcohol I'd ingested had failed to eradicate the image of Melody on the bathroom counter, Hunter on his knees with her legs thrown over his shoulders, his face so far up her crotch that if I didn't recognize what he'd been wearing I wouldn't have been able to identify him. He'd sent thirty-two text messages total, but I only read the most recent because the cheating rat bastard didn't deserve that much of my time.

Hunter: Will you please talk to me? I know I've hurt you and I'm sorry about how I reacted at the reception. Please give me another chance. I want you with me on draft night and every night for the rest of our lives. I love you.

Me: I'll be moving out of the apartment this week while you're at the combine. Don't contact me again.

Three little bubbles.

Shit, he had his phone.

Hunter: Is this because of Jackson? Did you let him fuck you?

The way he could go from groveling to onslaught spoke volumes.

If I were looking for satisfaction, I would have replied: "Sawyer gave me the best night of my life." It was the truth—and left it open for interpretation—but I chickened out and didn't reply at all.

Airplane mode was a screen tap away when a new text popped up, and I had to cover my mouth with both hands to squelch my laughter.

My Hottest Friend: Don't puke on the plane, Chuckles.

My thumbs flew across the screen at a record-setting pace.

Me: Who is this? I have so many hot friends I'm not sure who I'm talking to.

I chewed on the corner of my bottom lip waiting for his reply.

My Hottest Friend: It's me, the hottest one.

Me: Becca?

My Hottest Friend: Really?

Me: Oh wait, sorry! My bad. Brendan!!!! How have you been, you sexy beast?

My Hottest Friend: We're really doing this, Quinn?

Me: Shit. Not Brendan. Aidan?!?!

My Hottest Friend: I'm the guy you slept with last night. Did it mean that little to you?

I shook my head as though he could see me and felt the heat taking over my face.

Me: Good Lord, Sawyer. Stop it.

My Hottest Friend: Are you going to call me?

Me: What? When? Why?

My Hottest Friend: It's a function in your phone. Anytime you want. Because we're best friends.

Me: You really want to be friends? Don't you have enough friends, Tight End? Plus, my life just got flipped/turned upside down, not sure I'd be a great friend right now.

My Hottest Friend: Did you just make a Fresh Prince reference?

Me: What's it to ya?

My Hottest Friend: You just gave me a hard-on.

I pressed my phone to my chest and searched the faces of my fellow passengers. No one seemed to notice how my insides were melting, so I dared to look at my phone again.

I was considering my reply when a woman's voice sounded over the intercom, giving me the perfect excuse to wrap up this conversation before I made a total dork of myself.

Me: My flight is boarding.

My Hottest Friend: Are you blushing?

Me: Wouldn't you like to know?

My Hottest Friend: Okay, before was a joke—now I really am getting hard.

Me: OMG, Sawyer. Goodbye.

My Hottest Friend: Quinn.

Me: Sawyer.

My Hottest Friend: Have a good flight.

Me: Right back at ya, friend.

4

SAWYER

Three Years and Four Months Later

The door to Ellen's Stardust Diner closed behind me with a jingle. I heard her before I saw her. I'd recognize that sweet sound anywhere. Standing on the second-story balcony, there she was—Kennedy Fucking Quinn.

My best friend.

The hostess led us to an open table, and I couldn't take my eyes off Kennedy as she killed the Ariana Grande song. The real thing was way better than the YouTube videos and social media reels I'd watched on repeat.

Damn, I'd missed her.

We talked or texted almost daily, but it wasn't the same. She had no idea I was in Manhattan, and I couldn't wait to tell her why.

It had been over two months since I'd taken Kennedy and my mom to visit my sister in Paris. I'd planned the vacation because I wanted to celebrate that my mom's breast cancer had gone into remission with the three people who meant the most to me.

Five months ago, Kennedy had flown to Florida, and we'd attended the Super Bowl. We'd partied after the game like rock stars until Hunter Sterling and a couple of his compadres came around and one had the stones to refer to Kennedy as Hunter's sloppy seconds. It wasn't the first time I'd had to let my fist set some asshole straight about Kennedy in the past three years.

The feeling of protectiveness—*all right,* borderline possessiveness—I felt toward her was only growing, and that was exactly why for the first time ever, I'd made a life-altering decision with a woman in mind.

I sat down and nearly missed my chair because I was already drunk on the idea that I'd get to hold Kennedy in my arms soon.

"Careful, man—we don't need you getting injured before the ink is dry on that new contract you've yet to sign." Declan Walsh, my former OSU teammate, soon-to-be NFL teammate, and stud wideout for the New York Cougars, laughed until his gaze followed mine.

Then his eyes landed on Kennedy, and his jaw dropped.

"Hot damn. That's her?"

My mouth was dry—I couldn't talk. He took my silence as confirmation.

"She's fucking hot. You seriously haven't hit that?"

"No, I have not," I bit out. "And you won't be either."

Declan's head snapped back to me, the song ended, and the diner erupted in applause.

Clearly stumped, he asked, "You're not related to her?"

I shook my head. "No."

"Is she crazy?"

"Definitely not."

"Is she into chicks?"

"You can ask your quarterback that one," I quipped, and then backtracked. "Wait, never mind—don't talk to that asshat about her."

"Asshat, huh?" Declan frowned. "How's that going to work when he becomes *your* quarterback?"

I shrugged. "Haven't figured that part out yet."

Declan had a valid point. If all went as hoped, I'd be sharing a locker room with none other than the douchenozzle himself, Hunter Sterling—my new starting quarterback.

"What's the deal, then?" Declan asked. "Why have you never hooked up with her? Why *just friends*?"

If I had a dollar for every time someone asked me that question, I wouldn't have to worry about who my new QB was because I wouldn't need one—I could retire.

I rubbed the back of my neck. "It's a long story."

Declan smirked. "Good thing we're going to be roomies until that hot-as-fuck Realtor finds you a place—you'll have plenty of time to tell me all about it."

The Realtor was hot? I didn't even notice. Another sign that my very nonplatonic feelings for Kennedy weren't a fluke.

"Looking forward to it," I grumbled.

"Can I get you fellas started off with some beverages?"

Declan and I both turned to look at the woman eyeing us as she stood ready to take our order. Simultaneously, we pulled our caps a little lower on our heads. The likelihood of being recognized was high—even if we were sitting in a musical diner on a random Friday night during the off-season.

"Is it possible for Kennedy to be our waitress?" I asked, already feeling guilty that the struggling Broadway hopeful probably assumed my question meant she'd be missing out on a tip, but I'd make sure she received a sizeable one for being a good sport and all.

The waitress gave a knowing look. "She's impressive, isn't she?" I felt the heat rising in my neck and face, but maybe she didn't notice. "You're not the only one—every red-blooded male who walks through that door wants Kennedy to be his waitress."

Whatever. She'd noticed.

"She's like the main attraction around here. Honestly, I'm

not sure why she's still waiting tables—girl could have scored a sugar daddy or two by now if she wanted."

She dropped that truth bomb as if my blood pressure hadn't spiked enough.

The waitress strolled away, and Declan watched me closely. A telling chuckle rolled off him.

"What?" I demanded.

"Nothing. Nothing at all, man."

We were thumbing through the menu when the scent of Kennedy's strawberry body lotion hit my nostrils, and at the same time, her hand touched my shoulder, sending a surge of fiery adrenaline through my veins.

Her body arced the corner set by my chair. She was so close her upper body grazed my arm, and my hand went to her leg, my fingers brushing the back of her thigh just above her knee.

With anyone else, it'd have been inappropriate; with Kennedy, it was just us.

"What are you doing here?" she whisper-yelled.

She bounced in place, trying to contain her excitement, but it didn't matter because my self-control had checked out at "girl could have scored a sugar daddy."

In the next second, I was on my feet with my arms around her, holding her against me. Kennedy gripped my shirt and pressed her cheek to my chest. My head dipped, and my eyes closed. My nose nuzzled her hair as I tried to soak up every drop of her essence. There was no one else I was like this with. All that was missing was my mouth on hers and we'd have looked like a full-fledged couple who'd been apart for far too fucking long.

We each took a half step back, and she stretched on her tiptoes, guiding me down by my shoulders so she could plant a kiss on my cheek.

Her lips lingered a little too long. That tiny spot on my skin would continue to tingle long after she'd walked away to take the next table's order.

Reluctantly, I sat back down, reeling in my emotions and readjusting my game face. "We have a lot to catch up on, Quinn. What time do you get off?"

Her stunning smile, the one that was just slightly too big for her face, was unwavering as she stared at me without speaking. But as Kennedy said, that too-big mouth was the reason why she could hit those crazy-ass notes.

"Quinn?"

She blinked, appearing dazed. "Oh. Right—in about an hour."

My heart somersaulted in my chest. It was going to be a long sixty minutes. "We'll wait for you."

She nodded quickly, and then turned her full attention to Declan. "I'm so sorry! We're being so rude!" She extended her hand. "Kennedy Quinn, it's a pleasure to meet you."

Shit. I'd forgotten Declan was even there.

His wry grin told me he knew I'd blanked out on his presence. Then he gave Kennedy the same smoldering look that made the jersey chasers drop their panties. "Declan Walsh, and the pleasure is all mine. I've heard a lot about you—but Jackson left out the part about you being a total knockout."

She laughed her throaty laugh—the kind of laugh that made guys turn away from their wives and girlfriends just to see where that cock-hardening ballad came from. Declan looked back and forth between the two of us, that same smirk from earlier making a reappearance.

He focused on our knockout waitress again. "Will you be singing another song?"

Kennedy pressed a pen to her bottom lip for a moment then pulled it away. "I could. Do you have a request?"

"My niece is obsessed with *Frozen*. I've taken her to see it four times on Broadway. I'd love to record you singing so I can show it to her."

Fuck this smooth bastard.

Kennedy's shoulders relaxed with a sweet sigh, and she tilted her head to the side. "Oh my gosh, you're an amazing uncle to do that. What's your niece's name? I'll dedicate it to her."

Declan looked like a man under hypnosis. Once we were in the privacy of his apartment, I'd have to confirm that Kennedy was in fact real and not an illusion.

A One Direction song and a *Wicked* song later, Kennedy was back at the mic, her predecessor introducing her as "everyone's favorite princess." The title made me cringe; Kennedy was anything but a princess—at least not in the stereotypical sense. I'd never known anyone as down-to-earth, humble, and selfless as her.

She walked the first-floor catwalk beneath the Studio 54-esque disco ball. The black shorts didn't cover much, and the towering heels accentuated every muscle in her tanned and toned legs. Her sleeveless blouse was tucked in, showing off her trim waist. The top three buttons had been left open.

It was mid-July, but couldn't she wear just a little more clothing, for fuck's sake?

But while a part of me wanted to cover her up in a sleeping bag, another part was cheering her on as she unapologetically owned her sexual prowess. Her strict Southern Baptist parents had been less than supportive when their only child chose New York City as her landing spot after she'd graduated college. When their unnecessary guilt didn't engender the result they wanted, they essentially cut her off emotionally. The poorly timed rapid succession of Hunter's infidelity and her parents' misguided judgments had set up the kindest girl I'd ever known for an undeserving amount of heartache.

"This next song is for a special little girl. Delilah, the next time you visit the Big Apple, have your uncle find me and we'll sing this one together."

Kennedy looked over at us and smiled like the star she was. Then she started to sing, and everything but her faded into the background.

An hour and a half later, the three of us were tucked into the back corner of Hiatus, a hole-in-the-wall pub that Declan frequented when he wanted to hang out on the down low.

Kennedy took a long sip of beer from a tall glass, then tugged the elastic from her hair, letting her thick locks fall haphazardly. She finger-combed through the layers, giving them a shake, and the scent of her coconut shampoo wafted my way. Her hair was shorter than it had been in Paris. It used to go all the way down her back, but now it landed just below her shoulder blades.

I studied her, looking for any other changes, however subtle.

"Sorry I reek like fried food, guys," she apologized.

"You always smell fantastic, Quinn," I said, adding my charming grin.

She giggled and rolled her eyes—and yeah, three years later, the sweet sound still had an effect on me.

Declan leaned back in his chair as though he needed a better view of the Sawyer and Kennedy show. I could plan on getting so much shit for how whipped I was around her when we got back to his place.

"All right, Sawyer, how about you tell me what the heck

you're doing here, and why you didn't give me a heads-up so I could have taken time off from work." Kennedy propped her elbow on the table and rested her chin in her hand, batting her lashes at me with total sass attached.

Scrutinizing her face for a reaction, I asked, "How would you feel about us becoming neighbors?"

"Why? Did you lose all your money or something?" she deadpanned.

Declan laughed.

My head fell to the side. "Really, Quinn? I don't mean *literally* your neighbor."

Now I was concerned why she'd suggested that someone had to be destitute to want to live where she did. She'd moved into her new place when she'd returned from Paris, and my off-season workout schedule, designed to have me in peak condition to ensure my candidacy for a long-term contract, had kept me from visiting.

No more long-distance bullshit, pretty girl. I'm coming to you, and I'm staying.

"Is Hamilton Heights unsafe?" I asked, unreasonable paranoia wanting to make an appearance. "What about your building?"

Kennedy's smile was both sympathetic and troubled. She frequently reminded me that I worried about her "too much," but I knew my worry was relative to all the other emotions this girl made me feel.

Her fingers curled around my forearm, setting my skin on fire. "Don't worry about where I live. It's perfectly safe. Besides, I have two amazing roommates—one of whom is a big, strapping man with lots of muscles."

Was my heart still beating? I knew she had a roommate, but *two* roommates? And one was a *dude*?

"You're living with a *guy*? Who? Do I know him?"

"His name is Andrew and he's wonderful," she said with a casual, single-shoulder shrug, like she'd just referred me to her hairstylist.

Fuck that.

I needed the guy's social security number, or at least a last name to work with. Who doesn't give their best friend these kinds of details?

Kennedy mindlessly settled her fingers between mine, our unified hands resting on the table. "You can meet him tomorrow night if you'd like—we're performing together at a piano bar uptown."

"You *sing* with him?"

Did my voice just crack?

Kennedy's chin dragged up and down with patronizing slowness as though she hadn't just polluted every fantasy I'd ever had of her singing by adding a dude to the once sensual image in my head.

"Yes, Sawyer, I sing with a *man*. He has a penis and everything. Not that I've seen it—*yet*—but I've heard the rumors and . . ." She bit her lip and rolled her eyes in a dreamy expression.

Declan laughed, like an asshole.

I wondered if I might hyperventilate. There was no doubt I wanted to strangle Declan and spank Kennedy.

I've wanted to spank Kennedy *a lot*. That was another fantasy I'd had.

One she doesn't know about.

When she realized I wasn't finding the humor in her admission, she sighed and cocked her head at Declan. "If you haven't figured it out already, Sawyer's a bit dramatic and overprotective."

Declan raised his glass and looked directly at me. "Oh, is that what he is?" he asked before taking a swig of beer.

These two . . .

She fake smiled and lasered her eyes on me. "Yes, he is. And my friend is getting off track—so, Sawyer, please explain why you want to be my neighbor."

Well, here goes nothing.

"I'm signing with New York, as long as I passed my physical. We're still waiting for the final word. So, no, I won't be your *actual* neighbor. I'll be crashing with Walsh until I can find my own place. And *yes*, I do want to meet your roommate with a penis, so tell me where to be tomorrow night and I'll be there."

Before Kennedy could respond, Declan chimed in, "We've got . . . uh . . . those plans tomorrow night with Jordan."

Fuck a goddamn duck.

I ignored Declan; I'd figure out that clusterfuck later.

Those "plans" involved a group date I'd been conned into with journeyman safety Chase Jordan, his wife, her sister, and a friend. And by "conned," I meant Declan asked me to do him solid since he really wanted to hook up with the friend and they needed one more single—and, therefore, presumed available—man to entertain the sister.

But Kennedy was my number-one priority. I would make time to meet the guy she was shacking up with somehow.

Kennedy was uncharacteristically silent; I'd expected at least a little enthusiasm over my announcement. But when I saw how pale she'd turned, I knew the thoughts invading her mind.

Pulling our clasped hands to my chest, I leaned in to ensure she looked me in the eye. "Don't worry, Quinn. It's all good."

She nodded, but her hand was clammy—a sure sign that she was nervous.

"Is this about Sterling?" Declan asked.

Kennedy and I both turned to look at him. I gave him a slight nod; Kennedy bit her bottom lip. I reached up and plucked it from between her teeth before she made herself bleed.

"You play for New York?" she asked Declan, her voice quiet.

He gave a sober nod. Most people with NFL connections had at least some knowledge about Sterling and Kennedy's very public breakup. After Seth and Abby's wedding, Melody had gone on a *Mean Girls* social media crusade against Kennedy, who'd endured the whole ordeal with her head held high like the fucking badass she was.

I ran my knuckles over Kennedy's soft cheek. "I still hate the fucker, and I always will. I don't give a flying fuck if he *is* my quarterback."

She huffed a despairing laugh. "See? That right there." She wagged a finger at me. "That's what worries me, Sawyer Jackson. Not the past coming back to haunt *me*—but it ruining *your* future. You can't go all vigilante again. You're going to get kicked out of the league next time. You deserve every penny of whatever they're going to pay you and I don't want you risking any of it defending my honor. It was three years ago. Get over it, okay? I have. Understand, Tight End?"

Knowing her adorable, fiery warning was coming from the right place, I replied, "I will be on my best behavior, Quinn—scout's honor."

I was never a Boy Scout, so I wasn't bound by shit.

She scowled and tossed her hair over her shoulder. Turning to Declan, she said, "All right, I'm enlisting your help in keeping this guy from throwing everything away. Got me?" She cocked a brow, waiting for his reply.

Christ, I could eat her right up when she got spunky.

She never had any idea what she did to the men around her. Though Declan's reactions weren't as caveman as most, it was obvious that he was more than interested. Soon, I'd inform him of my plans to woo Kennedy with all the boyfriend skills I had yet to master.

She's mine, bro.

"I got you. You have my word," he replied with a wink.

I drew in a frustrated breath. It wasn't his fault Kennedy was so goddamn desirable.

"Fantastic." She beamed at Declan and then turned to face me again. Her eyes shimmered with the promise of something bound to knock me on my ass. "Now that's settled, it's my turn to tell you *my* big news."

5

SAWYER

Flag on the motherfucking play.

"Chicago?" I had to force the lump in my throat down my esophagus just to get the word out. "I thought the whole point of getting a Broadway agent was to be on *actual* Broadway—you know, here in *Manhattan.*"

I realized I'd sounded like a colossal dick the moment the words rolled off my tongue. I didn't need Kennedy's hurt expression staring back at me to point it out.

Her eyes dropped to the table and then she tucked her hair behind her ear, silence enveloping us like an awkward blanket.

"I'm gonna hit the head . . . be back in a few."

I glanced up as Declan got to his feet. He gave me an inaudible *tsk*, shaking his head as he used the convenient excuse to give us privacy.

The moment he was out of earshot, I cradled the back of Kennedy's neck with one hand, forcing her to meet my eyes. "I'm sorry. I didn't mean it like it sounded."

She shook her head, her eyes watering. "No, I'm the one who should be sorry. This is about you tonight—your new contract—not about me. I shouldn't have brought it up."

Was she fucking serious?

"Quinn." I turned my entire chair to face her, prepared to haul her onto my lap if she didn't give me her full attention.

"You're signing with an *agent*. Do you know how fucking proud of you I am?"

She blinked back her unshed tears.

"Really?"

"Yeah. *Really.*"

Her gorgeous smile returned, and it took all my willpower not to crush my lips against hers.

"I'm just surprised that this agent is talking about getting you auditions in Chicago . . ."

She nodded in understanding, a slight shrug telling me she was going to downplay the whole thing now that she knew I'd been triggered. Kennedy had mastered me like the notes of the goddamn *Titanic* song. She could read me like an open book and was always prepared to soothe my overreactions before I'd even acknowledged them as my own.

"William just mentioned it as an option—apparently, he has reach there. Of course my dream is still to be on Broadway, but an Off-Broadway production of a major show would still be a massive step up from what I'm doing now. Sure, the diner and gigs pay the rent, but that's not my dream . . . know what I mean?"

William—I'd have to add him to the list of men in Kennedy's life that I'd started composing as soon as I'd learned that an *Andrew* existed.

Unable to resist, I pressed a chaste kiss to her forehead. "I do, Quinn. And you have my full support."

Just don't make me become a Chicago Bear—fuck those guys.

We spent the rest of the night reminiscing about our unconventional meeting and friendship with Declan. When my mind tried to stray to thoughts of the possibility that Kennedy could leave New York to fulfill her lifelong dream, I felt my heart stutter in my chest.

Declan hung on to every word, especially when Kennedy

did the storytelling. Eventually, he'd ask me the inevitable—because look at her, he would—and when he came to me to see if he could take my best friend out, my answer would be an unequivocal no. But I would need to back up my unrelenting stance, and that's when I'd disclose my master plan. I wasn't a complete novice when it came to this boyfriend stuff—okay, maybe I was—but I at least knew enough to know better than to assume Kennedy was going to welcome me into her bed with open arms without a little effort first—though a man could hope.

"I think I should take you home," I said as we stood outside the bar waiting for the Uber I'd ordered Kennedy.

Her cheeks were flushed from the alcohol, and her eyes were glassy enough that I knew she had a strong buzz going.

"I get myself home every night just fine without you, Sawyer Jackson. Go on. Order an Uber for the two of you. It's hotter than a sticky ballsack out here—get in some AC, friend."

That mouth of hers—oh, how I'd corrupted my once sweet Southern girl.

A silver Altima pulled up along the curb. I opened the door to confirm the driver was the nerdy-looking twig I'd selected on the app.

"We'll be just a second," I told him.

When I stood back up, Kennedy was moving into me. "Good night, Sawyer. Maybe I'll see you tomorrow night."

Fucking right you will.

She leaned up, her recently licked lips brushing against my cheek. Before I could wrap my arms around her for the embrace I desperately wanted, she'd turned to Declan, giving her back to me.

"It was so nice to meet you, Declan. I hope we can hang out again soon."

Then she kissed his cheek too, and something that felt

a hell of a lot like jealousy blurred my vision. Lucky for him, he had enough common sense to keep his fucking hands to himself.

I was too engrossed taming the green-eyed monster inside of me that I only caught the end of their goodbye.

"With Jackson crashing with me, it only makes sense we'll be seeing a lot of one another. I look forward to it."

With her hand on the car door handle, she paused and looked at me over her shoulder. "I'm so happy for you, Sawyer. You deserve this contract. Don't screw it up because of me, okay? Promise me?"

Her eyes searched mine, seeking my truth. So I gave it to her, at least part of it, anyway.

I moved closer and held her chin between my thumb and forefinger. "I'm not going to screw this up. You have my word."

Her breath hitched, and her lips parted.

Did she know I wasn't talking about my career?

The silent ride to Declan's gave me plenty of time to over-think what my next move should be. I needed to tell Kennedy how I felt about her, but the timing had to be right. I only had one chance not to fuck this up.

That's it—one chance.

If I failed, I'd lose everything, and the thought of not hav-ing Kennedy in my life—period—had been the last thing hold-ing me back from taking the next step.

Staying sane and positive while rehabbing my torn ACL two years ago and withstanding my mom's battle with breast cancer had only been possible because of Kennedy. She meant everything to me.

I knew the risk was extraordinary, but if everything turned out as I'd planned, the reward would be even sweeter.

After he'd handed me a beer, Declan leaned against his kitchen counter and crossed his ankles. "All right, she's not here—so, tell me why you haven't locked that down, because you better have a good reason. Otherwise, you're a fucking idiot."

Go on, tell me how you really feel.

I sat at the island holding the cold bottle between my hands. For a minute or so, I watched the condensation racing down the glass, placing mental bets on which drop would win. When it was evident that Declan was either patient as fuck or as stubborn as me, I replied, "You already know about Sterling."

Declan set down his Guinness and folded his arms across his chest. "Yeah, but she even said it herself, that was three years ago, dude. She's over it."

"Well, we've been living in different states for another thing..."

Declan shook his head like he expected more from me and scuffed the back of his heel against the toe of the opposite Yeezy. He didn't need to say another word. He was going to wait me out until I was ready to be brutally honest with the both of us.

Definitely as stubborn as me.

I tilted my drink back and chugged until I'd downed half of it. Then I went back to staring at the amber bottle.

"Kennedy could never be a hookup or a fling. She's ..." I struggled to keep my tone even and steady.

"The girl you marry, not the one you fuck and forget. Am I right?"

I slumped on my stool, my forehead resting on the cold marble countertop. Realization had my bones feeling as though they'd turned to rubber. "She is." I groaned in agreement. "And I'm not even fit to be her boyfriend, never mind her *husband*."

Declan chuckled as he moved to my side, clapping me on the back.

"Take your time—do it right. She's incredible. If you get the chance to be with her, don't fuck it up."

Kennedy always reminded me that repetitive thoughts unconsciously become our mantra. If she was correct, then "Don't fuck it up" was most definitely my mantra as of late.

I needed DFIU tattooed somewhere on my body.

"But don't take too long—I think she likes me."

My head snapped up so fast Declan jumped back, raising his hands in mock surrender. Then he laughed. "Dude, you should totally see your face right now. Mean mug whoever you line up against on the field like that, and they'll clear a path for you straight to the end zone."

It wasn't that the bed in Declan's guest room was uncomfortable, I just had too much on my mind after spending a few hours with Kennedy for my brain to power off. After I'd tossed and turned for an unreasonable length of time, I gave up on sleep and picked up my phone.

I scrolled through my photo gallery. The only pics and videos I'd spent energy organizing were the ones with Kennedy; she ranked higher than football these days. She smiled in almost all of them, but there were many I'd taken when she hadn't realized I was watching her, and some of those were my favorites of all.

Jesus Christ, you sound like a fucking stalker.

After going through three years of captured memories, I couldn't fight back the urge to text her. I wanted to hear from her—something. Anything.

Me: Sleeping yet?

Three dots appeared instantly, and I sat up.

Quinn: Nope. Just got into bed. One of my roomies got a callback so we had a mini celebration for her and for my agent thingy news.

My shoulders stiffened as my mind immediately conjured images of Kennedy arriving at her apartment tipsy, greeted by a guy ready to "hang out."

Me: You're hanging out with that guy?

My thumbs stabbed at the screen like it'd killed my dog.

Quinn: He has a name, Sawyer. It's Andrew. Remember? Yes, he's here. My other roommate, Brooke, she got the callback. You'd probably fall head over heels for her. She's tall, blonde, and bonus—her ample boobs are the real deal.

Why did she have to do that?

The back of my head hit the headboard. I wanted to tell her that all I wanted was the short brunette with green eyes, and I didn't give a fuck what size her tits were.

But because I was a coward with no game when it came to Kennedy, and I felt her applying liberal amounts of her Sawyerblock SPF 10,000, I volleyed back with something that bordered on hurtful.

Me: Will the hot blonde be there tomorrow night?

I regretted it as soon as I sent it.

But Kennedy was mostly immune to my occasional ass-holeness, and knew how to hand it right back to me.

Quinn: No, Sawyer. Even if she was—you're not allowed to bone my friends. I was being facetious.

Me: Just kidding, Quinn. By the way ... about tomorrow night ... I kinda have a "date." Not a real date, but something I'm doing for a friend. I'm going to see if I can convince everyone to go to the piano bar, so send me the address.

Are there twenty-four-hour tattoo shops in NYC? Asking for a friend.

Quinn: Sawyer Jackson, did you just use the word "date"?

Me: It's not a real date.

Quinn: Hang on, I need to check CNN—is anyone checking on Hell?

Me: IT'S NOT A REAL DATE.

Quinn: If this isn't a punk and if you really do have a D-A-T-E, you are not allowed to bring her to watch me sing. Do better.

Me: Christ, woman. It'S nOt A ReaL DaTE. Besides, I'll tell her we're friends.

Quinn: You really don't understand women at all, do you?

One thing I'd recently learned about women: some women have the eyesight of a goddamn bat.

Me: What? What's wrong with that? She'll understand.

Quinn: Not all girls are as cool as me, bruh. They won't all understand.

My heart seized, and I chuckled out loud to the empty bedroom.

Quinn: As the unofficial spokeswoman for the mythical All the Single Ladies Alliance, I forbid you to bring your date to watch me sing tomorrow night.

I frowned even though she couldn't see me.

Me: WTF Quinn???

Me: Then you're not allowed to date my friends either.

Quinn: Huh? Did you just change the subject like a psycho?

My ears were hot and itchy. An emotion I couldn't label swirled in my chest.

Me: Sure. Consider the subject changed. If I can't bone (your words, not mine) your smokin' hot roommate then you can't date my friends either.

She's right—you are a psycho.

Quinn: There's a distinct difference between boning and dating.

Me: Are you saying you want to date one of my friends?

Christ, you sound like a chick.

Quinn: Are you trying to mindfuck me right now? For the love, Sawyer. I don't know! Maybe? Or I could just let them bone me instead.

I tap out.

Me: What? Fuck no!

Quinn: What's Declan's number?

Me: Quinn.

Quinn. Sawyer.

Me: Please tell me you're kidding. You're kidding, right? This is you giving me a taste of my own medicine?

This shit had spiraled out of control, and my anxiety was palpable now.

Quinn: Good night, Sawyer.

Me: Quinn?

I waited five minutes—no reply.

I pulled up my contacts, my thumb hovering over her name.

I went back to my texts.

Breathe, motherfucker.

Me: It's. Not. A. Real. Date.

6

KENNEDY

I woke up with a mild hangover after the night out with Sawyer and Declan followed by celebratory shots with Brooke and Andrew. Deciding to take advantage of my day off from the diner, I spent the morning lounging in bed while reviewing the contract that had been sitting in my inbox since yesterday afternoon.

Three years after moving to Manhattan, I was signing with one of the most sought-after Broadway agents, William Abreu.

William was in the top echelon as far as agents went, and was known for his *intensity*—for lack of a better word. When I'd submitted my portfolio, I had zero expectations that I'd ever hear back from the spectacularly demanding agent.

Now here I was reviewing a contract, ready to sign on the dotted line and commit every waking moment to doing whatever it took to land a role on the big stage.

Vocal conditioning. Audition prep. Acting classes. All of it. This was my life now. I would eat, sleep, and breathe Broadway. I was at the mercy of the one and only William Abreu.

After William and I ended our phone call yesterday, I knew who the first person I'd share my life-changing news with would be. So imagine my surprise to find said person occupying one of my tables rather than being 1,200 miles away in Florida where he belonged. And imagine my even bigger surprise when his reaction was that of a man who'd just been informed he was about to lose his right testicle.

Sawyer Jackson.

What was I going to do with that man?

My phone vibrated on the nightstand. I leaned over to catch a glance at the screen and immediately sighed.

Speak of the handsome devil.

I reminded myself I was supposed to be mad at him and sent him to voice mail.

What began as two strangers thrown together by what Sawyer had labeled "fate"—he was totally teasing when he'd said it—had evolved into something I treasured deeply and feared losing even more.

As unlikely a pairing as we may have been in the beginning, we were now as close as any two friends could be—closer, maybe. And though our relationship had always been impregnated with innuendos, relentless banter, physicality that left my body in need, and endless moments of juicy sexual tension, we'd always remained "just friends."

Because it was for the best—right?

Right.

I was nothing like the sexually liberated women who chose to enjoy Sawyer's company for exactly what he had to offer—a night they'd never forget followed by a swift slap on the ass as he sent them on their way without so much as a phone number exchange.

With Sawyer being in Florida, I'd managed to keep a healthy distance between myself and his promiscuous lifestyle, choosing "ignorance is bliss" as my mantra, and forbidding myself from reading certain media outlets.

How's that gonna work with your blue-eyed devil living in the same city?

I liked to consider myself a rational, nonjudgmental

woman, capable of accepting her best friend's standards and choices. Besides, I had far more important matters to spend my time on, and policing Sawyer's sex life wasn't going to derail me.

When my phone vibrated a second time, I reluctantly crawled out of bed and left the room.

Now you're being bullied by your phone?

Sawyer was an addicting distraction I didn't have time for. I had files to gather and send to William, a contract to read for the forty-ninth time, and a gig to prep for.

As I showered, Brooke sat on the bathroom counter painting her toenails bubblegum pink. I'd met Andrew first at a party, and a month later, he introduced me to Brooke. We'd become three fast friends, each of us well aware of what life as a Broadway wannabe entailed. When we were all looking for a new apartment at the same time, it had felt a bit serendipitous.

Brooke raised her voice so I could hear her over the running water. "When do I get to meet *the* Sawyer Jackson?"

Good grief.

Maybe *this* was my life now.

Squeezing the excess water from my freshly shampooed and conditioned hair, I replied, "I'm sure you'll meet him soon enough. Sawyer is on a mission to get up close and personal with everyone in my life."

"I will *gladly* get *up close and personal* with your football player, but if I get the part, I'll be too busy, so you better get on it, sweet cheeks."

"He's not *my* football player." I turned the faucet off and stuck my head out of the shower curtain. "And you mean *when* you get the part."

Brooke flipped her long blonde locks over her shoulder. "I wish I shared your commitment to the power of positivity, Kennedy."

The bathroom door creaked open, and a draft of cool air moved in.

Andrew's husky voice cut through the steamy room. "What's our little Law of Attraction specialist manifesting now?"

Brooke greeted him first. "Morning, sexy." She had some gift; everything that came out of her mouth sounded like an invitation.

I grabbed my towel and wrapped it around myself, tucking it in at the top before stepping out onto the bathmat.

"Kennedy was just reminding me that if I *will it* hard enough, I'll be the next Kristin Chenoweth." Brooke used her teacher voice, and I rolled my eyes.

My nose lifted into the air, I twisted my hair and clipped it on top of my head. "Make fun of me all you want, but it works."

Andrew squirted a dab of toothpaste on his toothbrush. "Ah, yes. If either of you lovely ladies care to will something on my behalf—I'd like to be the next Leslie Odom Jr."

His platinum hair had a serious case of bedhead, but his hazel eyes were bright. He smiled wide at our three reflections in the mirror, showing off his perfectly straight white teeth, just before shoving his toothbrush in his mouth. His pajama bottoms hung low on his hips, and he was shirtless, highlighting an array of mouthwatering tattoos.

All six-foot-something of Andrew was solid muscle. His perfect pecs and washboard abs led a trail right down to the V-shape that lured me in every time he walked around the apartment looking like a Viking god front man for a rock band. Once he parked God's sexy work of art behind a piano or picked up his Gibson, it was only a matter of seconds before there wasn't a dry pair of panties in the house.

Lord help me. I needed to get laid. It'd been too long.

Andrew?

Not going there.

Sawyer?

No, Lord. Refer back to my previous answer.

"What time do you want to meet up tonight?" Andrew asked with a mouth full of foam and a smirk. He'd totally caught me checking him out in the mirror.

It was harmless.

My face was hot, and not because of the thirty-minute shower I'd just taken. "You want to meet there?" I asked, avoiding his heated gaze before I did something totally repulsive—like drool.

He nodded and spat. "I have to work today, so I'll go straight to the bar. We're on at eight, so let's try to be there by seven fifteen."

"Sounds like a plan, man," I said with forced casualness, tossing my hairbrush in my tote.

For the first time since we'd found out about the gig, an unsettled sensation kneaded at my core. It had been a while since I'd performed anywhere other than the diner, weddings, and other private events, and William had mentioned that he'd stop by if he had time.

Brooke looked back and forth between the two of us and pouted. "I wanna go watch you guys. No fair."

Andrew was messing with his hair in the mirror. "Your dad would kick my ass if you blew him off to come watch us in a piano bar."

I'd never met Brooke's father, but she and Andrew grew up together in Manhattan, attending the same private academy. They'd even been friends with benefits in the past, though they'd sworn off roommate sex when we all moved in together.

She wiggled her freshly painted toes and slid off the counter. "You're right—but I can still whine about it. I'd much rather spend my night watching you two hotties than attending another fundraiser with my father." With her petulant expression still in place, Brooke exited the bathroom, smacking Andrew's butt on the way out.

"Good luck today!" Andrew and I called out in perfect harmony as though we'd practiced it.

Brooke yelled back, "I don't need luck! I've got Kennedy!"

"It doesn't work that way!" I reminded her before securing her abandoned spot on the counter.

"Hey, Drew?" I asked, my tone clearly shifting from banter mode to I-need-a-friend-right-now mode. "Can I talk to you for a minute?"

He turned away from the mirror and rested his hip against the vanity, crossing his arms. "What's up, Buttercup?"

I'd have asked him if he wanted to put on more clothes, but after two months of living with Andrew, I wasn't sure I'd ever seen him in the apartment longer than five minutes before he lost his shirt.

After my texts with Sawyer last night, I knew I needed to warn Andrew that he might be walking into the lion's den should Sawyer not heed my fair warning and show up at our gig. Even with his it's-not-a-real-date in tow, there was still a risk of Sawyer being obnoxious, and Andrew didn't deserve that.

I really hope William is busy tonight . . .

I wasn't sure I had the emotional wherewithal to handle a Sawyer and Andrew exchange. A Sawyer and William exchange would probably be the end of my existence as I knew it. Sometimes—who the heck am I trying to kid here—*allthe-times*, it was an exhausting effort to play interference between Sawyer's misplaced claim to my honor and other men.

"You know I'm friends with Sawyer Jackson, right?"

Andrew grinned. "Go on, rub it in. You know I'm a fan. I'm still counting on you introducing us someday."

A sarcastic chuckle whispered through my lips. "Be careful what you wish for."

Andrew's mouth drew a straight line, and his eyebrows came together. "Talk to me, Kennedy."

It was better to just rip off the Band-Aid. I let out a deep breath and straightened my spine. "Sawyer may be there tonight, possibly with some of his teammates. I think they're going on a group date or something like that."

The grin was back, bringing a dimple along for the ride. "That's cool—at least we know we won't be singing to an empty room. Why so glum, then?"

Oh, Andrew. You're so cute.

"Just a heads-up—Sawyer can be a bit overprotective at times."

His pecs winked at me as he shifted his stance. "How so?"

Put on a shirt, man.

"Well, let's just say being overzealous in defending my honor hasn't always turned out so well for him. And he is less than thrilled that I am living with you."

Andrew's eyes narrowed. "Is he jealous? I thought you said you guys are just friends."

If the phrase "just friends" were a drug, I'd sell it by the gram.

And dear God, would I be rich.

"We *are* just friends—we've never been anything more than friends—but after Sawyer's father died when he was young, he sort of grew up as the man of the house. As soon as he was old enough to do so, he started taking care of his younger sister and mother. And now . . . well, now we're like family too, I guess. He thinks it's his role to look out for me. What I'm trying to say is, don't take anything he says personally. He really *is* a good guy."

Andrew held up his hands. "Hey, you won't get any

blowback from me. I'm glad you have someone who cares about you so much." He stepped closer, resting one of his hands where my towel ended and my knee began. "And for the record, you've got me too." He dipped his chin in commitment. "I know you've been through some fucked-up shit with your ex and your parents. I've got your back too."

A single tear trickled down my cheek, and he wiped it away with the pad of his thumb. "Thanks, Drew."

Andrew motioned his head toward the open door. "Now get your sweet self out of here so I can get naked. Wear your red dress tonight, and I'll wear a matching tie."

7

KENNEDY

"Hey, you okay, Buttercup?"

I took a sip of water, and my shoulder blades eased down my back. "Yes, I'm fine. Just eager to get started, that's all."

Which was a total lie.

Ever since Sawyer had sent me a text suggesting that after my gig, we should "talk about us," I'd been having hot flashes like my mother when she hit fifty.

What exactly did he mean by that?

I don't know. I didn't ask. After he clarified that he'd indeed meant "us" as in *us-us*, and not the United States, I did what any other dignified millennial would do and "forgot" to reply.

Simone's was packed to the hilt. I glanced around the East Village speakeasy as I ran my sweaty palms down my red satin dress for the hundredth time. Andrew stepped in front of me, the gold flecks in his eyes twinkling under the bar lights. A slow, sultry smile unfurled on his lips, and then he dropped his mouth to my ear.

"Breathe."

Easy for him to say—he'd just robbed me of the last of my air.

Leaving me on the brink of panting, he moved to the piano, lowering himself to the bench with the grace of a dancer.

I shook my head lightly, and my loose curls fell into place. A pearl-trimmed comb drew back one side of my hair, and I pulled the rest over my opposite shoulder.

Andrew looked at me, the piano, and then back at me as though sizing up the situation. He stood abruptly and then his hands were on me.

"Hang on, Buttercup."

He lifted me from my waist, and in one smooth move, he had me perched on the piano.

I gave him a silent look that said, "Dude?" and he shrugged with a wink.

A woman at the table directly in front of us let out an audible sigh as she fanned her face with her hand. "Wow. That was *hot*."

She didn't exaggerate; Andrew was sex on a stick if that were such a thing.

My partner chuckled behind me as he returned to his seat.

I felt a poke in my ribs and glanced over my shoulder. I wanted to give him my meanest scowl—but come on, it was Andrew. I shook my head at his silliness, and then turned back to the crowd, scanning the sea of expectant faces for one that looked familiar.

Maybe he changed his mind. Maybe his "date" turned out to be the real deal after all.

Undiluted disappointment prodded at my weighted heart.

What do you expect? You warned him not to come tonight, and you ignored his text.

My brash reactions had been automatic, shaped by years of conditioning to thwart any attempt by my heart to acknowledge the longing for Sawyer that burned deep in my core. The man who owned my heart was the very one I had to protect my heart from the most. Did I believe he loved me like a friend, or a sister maybe? Of course. Did I believe he had the capacity to love me as anything more? Much to my heart's dismay . . . no. No, I did not.

Three years later, I was still not the hit-it-and-quit-it type of girl that Sawyer bedded. And no-strings-attached physical satisfaction à la Brooke and Andrew was off the table for this monogamous-as-a-penguin girl.

Behind me, Andrew's masterful fingers floated across the piano keys with precision, drawing me into the present. I raised my mic.

I needed to push Sawyer Jackson to the back of my mind, where I intended to store all my *friends* for now, because I had a job to do and dreams to chase.

We were halfway through Demi Lovato's "Give Your Heart a Break" when I spotted Sawyer and his friends. They sat at a table near the front and off to the right. They'd scored quite possibly the best seats in the place.

I wonder who he had to pay off.

He looked delicious in a fitted gray button-up with the sleeves rolled up his muscular forearms. His dark hair was tousled like he didn't put in any effort, yet knew it was a hot look. Even from a distance, I could tell he was freshly shaven, and he probably smelled like spices and leather.

Seeing Sawyer was both thrilling and terrifying, but don't they say that the best things usually come packaged that way?

His back was to the wall, and a willowy woman with gorgeous blonde spiral curls sat on his right. That's when I realized that Sawyer may need to have the definition of "date" spelled out for him. The blonde ran her fingertips down his chest, her body positioning giving off the vibe that she was trying to get his attention. Sawyer's gaze never left me as he said something with a straight face. The blonde giggled and leaned in like she was inspecting his pores and then nipped at his jawline. It looked like a reenactment of an episode of *The Bachelor* I'd watched with Brooke the other night, and I had to turn away.

Damn Sawyer for toying with my emotions.

And damn myself for allowing my thoughts to even go there, no matter how brief the consideration may have been.

Just when I'd felt the Kevlar-grade anti-Sawyer shield around my heart starting to surrender, reality hit me like a well-aimed bullet, and I was reminded why I could never trust him with the most sacred part of me. After Hunter, I learned to tread carefully with matters of the heart, and Sawyer's blasé attitude toward sex and women would never resonate with my soul.

Turning my attention away from Sawyer, I sought grounding in Andrew, who cocked his head to the side to make eye contact. His gaze infected me with his passion, and his raspy voice stoked the energy between us. Giving in to the moment, I poured all my emotion into my next lines and watched Andrew's face light up with pride.

I slid off the piano, and his little nod said, "You've got this, Buttercup."

On steady feet, I glided around the edge of the instrument as we continued to hit every note as though God had created us for the sole purpose of singing that very song. When I moved behind Andrew, I dragged my fingers along his shoulders seductively. Andrew and I were both excellent performers with an uncanny ability to lay on the sex appeal real thick while still keeping it professional. He winked at me in encouragement, and I lifted my chin as I hit my run.

We fed off the crowd, and our performance grew steamier.

My gaze never found Sawyer's again, and thoughts of him and his date were long forgotten as the music I was creating with Andrew carried my heart to another time and place.

During "Shallow," I sat on the bench beside Andrew, and we shared the same mic. It was no coincidence that there was a whole lot of kissing and touching happening all around us.

We tried to close with "Endless Love" by Lionel Richie and Diana Ross, but the crowd insisted on an encore. Andrew took a suggestion from the same woman who'd swooned over him in the beginning. She'd been flashing him her breasts and upper thigh all night, and now she wanted us to sing Bonnie Raitt's "I Can't Make You Love Me."

She got her wish.

The song ended, and Andrew rested his sweaty forehead against mine while mumbling something indistinguishable due to the deafening applause. Getting to his feet, he took my hand and led me into the low-lit hallway and toward a room assigned *Employee Use Only*.

He stopped short of the door and cupped my face with his long, elegant fingers—musician fingers.

"You are too fucking gifted to be singing in bars and diners, Buttercup."

My hands found purchase on his wrists. "You're one to talk, Mr. Juilliard."

I couldn't alter my exaggerated grin.

Before he could respond, a throat cleared loudly behind us. Andrew and I turned at the same time, ending our physical contact.

Sawyer stood there with his hands shoved in his pockets, snapping me out of my blissful state—a state where Sawyer and his date didn't exist. I couldn't read his expression in the shadow-heavy lighting, and he didn't make an effort to come any closer.

He just stood there, remaining obscure and silent.

Maybe he knows you're annoyed.

Maybe he thinks you just behaved like a hooker.

Maybe he wants to kick Andrew's ass.

Maybe you should just walk your own ass right over there and find out.

"You good?" Andrew's genuine concern snapped me out of my thoughts.

I cleared the emotion that had lodged itself in my throat and nodded.

"I'll be in here for a bit if you need me." He squeezed my shoulder before disappearing into the room behind me.

I wanted to resist the need to be close to Sawyer, but my irresponsible heart triumphed over my mind the moment he took a step toward me. Wordlessly, we moved like a pair of magnets, taking deliberate strides to close the gap between us. Our bodies bumped lightly when we connected, drawing a small gasp from me. The high I'd just felt after taking a hit of performing with Andrew was nothing compared to the euphoria I felt when I shared air space with Sawyer. He held me by my elbows, his hands scaling my bare skin, creating goose bumps, until he stopped to grip my upper arms.

My head tilted back, and Sawyer's disarming gaze raked over my face as though searching for something he was desperate to find.

"Quinn." The gravel in his voice and the whiskey on his breath had me clenching my thighs together.

"Present and accounted for," I breathed.

"That was . . ." His Adam's apple moved when he swallowed.

"Over the top?"

He shook his head.

I cringed. "Slutty?"

His head drew back as though I'd slapped him. With a slanted smile, he said, "I was thinking more along the lines of—*intense*. That was intense."

"Uh-huh," I mumbled, unsure if that was a cop-out or not.

I needed to be closer.

My hands slid up his chest and settled on his shoulders as his arms enveloped my waist. Sawyer held me so close my toes barely grazed the floor.

"I am so proud of you, Quinn," he whispered against my temple. His lips pressed a tender kiss there, and I closed my eyes in longing.

His embrace tightened around me even more.

I reciprocated.

We held each other closer and longer than friends should for a few beats, and then he loosened his hold enough that I slid down his body to find my feet. His hands traveled my back, and his thumbs landed on the edges of my hips, leaving the rest of his ridiculously massive hands with few options.

So yeah, he was basically holding my ass.

A shudder moved through his body, and the throb between my legs grew stronger. My hardening nipples wanted in on the action. I leaned into him, searching for friction.

"Quinn," he growled low and dangerously.

"Sawyer."

His fingers gripped a little harder. "We need to talk. Not right now, but later."

It wasn't a question.

"What specifically do you want to talk about?" I'd promised myself I wouldn't ask—but alas, I'd lied.

His eyes twinkled, and the panty-dropping grin that he saved for special occasions spread across his face. "The United States."

My face burrowed into his chest, and my entire body shook with laughter. Sawyer held me to him, and his warm chuckle caressed the top of my head.

A throat cleared to our left, interrupting our moment.

Shit, Andrew.

Sawyer and I pulled apart, but we didn't let go of each other. His fingertips dug into me, enticing me to grind against him. My hands slid down the smooth planes of his chest to rest on the defined abs I could feel through his shirt.

Snapping out of whatever state we'd both fallen into, Sawyer released one hand, and his other hand glided across my lower back until he could claim my opposite hip. He pulled me tightly to his side.

We stole one last private grin at each other before turning to face . . . not Andrew.

Christ on a cracker.

It was William Abreu.

8

SAWYER

Kennedy evacuated my embrace like she was a lit match and I was a busted propane tank. She put enough distance between us for the Father, the Son, the Holy Ghost, and then some.

"Mr. Abreu." She clasped her hands together in front of her, going from smokin' hot temptress to girl-next-door all before I could size up the Armani-clad man standing beside us.

"Please, call me William."

Ah. So this is William.

William in his expensive suit and with his French accent turned to me, extending his hand with a stiff smile. "You must be Kennedy's boyfriend. William Abreu."

I was processing the number of silver hairs on his head to theorize an age range when a high-pitched, nervous laugh bounced off the hallway walls.

"Boyfriend?" she squeaked. "Oh, no. No, no, no, no, no." Her head continued to thrash like she'd short-circuited.

Forgetting to accept her agent's greeting, I placed a calming touch on Kennedy's shoulder. She stopped moving, blinked twice, and then plastered on that award-winning fake grin she was so fucking good at.

"No—*definitely* not my boyfriend."

One more time for the people in the back, Quinn.

70

With robotic movement, I finally accepted William's handshake. "Just a friend," I gritted through my teeth. "Sawyer Jackson."

My grip tightened around his, and I think I felt him wince just slightly.

Kennedy's fingers knotted together as tension filled the narrow hallway. The same strung-out smile played across her face. Then her lips were moving, and consciously, I was aware that she and William were having a conversation, but for the life of me, my ears were useless. People had wrongly identified us as a couple in the past, and never once had she reacted like she'd been accused of a hate crime. What had changed? Why was she suddenly acting as though being my girlfriend would put her in the same category as Kardashian fans?

Looks like you have your work cut out for you.

I shook off the thoughts that were creating a riot of emotions in my chest and caught the tail end of their conversation: "Right then. Monday, my office, nine a.m. I'll see you then, Ms. Quinn."

William strode away, and I resisted my need to touch Kennedy. A few beats passed, and then she looked up at me, her expression unreadable.

I inclined my head in the direction of the bar. "Can your *definitely-not-your-boyfriend* buy you a drink?"

She cocked an eyebrow in true Kennedy fashion, and my heart rejoiced in the familiar. Then she raised her chin in opposition. "That seems less than appropriate, *friend.*"

I took a step into her, daring her to metaphorically push me away any more than she already had tonight. "And why is that, *friend*?"

"Because you're clearly on a *very real* date. That's why, *genius.*"

The dig at the end wasn't enough to distract me from the

hurt reeling in her eyes. My heart stumbled into my sternum, and I moved in closer, her taut demeanor crumbling under our proximity.

"Quinn . . . I . . ."

A door closed somewhere behind us, and I glanced over Kennedy's head to see Andrew striding our way. Even in the low light, I could see the jovial vibe rolling off him as he approached.

For fuck's sake.

"What are you two still doing out here?" Andrew asked as he slung an arm across Kennedy's shoulders, encouraging me to take a step back. He grinned back and forth between us like he hadn't just interrupted a potentially significant moment before zeroing in on me. "Sawyer Jackson in the flesh," he pointed out. "Let me buy you a drink."

The way this night had gone so far, he'd better make it a double.

I needed to get Kennedy alone. I had to talk to her before I lost my courage.

I'd woken up this morning determined to tell her how I really felt about her, even texting her to ask that we *talk* tonight. Okay, maybe bringing along the chick sitting next to me right now wasn't the savviest move I could have made. But making my way out of Kennedy's friend zone and into her heart's end zone was shaping up to be a fuck of a lot harder than I'd realized. And it didn't fucking help that her attention was being intercepted like an overthrown ball by other men every time it felt like something deep was about to go down between us.

Maybe there's a playbook you could study.

Surely, she was in a hurry to leave this place too. I mean,

that whatever it was—a *moment* I guess you could call it—was unlike anything we'd ever shared before.

But as I looked at her across the table, I wondered if it had all been a dream, and sadly, I'd woken up.

"There's no way you're not sleeping together! No way!" Declan's date, Dominique, exclaimed. She leaned over him so she had a better view of the two people shaking their heads and dispelling every romantic theory in her Brazilian—or was it Colombian—mind.

Andrew held his hands up. "God's honest truth. Kennedy will tell you—she thinks I'm a 'D-list kisser.' Those were the exact words she used. Didn't you, Buttercup?"

That got my attention.

Thirty minutes ago, I'd shaken Andrew's hand after conceding that even though his little performance with Kennedy had been more convincing than some of the soft porn I'd watched as a teenager, he was still a good dude and worthy of being Kennedy's friend.

Now, I was beginning to rethink whether or not I wanted to break his perfectly symmetrical face.

Dominique smacked the table with her hand. "What! Now you *must* explain!"

I shot Declan a look that I wanted him to interpret as: "For the love of fuck, shut her the fuck up!"

He merely hiked a shoulder in return. The bastard didn't even bother trying to look apologetic.

My fist clenched and unclenched repeatedly under the table, and I ordered another round of drinks.

Jordan and his wife, Sarah, were also following along with Dominique's interrogation, but they were more interested in the duo's musical talents than if they were getting it on in the backroom between sets.

Then there was my *date*, as Kennedy so aptly reminded me, Annie.

I'd barely acknowledged her all night because the instant I laid eyes on the goddess that was Kennedy Quinn dressed in a snug red dress that had lust written all over it and singing like an angel, I'd been spellbound.

Andrew propped his arm over the back of Kennedy's chair. "Do you want to assassinate my rep for everyone to hear, or do you want me to do the honors?"

She rolled her eyes and let out a breathy laugh. It wasn't her usual giggle; she sounded tired. Stressed.

"Go ahead, Drew . . . you tell it better than I do."

Andrew, or *Drew*, looked down at her with the same adoring expression he'd used all night, but she didn't meet his eyes. Her arms rested across her stomach, and she raised a hand to inspect her fingernails. His gaze lingered, and he squeezed her shoulder with his hand.

Kennedy looked up, and I think he mouthed, "You okay?"

Dominique's incessant chatter had everyone preoccupied, but I saw the exchange between Andrew and Kennedy, and it took every drop of willpower I owned not to haul her little ass over the table and set her down on my lap where I could wrap her in my arms and make sure she was indeed okay.

Soon—be patient.

Annie followed my line of sight and started watching my best friend with the same intensity that I was.

I swore I could see the wheels turning in that head of crazy blonde corkscrews.

Please don't ask about Kennedy.

Dominique made another plea to hear the fucking kissing story.

Andrew shook his head half-heartedly. "The abridged version goes: we met at a party about a year and a half ago, I was super drunk, she wasn't. I kissed her, and she says my tongue went up her nose, and she called me a 'D-list kisser.'" Andrew shrugged.

Kennedy wrinkled her nose and nodded to confirm, and a chorus of laughter broke out around the table. I even managed to crack a smile.

But Christ, she's known him that long and never mentioned him?

"You guys never tried again?" Dominque asked pleasantly enough, but I still didn't like it. Her question was insulting and unwarranted, even if it wasn't directed at me. What was she thinking?

Calm down, big guy.

Both Andrew and Kennedy shook their heads with the same degree of decisiveness.

Andrew was the one to answer, his tone solemn for the first time tonight. "The chemistry we share on the stage is rare, so why would we risk fucking it up?"

The warning of his last several words rang in my ears.

My chest tightened, and I rubbed my knuckles across my left pec.

"What about the two of you?" The airy voice beside me suddenly sounded like a blow horn attached to my eardrum.

Mother fuck.

I turned to see Annie's doe eyes looking back and forth between Kennedy and me, her question crystal clear.

Kennedy blinked several times, and her face paled. She looked like she was going to be sick.

At least she didn't break into song and dance about all the reasons why you've never been more than friends.

She'd warned me not to bring a date tonight, and like an arrogant ass, I'd done it anyway. I needed to shut it down quick.

I directed all my attention at Annie, hoping I could get

her to back off. "As I explained earlier, Kennedy and I are *just friends.* There's no history there. She has no idea what an exceptional kisser I am."

Everyone laughed.

If Andrew was going to use charm—so would I.

High on finding my rhythm in the conversation, I opened my mouth and inserted a shit-covered Frodo foot inside. "But in a few hours, you'll be able to tell the world just how gifted my tongue is."

An excited and sultry smile crept up Annie's face.

This time, no one laughed.

What. The. Fuck.

Whatthefuck did I just say?

I turned to Kennedy like I was facing a firing squad, which would have been less painful than seeing the sheer look of fury and horror on her face.

I deserve trial by combat.

Her bottom lip trembled, and she caught it between her teeth. I swear I saw flames in her eyes—and not the good kind that accompany passion and desire.

Nope, Kennedy's eyes wanted to burn down the bar with me trapped inside and the city's water supply turned off.

She pushed back her chair and got to her feet, wobbling slightly before Andrew steadied her. He was right there at her side with his piano-perfect hands all over her.

Of course he was.

"It was really nice meeting all of you," she said quietly. "Thank you so much for coming. We really appreciate it. I'm exhausted, though, and I need to get going."

Kennedy made eye contact with everyone at the table, including Annie—everyone but me, that is.

Andrew shook everyone's hand, and when he shook mine, he gave me a look that said, "Nice, asshole."

Then she was gone.

My heart hung heavy in my chest, and a tremendous sense of emptiness echoed through my body. I wished for a black hole to open beneath me and draw me into oblivion.

When the three ladies excused themselves to the restroom, I finally felt as though I could let my guard down.

I buried my face in my hands with a groan of self-disgust.

"What the fuck, dude?" Declan cuffed the back of my head.

In twenty-four hours, he'd become a proud member of the Kennedy Quinn Fan Club.

I ran my hands through my hair, tempted to pull it all out if it would divert the nagging stab of pain in the center of my torso.

"I don't know why I just said that—wait, yes I do—because I was trying to get Annie to stop asking questions." I slammed my fist on the table. Fortunately, the bar was too loud for anyone but my two-member jury to notice. "Fuck me."

Jordan used a hand to smother a laugh. "You mean *Anna*, bro?"

Christ. It was an *A* name—close enough.

"Do you love her?" Jordan asked.

"Who? *Anna*? Jesus fuck! Fuck no!"

Okay—maybe that had been a little harsh.

Jordan's expression confirmed he found me as appalling as I did. "Not Anna, numbnuts—Kennedy. The way you look at her is kind of pathetic—either do something about it or inquire about getting your balls back."

Declan flicked a coaster at me. "That's what I've been telling him since last night."

My hands scrubbed my face as though they could erase the last fifteen minutes. "Yeah, assholes, I know. What do you think I'm trying to do?"

Jordan emptied his beer glass before giving me his two cents. "If you want some advice from a happily married man, maybe start by not bringing a date to meet the woman you love. And I'd recommend you stop insinuating you're going to go down on another chick."

I needed alcohol.

Large, vast amounts of alcohol.

Jordan moved his chair closer to the table and lowered his voice. "Let's stop talking about your supersized fuckup for a minute. So what's the story with your girl and Sterling?"

Bile encroached my throat. Not because he'd referred to Kennedy as my girl, but because I wasn't sure if rehashing my history with Sterling was helpful at this point. Then again, these guys were going to be my new teammates and quite possibly the peacekeepers in the locker room. It wasn't something I'd be discussing with everyone on the team—most had loyalty to Sterling. I had no intention of dividing the locker room, but for the few I considered true friends, I guess I wanted them to understand where my undying hatred for our star QB derived from.

My eyes drifted in the direction of the restroom.

Declan answered my silent question. "They're heading over to the dance floor."

Nodding, I cleared my throat. "It wasn't enough that he cheated on her and made their breakup so public, he couldn't even rein in his new chick when she went after Kennedy on social media. She spun the whole thing, claiming that it was Kennedy who cheated with none other than yours truly. She went from being college football's darling to . . . well, you know what's been said."

"Yeah, but anyone close to the situation knows the truth," Declan offered.

Jordan held up a hand, hitting pause on the conversation.

"Hang on—why do you call her Quinn, but refer to her as Kennedy?"

I smiled to myself, remembering the first time *Quinn* rolled off my tongue. "It started as a joke, and it just stuck. She's always been and always will be Quinn to me."

"Got it. Continue."

"Her fucking parents believed that lying bitch over their own daughter." My words sparked memories of Kennedy calling me in tears, her words unintelligible, but her pain obvious.

My hands balled into fists, and I forced down the pit of suppressed anger I'd tapped into. How her parents could surmise that Kennedy choosing a liberal lifestyle was somehow synonymous with being an immoral cheater was beyond me.

"Jesus, that's rough." Jordan rubbed the back of his neck and let out a low whistle.

Declan rocked back in his chair. "And to think that even with all that bullshit, she still didn't ditch your ass. She stayed friends with you even when the optics were not in her favor. She's got one hell of a backbone, either that . . . or . . ." He hesitated and took a gulp of beer. "Or your feelings aren't quite as unrequited as you think."

I was relishing in the possibility that Declan may be on to something when Jordan leaned into the table.

"But, dude . . . Franco? You broke his fucking jaw and got suspended for three games."

"Franco deserved more than a broken face after what he said," I growled, my mind flashing to images of the loose-lipped cornerback getting in my face after I'd burned him on several routes. I'd listened to him chirp for nearly four quarters without so much as a "Fuck off," but when he dropped Kennedy's name, I saw red—and then he bled red.

Not much is secret in the NFL, and once word spread that Kennedy and I were indeed close, though not as intimately as some believed, opponents saw it as a way to rattle me and fuck up my game. Especially if they were Team Sterling. Franco and Sterling had been teammates at Boston College, which apparently made him Sterling's bitch.

Declan placed a supportive hand on my shoulder. "Dude, you know there's going to be shit said on the turf. We can manage the locker room—I seriously don't anticipate any issues there. But out there on the field, don't get baited, man. We're going to need you this season."

I knew Declan was right, and Kennedy expected me to heed his advice. After a moment of silence, I nodded in agreement.

It felt good to get everything off my chest. The only people I'd ever discussed it with until now were my mother, sister, and my agent. Of course, my mom and sister wanted to claw the eyes out of anyone who dared breathe a negative word about Kennedy, and Trek had a soft spot for Kennedy too.

Jordan sat up, an almost business-like expression on his face. "So, what's the play call?

"Play call?" I questioned.

"Yeah, how you're going to advance toward the end zone. Because there's nothing worse than having a lovesick, blue-balled teammate, and training camp is about to start."

"I have no fucking play call," I admitted, realizing that as confident as I was in my abilities to do the tangible, it was the sentimental and soul-stirring moments in between that gave me pause and made me question my adequacy.

Declan grinned. "How about you start by going to her apartment right now and apologizing for being the world's biggest douche?"

Jordan raised his glass in agreement. "Hear! Hear!"

I ran my hands down my jeans. The last time I'd been this nervous was the night of the draft. That night had changed my life forever; maybe tonight would too. "Any chance you can cover for me so I can get out of here? I know it's a real dick move to leave Anna."

Got it right that time.

Jordan waved his hand toward the door. "Go. Anna's with us—don't worry about it."

"What are you going to tell her?" I asked, not sure I really cared, but also hating being "that guy."

"We'll tell her the truth—something really important came up and you had to leave." Declan was quickly mastering the role of BFF number two. He'd never have a shot at spot number one—that one was indefinitely claimed by Kennedy.

"I owe you one, both of you." I stood up, opened my wallet, and tossed some large bills on the table—more than enough to cover for everyone's drinks and tips. "Wish me luck."

"Don't fuck it up," they said in unison.

9

KENNEDY

What. A. Night.

Andrew and I had been *ah-mazing.*

The crowd had loved us.

We'd been rebooked.

Something had happened with Sawyer.

Then he'd proceeded to seduce his date right in front of me.

I groaned and covered my head with a pillow. "Eff my life."

Why was I allowing Sawyer and his predictable antics to affect me like this? I had a pivotal meeting with William coming up, and Sawyer's drama was only sidetracking me.

There was a courtesy knock on the door, and then it swung open. I tossed the pillow aside to see Andrew stalking into my bedroom.

Thank the gods he was fully dressed.

Between vocal foreplay with him and whatever-it-was with Sawyer, my hormones were hosting a rave, and my hand wore the glow-in-the-dark stamp to prove I was attending. I wondered how long Andrew planned to infringe upon my sulk fest because the likelihood that I'd need to use my battery-operated lover was increasing with every whiff of the heady pheromones he was giving off.

"What's up, Buttercup?" He landed on my bed, and I bounced a couple of inches.

He appeared to be in a gregarious mood.

I groaned again. "Not much. Just trying to figure out what to do with my life. You know, nothing too serious." I sounded as flatlined as my sex life.

Andrew folded his hands on his chest and looked up at the ceiling. "When you've figured out what you're doing with your life, can you figure out what I'm doing with mine and get back to me?"

I rolled my head over my pillow and grinned at him. "Sure thing, darlin'. I'll have my people call your people."

Andrew reached over with one hand and patted the top of my head. "Darlin', huh? Just how much did you have to drink tonight, Miss Kennedy?" He added a heavy Southern accent to the "Miss Kennedy" part.

"Not enough, that's for sure."

"I'm only asking because your accent only comes out—"

"I know! I know!" I shook off his placating hand and bared my teeth in a goofy snarl.

Andrew sat up, the right side of his mouth hooking upward. "I bet I know who else says that about you." He waggled his eyebrows. Then he leaned over me, his voice growing huskier. "Maybe the tall, dark, and handsome football player who was grabbing your ass and eye-fucking you tonight."

I braced his chest with my hands. A slight whimper might have escaped me when I felt the hard dips and valleys between his sculpted muscles.

"Shut up before I throat-punch you," I gritted through my teeth. "You won't be any good to me with a busted windpipe."

Andrew collapsed beside me, and the bed shook. With all my might, I brought the pillow crashing down on his face, but he only laughed harder and snatched it away.

"What's gotten into my sweet girl?" he teased.

My "think before you speak" mode turned off, I replied, "Your sweet girl is confused, irritated, and sexually frustrated."

Silence fell across the room. Andrew's mouth opened like he was about to speak, and then he snapped it shut. When our mutual laughter died, he said, "If that's all it is, Buttercup, I'm sure I could help you out."

I wasn't sure if he was kidding or not, and I didn't dare make eye contact and find out.

"Is Brooke coming home tonight?" I asked.

The bed shifted, and Andrew propped his head up with his hand. His eyes roamed over my body before he answered, "You want *Brooke* to help you?"

In his dreams.

"No, Drew. I'm just wondering if Brooke is coming home tonight in general. I'm just asking a simple question, perv."

"Well, in that case, I don't know—she texted me that she met someone, and she may or may not be bringing him back here."

"Was she sending us a warning or something? Are we supposed to make ourselves scarce so they can have wild monkey sex throughout the entire apartment, leaving their bodily fluids everywhere?"

Was that jealousy in my voice?

"Jesus, Kennedy, you really do need to get laid." Andrew still looked amused when he asked, "Is this all about Sawyer?"

"No. Yes. Maybe. I don't know. Don't ask questions I can't answer."

Andrew laughed as he slid off the bed, grabbing my hand along the way. "Take it from me—the fastest way to kill your libido is to get tanked. We were fucking stars tonight and there is a bottle of vodka with our name on it."

With little reluctance, I followed him to the living room.

"Don't think I'm going to let you kiss me. You kiss like shit when you're drunk."

Andrew chuckled. "Yeah, so I've been told."

"You suck at this," I complained many shots later.

"You try doing this with your fingers when you're hammered," Andrew sassed back.

"I'm sure I could do a better job than you're doing," I quipped.

"Fine. Let's switch places."

"No. We can do this. We're capable adults—just try harder."

"This is embarrassing," he muttered.

"Relax. It's easier if you don't overthink it."

"I went to fucking Juilliard, Kennedy. I should be able to play *Rock Band* with my eyes closed and one hand tied behind my back."

Andrew's bravado and the indignant expression on his face had me on my knees in a total fit of giggles. He dug his toes into my ribs just as our door buzzed.

Our laughter dried up, and we looked at each other.

"Did you order takeout?" Andrew asked.

"Nope."

Andrew scaled the back of the couch to answer the door rather than take the simplest route and walk around it. He slapped the switch and called into the intercom, "Yo."

There was a slight crackle followed by "Andrew? Hey, it's Sawyer. Is Kennedy home?"

Without asking whether I wanted company, Andrew replied, "Sure, man, come on up."

Bro code at its finest.

What about roommate code?

Andrew climbed back over the couch, stretched out his long, pajama-clad legs, and rested his bare feet on the coffee table. "This is going to be interesting."

"Why did you let him up?" I spat.

He pretended to flick invisible lint off his naked shoulder. He'd lost his shirt somewhere between "Billy Jean" and "Black Hole Sun."

"Because you, my beautiful little friend, need an orgasm or five tonight. I've never seen you in such rare form."

"I'm too drunk for this! You have no idea what you just did, Drew!"

"Why are you stage-whispering at me? We're the only two here." He held his arms up and looked around the apartment to prove his point. "Well . . . for the next thirty seconds, that is," he added with a Machiavellian smirk.

"You are no longer my favorite roommate."

"Hey, I'm just trying to get you laid. I told you I'd help, but if you want to keep our status as is, I guess Sawyer isn't a bad second option."

I growled at him and went to the door.

Fueled by liquid courage and roommate betrayal, and still unable to get images of Sawyer using his tongue on his date out of my head, I threw the door open just as Sawyer raised his hand to knock.

Whoa.

Sawyer looked . . . blurry.

"What are you doing here?" I snapped. I looked at my empty wrist. "Doesn't your tongue have someplace to be?"

"Watch is on your other wrist, Quinn."

Damn, Sawyer.

"Can I come in?" he asked, his expression set on regretful, his hands shoved in his pockets.

Why not? If I was going to tell him what a manslut he was, I didn't need my neighbors bearing witness.

I moved back and held my arm out to welcome him in.

Sawyer stepped forward, and his eyes scanned the living room. The television was paused on "Sweet Emotion" and the *Rock Band* guitar and drums were on the floor. A bag of pretzels and an industrial-size container of Sour Patch Kids sat next to a nearly empty bottle of vodka, half a jug of pineapple juice, and a couple of red plastic cups.

Because Andrew and I were classy like that.

Sawyer spun around to face me. Now he looked giddy.

He also looked so innocent with his hands still in his pockets that the ice around my cold, dead heart started to melt.

He grinned like the Cheshire Cat. "You're seriously drunk."

"No, I'm not," I lied.

"Oh yes, you are—you are so wasted, Chuckles." Sawyer moved closer to me. I could smell his mint gum. I guess he wanted to freshen his breath after doing God only knows with his tongue.

He lifted his chin and winked at me, and I didn't know if I wanted to slap him or wrap my legs around his head.

"Am not," I repeated with defiance.

"Are too," Andrew offered.

I gave him a death glare. "A throat-punch is still on the table, Drew."

Sawyer laughed, and my eyes traveled back to him, the subtle motion causing a wave of dizziness to wash over me.

Sounding fascinated, Andrew asked, "Tell me, Sawyer, did you know about this dark side of Kennedy?"

Sawyer was unable to hide his approval. "Oh, you mean her *inner tiger*? Yeah, I've seen it come out a few times when she's blitzed."

"Why are you boys talking about me like I'm not here?" I had an urge to stomp my foot, but I was an adult.

A drunk adult—but still an adult.

"*Boys?*" they said in unison.

Andrew stood up from the couch and rested a hand on Sawyer's shoulder. "I'll leave you to it, man. Good meeting you—hope to see you again. Thanks again for coming tonight and bringing your posse—we appreciate it."

Sawyer replied, but I didn't pay attention to what he said. I was too busy shaking off my traitorous roommate as he ruffled my hair. "Good night, Buttercup. You were a fucking dream on the mic tonight."

"Night, Judas," I shot back.

When the bedroom door clicked, Sawyer took Andrew's vacant spot on the couch. He looked as handsome now as he had in the hallway at the bar, and here I stood in his Ohio State hoodie, my hair in a messy bun, and reeking of vodka with Sour Patch Kids debris on my lips. He waved me over, and I walked the few steps to stand in front of him, my arms crossed with rebellious intent.

My anger or whatever it was—jealousy, perhaps—quickly faded the longer he smiled at me like I'd hung the moon.

"How drunk are you?"

I doubled down. "I'm not drunk."

"Quinn."

"Sawyer."

"How drunk are you, Quinn?" he asked again, his soothing voice unchanging.

"I'm a lot drunk, Sawyer."

His smile grew even bigger. "I thought so."

"Are we still going to talk about the United States?" The words were out before I could stop myself.

He patted the couch cushion beside him. I refused his invite, and he did it again.

"Quinn, just sit down. You can still be mad at me if you want, just do it sitting down."

So that's exactly what I did.

Sawyer studied my face; I could tell he was trying to suppress a laugh.

My eyes narrowed. "What's so funny?"

"You. You're adorable when you're mad at me."

I rolled my eyes.

He reached over and coiled one of the hoodie strings around his index finger. "When did you steal this anyway, little klepto?"

My cheeks turned OSU red. "Super Bowl weekend," I admitted.

"It looks better on you."

I didn't look up, but I could hear the smile in his voice.

When I didn't react, he dropped the string and peeled one of my arms away from my stomach so he could hold my hand.

"I'm sorry about what I said at the bar," he said with a heartfelt sigh.

He was sincere, and for some reason, that almost made it worse.

I fought back the tears forming behind my lids. "You don't owe me an apology. You were on a date. You can talk to your date about your cunnilingus skills all you want—that's your prerogative."

Cunnilingus? Good grief, Kennedy.

"Did you just say cunnilingus?" Sawyer choked out a laugh.

"Shut up, Sawyer."

"Oh, Quinn, come here." Continuing to laugh at my embarrassed expense, Sawyer snaked his arms around my waist and hauled me onto his lap, positioning me sideways. "I'm sorry," he reiterated, forcing the corners of his mouth into a straight line.

"So you say," I deadpanned.

"Wow, you're really going to make me work for this, aren't you?" His eyes twinkled with a cockiness I found addicting. He leaned in. "Keep being a brat," he breathed against my ear. "You have no idea how sexy your angry face is."

I typically worked really hard to ensure that Sawyer never realized how his shameless flirting affected me the same way it did every other woman, but tonight I was failing myself in spades.

Feeling like a total loser for being so weak and pathetic over him, I laid my cheek on his shoulder with a deep sigh. *"Sawyer."*

He held me tighter and rested his chin on top of my head. "Yeah, baby?"

My eyes pressed shut, and my whole body relaxed into him.

Baby.

He didn't use the endearment often, but when he did, for those few moments I felt like I was his and he was mine. That we truly belonged to each other in every sense.

"I drank too much vodka," I said, because I couldn't tell him what I was really thinking.

"Hmmm . . . ya think?"

The booze kept on talking. "Yes, and I really, really want to use my vibrator, but I think I'm too drunk now."

Sawyer's entire body went rigid, and he gently pushed me away from where I'd been snuggled so nicely. The absence of his body pressed against mine made me cry on the inside.

"Jesus Christ, Quinn." He sounded breathless.

Who am I, and what happened to sweet Buttercup?

Inebriated Buttercup is in charge now, and she's horny.

Because my filter was clearly impaired, I kept talking. "Andrew offered to help, but I was really looking forward to just handling it myself, know what I mean? Oh right, you don't— because you *never* have to handle that kind of thing by yourself, do you?"

His Adam's apple bobbed, but no words came out.

I buried my face in his shirt. "Blah. Forget I said that. I'm just drunk and moody."

"We're both tired. Let's get some sleep and talk tomorrow when you're not drunk and I'm not in the doghouse."

I removed my face from its hiding spot and looked up at him. His jaw was just inches from my lips, and thoughts of kissing him spurred on my mind and heart. "You're not in the doghouse."

Sawyer's chin dropped, and he held my gaze. "So you say," he drawled.

He so loved stealing my lines and throwing them back at me.

"Come on, let's get into bed and go to sleep, before you really do turn into Chuckles. You're too drunk to take advantage of me, so I guess we can share a bed tonight."

We'd shared a bed more times than I could recall, so I pinched his pec in retaliation for the jest.

"Are you going to take me to brunch?" I asked, rubbing my hand over the spot where I'd just wounded him. It was hard enough that I'd probably left a mark.

He cradled the nape of my neck. His warm fingers brushed against my pulse in doing so, and I felt it all the way down to my core.

"Absolutely," he replied.

"I don't have to work until four; can we spend the day together?"

He pulled me against him, removing all space. "There's

nothing I'd rather do," he whispered as his lips lingered on my forehead.

I swallowed the golf-ball-size lump of yearning and desire in my throat. "Can you wait out here for like ten minutes so I can use my—"

Sawyer's hand swiftly covered my mouth. "Don't finish that sentence. The answer is a hard no."

I tried to talk, but he muffled my voice again, and I giggled instead. His body shook beneath me. At least he was laughing too.

"If I take my hand away, are you going to stop talking about rubbing one out?"

I laughed so hard I snorted in his hand, and then I shrugged playfully.

"Not good enough." His free hand tickled my waist, and I screeched.

Using both hands, I pried his hand off my face. "Okay! Okay! I give! You win!"

Sawyer's head fell back against the couch, and he crushed me to him in a dramatic gesture. "Can we go to bed now? *Please,* woman?"

"Wait." I held up a finger. "There's something you should know."

Sawyer's head snapped back up, and he eyed my finger like an appetizer. He wrapped his hand around mine, brought my finger to his mouth, and nibbled at it. "Is this when you tell me I can't stay the night because you're married?"

"No, but if I spontaneously combust due to lack of orgasms, you're gonna feel real guilty."

He scoffed. "Highly unlikely—I'll take my chances." He kissed my finger, and then gave me a slight nudge off his lap. "Let's go, drunk girl."

10

SAWYER

"Keep your pants on, Quinn."

Words I thought I'd never hear myself say out loud.

She rolled her eyes and hooked her thumbs into the waistband of her yoga pants, notching them down enough to give me a glimpse of the boy shorts she wore underneath. She'd already tossed my OSU sweatshirt aside like a jilted ex in favor of the world's tiniest tank top.

"Dude, it's Africa hot in my bedroom," she declared. "Besides, you've seen me in less. My bikinis are more revealing."

She proceeded to defy me, and my hands wrapped around her wrists mid-shimmy.

"Not happening, Quinn."

I took it upon myself to rectify the situation and yanked her pants back up, causing her to yelp and glower at me.

"You're a disgrace to men everywhere."

I ushered her to the bed and tossed back the covers. "Mhmm."

She dragged herself across the bed on her hands and knees. "I'm not going to be able to sleep now, thanks to you," she shot over her shoulder, but the teasing grin did little to persuade me that she was truly angry.

"Not with that attitude, you're not."

She bit her bottom lip and for the moment, fell silent, even though I knew she was on the threshold of an epic drunken giggle fest.

She tumbled back into the plush bedding with a frustrated sigh. "I need an orgasm like Tom Brady needs to drink half his body weight in ounces of water per day."

Mother fuck, this girl.

I tucked my hands safely behind my head where I could fucking control them. "Are you done yet?"

Please God, let this be her last appeal—a man can only withstand so much.

"Fine, I'll stop now."

She curled into my side, and my self-restraint cracked. My arms dropped to encircle her, pulling her against me. "Well, come to think of it . . . I am curious about one thing . . ."

She yawned, nuzzling against my chest. "Oh yeah? What's that?"

"Why did Andrew offer to help you with your, uh, lady issue?"

"Really, Sawyer?" She sighed and blatantly rubbed her nose on my shirt. We were boogers-level comfortable with each other. "He was just kidding. It was a joke. After that one and only god-awful kiss, Andrew and I have never even come close to scratching each other's itch. Okay?"

Christ, this girl knew how to put fucked-up images in my head like she'd been paid to do so.

"You've known him for a while . . . how come you never mentioned him?"

I knew I was taking a risk in asking, but the fact that she'd kept Andrew a secret didn't sit right with me.

"I don't like you worrying about me . . . I knew if you knew I was hanging out with a guy, you'd assume the worst in him and think he had ulterior motives when he doesn't." Her fingertips danced along the crewneck of my T-shirt when she talked, making my skin tingle with anticipation. "And, Sawyer . . . I met him when your mom was going through her last round of chemo . . ."

My eyes had adjusted to the darkness of Kennedy's bedroom, and when I glanced down, I could see the outline of her slightly turned-up button nose as she kept her cheek pressed against my heart.

"Understood, but it's my job to worry about you. The same way I worry about my mom and Maddie," I replied. Then I bit my tongue before I said anything else that could give away my lovesick status. That'd have to wait until she was sober.

Was I in love with Kennedy Quinn?

Fuck yeah, I was.

"Did you have sex with that pretty girl tonight?"

Her fingers curled into my shirt. I didn't know if she realized she was doing it or if it was an involuntary reflex.

She'd never directly inquired about what I did or didn't do with women.

Tell her the truth, man—the whole truth.

"No, baby." One of my hands covered hers, and the other ran through her hair. "I left everyone at the bar, and I came right here. This is where I want to be."

She didn't say another word, but she snuggled in even closer than she was before.

One of my most rewarding pastimes was watching Kennedy sleep.

Most of the time when we were together, we preferred to sleep in the same bed, so I knew her sleeping habits as well as my own, including the fact that she was a fucking bed hog.

The morning after the piano bar fiasco, Kennedy was on

her back in the middle of the queen-size bed. Her arms were flung wide, her right one resting on me. Her hair was spread across her pillow, and her lips were slightly parted as she breathed rhythmically. It all made her look so pure and sweet.

I had a perfect view of her breathtaking face, and all I could do was stare at her.

Like I said—rewarding as fuck.

Sometime in the night, Kennedy had turned feral, and now I had run out of real estate on my side of the bed. I rolled her onto her side, moved up against her, and settled my arms around my little spoon.

Two more hours passed, but I enjoyed every moment of closeness with my girl. Eventually, though, I needed to take a piss. I hated leaving her, but if I didn't, there was going to be a situation.

I exited the bed as carefully as I could, and she didn't even flinch. I pulled my jeans over my boxer briefs, leaving on the undershirt I'd slept in. As I padded to the bathroom, I heard noise in what I assumed was the kitchen. Andrew was up, or maybe it was the other roommate. I think her name was Becky.

No, Brooke. Her name was Brooke.

After relieving myself and borrowing some mouthwash, I decided to go to the kitchen in search of water.

Andrew was spreading something on a bagel when I entered. "Yo. Mornin', man." He didn't seem surprised to see me.

"Morning," I replied.

"Coffee and bagels on the counter—have at it."

Andrew was all right.

He was also shirtless again, and I was starting to get a complex. I obviously needed to reconsider the effort I put in on ab day. This stud was sleeping in the room next to Kennedy's.

"How's Buttercup this morning?" he asked, taking a bite of his breakfast.

"She's still dead to the world." I grinned, thinking about her as I poured myself a cup of coffee. I used the *Hamilton* mug I'd gotten Kennedy, the one that said "Rise Up." When I gave it to her, she'd been in the thick of the Hunter and Melody saga. The gift had made her cry, but she'd claimed she loved it and that it was the only mug she'd ever drink out of again.

"Do you call her Buttercup because of *The Princess Bride*?"

Andrew would have laughed audibly, but his mouth was full of carbs. After he swallowed, he replied, "I'd never thought of that before, but no, I started calling her Buttercup because I was too drunk to remember her name when I first met her. She was wearing a bright yellow dress and was so sweet that all I could think of was Buttercup. I guess it stuck."

Looking down at my coffee, I wondered if it was the same dress she'd worn the first night I'd met her at the dive bar in Puerto Rico.

Wearing a bright yellow dress and sweet—sounds just like my girl.

My heart did that funky thing in my chest again, and I rubbed my knuckles at the spot. When I looked up, Andrew was watching me with a thoughtful expression.

He cleared his throat and continued to make eye contact. "Just so you know, Kennedy and I are just friends."

I had to laugh, and the way Andrew laughed with me told me he got the irony of it all.

"No worries, man," I said.

"What's so hilarious?" A raspy female voice carried through the kitchen as a striking blonde wearing a pink lace bra and men's boxers appeared.

This must be Brooke.

Brooke stopped short of the fridge when she spotted me. She sized me up like she was a team scout and I was back at the NFL Scouting Combine.

"Drew, I didn't know you were bi." Her eyes continued to rake up and down my body with undeniable scrutiny, and then she hitched one shoulder. "You've got decent taste, I'll give you that."

Leaving me speechless, Brooke opened the fridge door and snagged a bottle of water before pulling up the stool next to Andrew. I'd come in here for the same thing, and now here I was, the guest role in an awkward improv scene.

Andrew came to the rescue.

"Brooke, meet Sawyer. Sawyer, meet Brooke, the girl with no filter."

Brooke snapped her fingers and pointed at me. "Ah-ha! Kennedy's man! Didn't recognize you—not a football fan. Sorry, not sorry."

I opened my mouth, but she cut me off with a careless wave. "Don't even bother with that lame-ass 'we're just friends' bullshit. You're her man. So there, I said it. You can thank me later."

I wanted to spike my mug and break out in a touchdown dance, but instead, I nodded at the relationship whisperer. "It's nice to meet you, Brooke."

At that moment, a disheveled man looking a decade-plus older than Brooke walked up behind her as he slipped on a suit coat over his wrinkled dress shirt. He glanced down at Brooke's bottoms and grinned.

The new guy would be going home commando.

"I've got to get going, but how about dinner tonight?" he asked loud enough that everyone could hear.

Brooke never looked in his direction. "Sorry, I have plans. How about I text you later?" she said before taking a sip of water.

The guy's neck turned red. "Yeah. Sure. Did I give you my number?"

"Sure." Brooke took another sip.

She did not have his number, said the narrator.

Taking the hint, the guy gave a stiff single nod to Andrew, and then his curious gaze lingered on me. He opened his mouth to speak, but Brooke waved him away.

"Time to go," she said, her voice laced with warning.

Once the front door clicked shut, Brooke snatched the other half of Andrew's bagel and went to town on it.

"Did he suck in the sack?" Andrew asked.

Brooke sighed, finished chewing, and swallowed. "More like all he wanted was for me to *suck him* in the sack." She dusted the toasted poppy seeds from her hands. "Dude left me high and dry. I've been waiting for him to leave so I can finish myself off."

Damn—this was locker-room talk.

I wondered how Kennedy fit into these dynamics. Her roommates were anything but boring.

"Hey." A soft voice made my mouth go dry. I turned to see Kennedy standing in the archway separating the kitchen from the living room. I extended my empty hand, and she took the invitation, moving to my side and circling her arms around my waist.

Every part of my being woke up and acknowledged her presence.

"Thanks for taking care of me last night, friend."

Friend.

My heart took a nosedive.

Calm down, you haven't had the talk yet.

"Anytime." I kissed the top of her head and closed my eyes, praying the alcohol hadn't left her with amnesia.

We'd had some moments last night, right?

"I see you've met Brooke." Kennedy pulled away before I was ready to let her go.

"I did." But I had more pressing thoughts on my mind. "Ready to go to brunch?" I asked, wanting to get this party started.

"Ooh! Brunch! Count me in!" Brooke bounced off the stool, stretching her arms above her head. She had to hike the boxers back in place before she gave us all a show. Though based on my brief interaction with Brooke, I had a feeling this girl was comfortable enough in her own skin that it wouldn't faze her one bit to waltz around the apartment naked with an audience.

"We've got plans, Brookey," Andrew chimed in.

Brooke wrinkled her nose. "We do? What day is it? And when did you become the boss of me?"

Andrew slid off his stool, his arm enveloping Brooke's neck in a playful chokehold. "Today is the day you start taking social cues." He lowered his voice, but Kennedy and I could still hear just fine. "And you like it when I'm the boss—admit it."

Maybe Andrew and I would become BFFs too.

But only if he reserved those kinds of comments for Brooke. He wasn't allowed to talk to Kennedy like that, not even if he *was* kidding.

Defying the stereotype, the blonde gave us a knowing smile. "Ah, okay. I see how it is."

I looked at Kennedy. Her cheeks were bright pink, her lips had flushed cherry red, and I wanted to eat her right up.

But that would have to wait, because first—brunch.

We never made it to brunch.

After we'd both showered and I'd borrowed a pair of joggers and a T-shirt from Andrew, we left the apartment in search of food. We'd only reached the end of the block when Trek called. I was tempted to send him to voice mail, then text him to tell him I would get back to him soon, but with the results of my physical hanging in the balance, I knew I'd better pick up.

I stepped into the doorway of a closed storefront while Kennedy gave me privacy and went to check out the knock-off handbag vendor. I didn't care if she listened to my conversation, but she was always polite and respected my career. Any other girl I'd ever spent time with always took my being on the phone as an invitation to crawl all over me, rub her tits against me, and whisper in my free ear.

Fuck, am I glad to be done with that chapter of my life.

"Hey, Trek. What's up, man?" I answered.

Bypassing the usual "Hey, mate," Trek went right into business mode. "Jackson—glad I caught you."

"Yeah, about that . . . I'm kinda in the middle of something, can this wait till later?" I almost hated to ask, given the timing of everything, but the beautiful brunette holding the fake Fendi had my mind on anything but football.

"Sorry, not possible. Can you be at my place in say . . . an hour?" Trek's words poked holes in my daydream. Getting to Tribeca wouldn't be a problem. Tearing me apart from Kennedy right now was the obstacle.

"Jackson, we need to talk, face to face."

Trek Evans had been my agent since before the draft six years ago. The man was the consummate professional and always had my back, and I considered him a good friend. If Trek insisted we meet now, I knew he had a legitimate reason.

When I hung up, I told Kennedy that I had to cancel on her.

She looked up at me. The sun reflected in her eyes made them look as turquoise as the Caribbean waters that had surrounded us the first night we'd met.

"If Trek needs to talk to you in person, you need to go."

She pressed a kiss to my jaw. "The fate of the Cougars' fan base depends on you, and as a New Yorker, I know that's some serious business."

Reason #731 why Kennedy Quinn was the perfect woman.

Her dewy skin glowed, and I had to touch it. She didn't wear a drop of makeup; she didn't need it. I traced my fingers along her forehead and down the side of her face to tuck her hair behind her ears. All the sensations I'd felt last night at the bar watching her sing, holding her in the hallway, and curled around her while she slept came flooding back, and I found it hard to breathe.

"But I told you we'd spend the day together. I owe you brunch."

And so much more, I thought to myself. Acknowledging my unfulfilled promises out loud made me feel even worse.

Pedestrians pushed by, but neither of us made an effort to move. "I'm really sorry, Quinn." My voice was just above a whisper. "I promise to make it up to you. Once my contract is finalized, it'll be better."

Kennedy leaned up a second time. Before kissing my cheek, she whispered, "We've lived in separate states for three years and our friendship has survived just fine . . . it will now too. Go make your dreams come true, Tight End. You know I'll be right here waiting."

I cocked an eyebrow. "You will? Is that what you've been doing all this time?" I pressed, emboldened by the potential of her admission.

Her cheeks flushed. "You know what I mean."

I gripped her elbows. "Can I come by tonight?" When she hesitated to reply, I added, "I'll meet you at the diner when you get out, and then we can head back to your place. We still need to talk . . ."

She sawed at her bottom lip and something that gave the impression of guilt flickered in her eyes.

My heart was in my throat waiting for her response.

"I have an early meeting with William tomorrow." Her words sounded like an apology.

Realization dawned.

She had . . . priorities.

Same as you, so don't be an ass about it.

Maybe I didn't need to be an ass, but that didn't mean I had to enjoy being benched. My jaw spasmed. "Got it."

She tensed in my arms.

I was fucking this up.

I softened my next delivery. "Maybe another night this week, then?"

Her gaze rested on my chest, and she barely nodded.

I lifted her chin, so she had to meet my eyes. "We'll talk this week, okay?"

A faint smile formed on her face. "Okay. We'll talk this week."

The elevator door opened into Trek's penthouse, and I was hit with a visual reminder of why I was here. Not that I wanted a penthouse like Trek's, but I did want the contract that would allow me to have one if I ever decided that I did.

I knew the importance of securing your future with a lucrative contract as soon as you earned one. My father had been a top running back in college, destined for the NFL, until a car accident took his life when I was a toddler, and my mom was pregnant with Maddie.

At the age of nine, I began mowing lawns to help my mom pay the bills, and by fourteen, I had a worker's permit and a part-time job. Things got easier my junior year of high school once my mom finished her nursing degree. But it was the full scholarship that secured my place at a D1 college and my NFL rookie contract that paid for my mom's life-saving cancer treatment.

After I tore my ACL, no one wanted to give me a long-term deal, but Miami had been willing to keep me on a one-year contract to prove myself. I'd done that in convincing style, and now I was ready for and deserving of what the New York Cougars were offering.

I found the ever-tidy Brit in the kitchen dressed like he was ready for the boardroom. I looked down at the casual clothes I wore and chuckled to myself.

"Tea?" Trek asked as I entered.

"Only if you're adding copious amounts of sugar."

I leaned against the granite island, and Trek slid a glass bowl toward me. Then he offered me a steaming cup.

"Sugar cubes? Isn't this what you're supposed to leave out for Santa's reindeer?" I asked, inspecting the bowl before dropping one—make that three—into my tea.

"That shite will rot your teeth right out of your head."

"Then why the fuck do you have a bowl of it ready to go?"

"For prats like you." Trek grinned at me. His smooth features came alive when he did. "Come on, let's sit, shall we?"

Trek's penthouse was the most elaborate of any I'd ever been in—and I'd been in many. Between an illustrious football—the lame kind that involves a soccer ball—career in England and modeling, the dude had been set for life even before he'd taken rightful advantage of his dual citizenship and became one of the top professional sports agents in the United States.

He motioned to a white leather chair for me to sit, and he took the one across from me.

Normally, we talked business in his office, but even though Trek was dressed to the nines, he opted for the informal setting of the adjoined sitting room.

"Talk to me, Evans. Why the urgency? Did something come up in my physical?" I asked, an unsettled feeling crowding out the bliss I'd been experiencing just an hour ago.

On the ride over, I'd found myself vacillating between where I ranked in Kennedy's life and the potential cause of this meeting. I couldn't imagine failing my physical, but I also never imagined Kennedy would turn down an opportunity to hang out with me.

Holy ego, Batman.

Then again, you never know what a team will and won't find acceptable when a five-year deal loaded with hefty, guaranteed money is on the table.

Or what's going on in the fucking complex mind of a woman.

Trek rested his ankle on his opposite knee. "Your physical was spectacular. The orthopedist said your knee is tip-top, joints have zero wear and tear, and your pliability was off the charts. Of course, everything else . . . lab work etcetera, checked out as well." He inclined his head to the side, seemingly impressed by the news he was relaying.

I set my tea down and leaned forward. Resting my forearms on my thighs, I clasped my hands together. "All right. So then . . ." I opened my hands, palms up. "What's the meeting for?"

Trek straightened in his chair, set his own cup aside, and crossed his legs entirely, like the ridiculously formal bastard he could be.

"Sawyer." His expression was set to serious now, and he'd used my first name, so I was dialed in to every nuance of his body language.

"Ownership is absolutely thrilled at the prospect of you

joining the organization. They want you—they were ready to sign your contract the second the physician signed off."

"Okay, then why are the two of us meeting here and not at the clubhouse ready to sign some shit?"

He sighed, running his hand over the top of his meticulously groomed hair that hadn't moved since I'd walked in. "As I said, ownership is on board. Management, on the other hand . . . they want some safeguards in place, and they want them legally binding. Ergo, they're asking for an amendment to be made to the original contract."

I slumped back in my chair. I'd heard of others getting the same treatment heading into their first long-term deal. "Okay. What is it? Lay it on me. Performance incentives? Is that it?"

Trek's expression was almost pained. "They want to include a . . ." He cleared his throat.

This can't be good.

"A morality and ethics clause."

Come again?

"What the fuck is that?" I nearly spit the words out.

"Precisely—I'm getting there."

I needed Trek to make it there faster because I was close to telling New York to fuck off.

Kennedy would tell you to breathe and be rational right about now.

Kennedy also told me she didn't have time for me tonight.

Is that really what she said?

"Obviously, they are aware of the Franco incident and your three-game suspension from two seasons ago—amongst other things—and I want to point out that they did not hold that against you when negotiating your deal. I never would have stood for that. But it does make sense that they have some reservations given the terms of your deal."

I held my hand up. "Trek, you know what happened. You

know *why* it happened. And you also know I have no regrets. I'd do it again if the same situation presented itself."

"Sawyer." Trek's voice sounded a whole lot like he was channeling Kennedy. "You absolutely cannot take that approach with these people, otherwise the deal is as good as dead."

My mind was telling me that he was right, but my heart was telling my mind to get bent.

Trek continued, "Listen, mate, I know what that girl means to you. I know she's like family and—"

"*That girl?*" I growled, standing up. "*Like* family? Kennedy *is* my fucking family, *mate.*"

Then, as though I could hear Kennedy in my ear telling me to chill the fuck out, I took a deep breath and sat back down. It wasn't Trek's fault; he was just the messenger.

"I wasn't trying to be dismissive. Kennedy is a gem, and I know how much she means to you."

Nah, Trek. I don't think you do, bud.

"As your friend, I applaud how you've defended her. As your agent, it's my job to help you walk that fine line between loyalty and what lands you spending the rest of your life coaching high school football in your hometown." He paused, then landed the blow. "Is my understanding correct that your future plans do not involve Western Massachusetts and tracksuits?"

"I could think of worse fates."

"Don't be an arrogant bloke, Jackson."

My left leg bounced uncontrollably from the adrenaline sprinting through my body. I bit into my fist and raised my eyebrows, giving Trek the green light to put me in my place.

"Need I remind you that it was just this past February after the Super Bowl when you broke Sterling's former backup's nose? You're bloody fortunate that infraction didn't land you on the Commissioner's Exempt List and that the Cougars cut that guy before free agency. Even before Kennedy entered the picture, you were always a hair trigger away from unflattering headlines. Corrine Greene from your OSU days ring a bell?"

"No one ever told me coach's daughter was off-limits."

I knew I was testing the boundaries of Trek's patience, but I couldn't help myself. He'd riled me up, so he'd have to suffer the consequences.

"You were caught fucking her on her father's desk," he drawled as though he were bored. "*By her father*, no less."

I dropped my hands to my thighs. "Do you want to sit here all afternoon reminiscing about how many times I've fucked up, or do you want to talk about this fucking addendum?"

Trek stared at me, and the judgmental silence became too much to bear. A shred of composure grappled at me. "Why now?" I asked. "Why are they just bringing this up now? Why even go through the whole physical and everything else only to spring this on me now?"

"Steven Moran, the director of player personnel for the Cougars—I have it on good authority that he's on the hot seat. Ownership is ready to ax both him and Head Coach Daniels if the Cougars do not advance to the conference championship this season. A hotheaded tight end who lacks impulse control will only impede that vision. The last thing Moran wants to be dealing with is your ability to create unsavory headlines for the team."

Silence fell between us, and then Trek reached for a manila envelope I hadn't even noticed sitting on the end table and handed it to me.

"Please, mate, just read over the addendum and tell me if it's something you can agree to. If so, we'll get your deal signed today."

"Is . . ." I swallowed hard. "Is Coach Daniels having second thoughts about having me on the team?" Uncertainty and something like insecurity gnawed at me.

Trek's expression softened, and he shook his head. "No, I don't believe so. He's only spoken highly of you and expressed his eagerness to work with you. I'm sure it's unpleasant for him knowing that his job is on the line this season, but that's how the wondrous NFL system works, correct? Not 'what have you done for me lately,' but 'what can you do for me today.'"

I nodded in earnest; I knew the saying all too well. Just ask my surgically repaired knee that followed an Offensive Player of the Year season.

Just as I was about to take the envelope from his hand, he gripped it tighter. I looked up and met his eyes. "And just our luck—he doesn't have a daughter."

I shook my head, and it felt appropriate to crack a smile. "So Moran's the douche I need to keep an eye out for?" I felt the tension in my chest leaving as I breathed a little deeper.

Kudos to Trek for having the mind to have this conversation in person.

"I think your eyes could make better use of themselves by staying peeled for trouble, and when you find it coming for you, do us both a favor and head the opposite direction."

"Copy that."

I scoured the addendum, and it came up clean for any mention of Kennedy in particular. As long as I stayed out of trouble both on and off the field, everything would be splendid. But any misconduct on my part that brought unwanted negative attention to the team or resulted in league fines or suspensions, and the team reserved the right to unilaterally terminate my contract immediately.

"And what if Kennedy and I are together? As in *together*-together. What's Moran going to say about that?"

Trek cocked an eyebrow at me. "What kind of rubbish

friend and agent do you play me for, mate? I already told Moran he could piss off when it comes to your personal relationships. I suggest you put on your big-boy jockstrap, accept a copacetic relationship with Sterling, and don't let any blokes get under your skin. You and Kennedy together is bound to ruffle some feathers and cause quite a stir. Probably best if you keep it on the down low."

I felt the premature fine lines and wrinkles setting up shop on my forehead. "You mean . . . like she's my dirty little secret?"

Trek shook his head vehemently. "No, but you're a smart guy, Jackson. You know who to bring around her, who not to. Don't give the media something to talk about."

"Easier said than done, but I hear you."

"Do you require professional assistance?" He motioned over his shoulder toward the room I knew to be his home office with a smug grin. "I've got pages of contacts for therapists, anger management classes—you name the malady, and I've got a referral. You NFL players are a rather suspect and somewhat sordid lot if you're anything at all."

I chuckled at his good-natured ribbing, but knew there was truth behind those words. Trek had my back, no matter how scandalous the trouble was that would inevitably find me.

11

KENNEDY

On Monday, my mind was still reeling from my meeting with William when the Uber dropped me off in front of my apartment.

We'd spent hours poring over my résumé, dissecting it until William informed me that he had enough to get him started and I'd be hearing from him soon. In the meantime, I needed to reach out to his contacts to register for the lessons and classes that he felt were pertinent.

I punched in the code to the front door of the building and hitched my bag higher on my shoulder. It felt like it had gained about ten pounds since I'd arrived at William's office, a reminder that I still had hours of work ahead of me today. Trudging up the stairs to the second floor, I was lost in my thoughts when a voice startled me. "Hey, you."

"Jesus, Sawyer!" I jumped. "What the heck are you doing here?"

"Nice to see you too, brat."

That earned him a smile, and I came to a halt, dropping my bag at my feet.

Sawyer cocked an eyebrow at the audible *thud*.

I answered his unasked question. "Books. Paperwork. More books."

He bent over to snatch my bag off the floor with enviable ease.

I flashed him a cheesy grin in gratitude and moved past him to unlock the apartment door. "What are you doing here? How did you even get in here?"

"You ghosted me, so I texted Andrew and he gave me the code. It was safer to wait in here than on the sidewalk since every news source in New York City has my face splashed across it right now."

I pushed through the door, leaning back against it as I held it open. I was ready to scold Sawyer for being overly dramatic when the reality of his words hit me. "Wait—does this mean . . ."

I lunged at him, and he caught me in his arms as though I weighed as little as the bag he was still holding. He hoisted me higher, guiding my legs around his waist, and I finished my thought: "You're officially a Cougar?"

"Yes, I am. But more importantly, what does a guy have to do to get greeted like this every day?"

My cheeks flamed, and I buried my head in his shoulder to avoid both his question and stare. "I'm so proud of you, Sawyer."

His arms kept us pressed together as he breathed into my hair. "And your appointment with William?"

"Not important."

He dropped me back on my feet so fast I felt lightheaded. "Fuck that, Quinn."

"Fuck what, Sawyer?"

He grabbed my hand and kicked the door shut behind him in one smooth move. "I'm not the only one who had a big day today." Tugging me toward the couch, he continued with his touching tirade. "You're going to park your sweet ass right here and tell me all about it."

"Oh, I am?"

"Damn straight. You're going to tell me everything. No more omitting details, Quinn. No more making decisions for me. Tell me everything. I get to be the one to decide if it pisses me off and makes me worry about you or not. So if you're going to Chicago, just tell me now so I can figure out how to deal with it rationally."

He stopped abruptly, and my face collided with the rock wall that was Sawyer's back. No longer able to swallow the laughter, I let it out. He spun around and snared me in his arms before falling back onto the couch, bringing me down on top of him. Our eyes met, and I was relieved to see the humor there, and then he was grinning back at me.

"You're too much," I managed as he stroked my hair.

Our mutual laughter gradually subsided, and Sawyer's hands shifted to frame my face in a possessive, almost desperate hold. His eyes locked on mine, paralyzing my thoughts. His breath stuttered as anticipation tightened the air between us. "You're too perfect."

"Sawyer," I sighed.

"Quinn."

All thoughts of discussing either of our big days vanished.

The tip of my tongue trailed along the seam of my lips, and Sawyer's gaze lowered to my mouth. Our hearts thundered in sync as he lifted his head, bringing us closer. My eyes fluttered closed, and I awaited the first taste of my best friend.

"Date me."

What?

My eyes snapped open, and I shoved off Sawyer, but damn him and his Terminator physique, the guy didn't even budge. With my feet on the ground, I planted my hands on my hips and glared at him as he hesitantly righted himself on the couch.

"Don't say those things, Sawyer! It's not funny!"

As though he couldn't care less about what I'd just said, he chuckled and gripped the backs of my thighs, pulling me into the gap between his spread legs.

"Quinn, I didn't say it to be funny. What do you think I've been wanting to talk about? Did you forget we were going to talk about the United States?" He winked at me, and I pushed his shoulders away. Again, he didn't budge. Again, I cursed the untimely use of his brute strength.

He has a point.

Of course he did. And *of course,* I'd had at least a ghost of an idea of what our "talk" would entail—but either I'd been in denial or too caught up in the next steps of my career to consider the prospective developments of that talk. Hearing the actual words coming out of Sawyer's mouth—hearing him use the word "date"—well, it felt a bit apocalyptic if I'm being honest.

"Is this Armageddon?"

"No, baby. It's not."

"Huh."

"Huh?"

I flopped onto the couch cushion beside Sawyer. "Yeah, *huh.*"

I stared straight ahead at the coffee table, a state of numbness taking over my body.

Sawyer tucked me into his side and leaned back. It felt like old times.

Just a platonic embrace.

He leaned in and nuzzled his nose against my hair, and then he feathered tiny kisses down my temple and cheek, pausing when he reached the corner of my mouth.

"Date me, Quinn," he whispered, his lips now dangerously close to mine.

"You're insane."

His mouth curled into a devilish grin. "Maybe."

"No maybes about it—stone-cold facts."

"I didn't hear you say *no*."

I sighed and scooted back as far as he'd let me. I needed a clear view of Sawyer's face while we talked.

"Why? Why do you want to date me, Sawyer?"

"We belong together," he answered with an absurd amount of confidence. "I've told you before. We're kismet. Written in the stars, whatever you want to call it. It's you and me. You're mine. I'm yours. But I know I have a lot to prove, so date me. Let me *woo* you. Even if you do end up in Chicago. I don't care anymore; we'll figure it out. I make a fuckton of money and I'll spend every penny of it flying back and forth to take you on dates if that's what will convince you that this"—he floated a finger back and forth between us—"we're endgame, Quinn."

Whoa. That's a lot to unpack.

Sawyer's words cascaded over me in a tidal wave of declaration and intent. He was right about one thing—he'd expressed these sentiments in the past, but they'd always been filtered through an overlay of banter, and I'd stashed them under an umbrella of benign flirting.

But this felt different—Sawyer was different.

The staggering ambition and certainty rolling off him right now were enough to put my heart on notice and to make my mind question everything.

"Why now?"

One corner of Sawyer's mouth hooked upward as he pulled me back to him. When we were close enough that I had to tilt my head back to find his eyes, he cupped my face with his hands. His palms were damp, and his fingers trembled just slightly, suggesting that beneath the bravado at least a part of him was as tentative as me.

"I'm here now."

I winced. "So I'm a matter of convenience?"

Sawyer's ears turned red. "That's not what I said."

True—but he'd have to say more. I could wait.

When he realized my intentions, he continued, "I'm here for *you*, Quinn."

"You're here because you play for the Cougars."

He cocked his head and pressed his lids closed, then sucked in a composing breath. His fingers felt rigid against my skin now. When his eyes opened, a forced calmness displayed on his face. "I'm a Cougar because *you're* here."

My eyes narrowed. I wasn't quite following, but after a lengthy silence it was evident that Sawyer wasn't about to offer anything more unless specifically requested.

The question that felt too big to ask yet too big to ignore hung on the tip of my tongue until I couldn't keep it in any longer.

"Why me?"

My essential inquiry seemed to appease Sawyer, and an arresting smile bested his once restrained expression. His forehead dropped to mine. "Because there's only you. You're the only one my heart recognizes. That's how I know I'll figure out whatever the fuck it is that I need to figure out to make this work."

My heart felt on the brink of combustion from an overdose of emotions. I wasn't sure how much more of this I could take.

He was saying everything a girl could want to hear, but I was under no illusions; Sawyer and I had *reasons* with an *s* for putting boundaries on our relationship, and the thought of throwing caution to the wind had me wishing I had a fairy godmother to tell me what to do.

But I didn't have a fairy godmother, so Brooke was the next girl up.

"I need to think about it."

"What?"

He recoiled. The wake of his touch left me feeling vulnerable and abandoned, so I did what felt instinctive—I fled.

I rose to my feet again and began pacing the room in deliberate strides. I tucked my hair behind my ears. Brooke would be home soon; I'd talk to her then.

"*Think*, Sawyer. I know, it's a foreign concept when it comes to you and women. I realize you're not used to women stopping to process an actual thought before jumping into bed with you, but I think you know me better than that."

"Wait just a second, Quinn."

The tone of his voice had me faltering in my steps, and I paused my tour of the living room.

Here we have an incredibly hot, fertile man in his natural habitat, and he's been turned down by the opposite sex for the first time in his life.

"First of all, don't be mean, baby."

I crossed my arms over my stomach. "Fine. Consider my claws retracted."

"Second of all, were you or were you not just about to let me kiss you before I brought up the word *date*?"

As though I wasn't the OG of our absolutely-no-friends-with-benefits rule, I shrugged. "It would have been just a kiss."

Sawyer's jaw dropped open. "Just. A. Kiss? Are you for fucking real?" He buried his face in his hands. "I *do not* understand women."

That makes two of us right now, friend.

Moving like his body was made of lead, Sawyer stood, ran a hand through his hair, and looked around as though his world had been rocked so hard, he was no longer sure of his surroundings.

"I don't get it, Quinn. I mean—I'm fine with you taking time to think about it—cool, fine, whatever. But what I don't get is your reaction—your reaction the other night when William thought I was your boyfriend, or your reaction now as though dating me is the equivalent of getting a root canal by Stevie Wonder with no sedation on your birthday."

Any other time, Sawyer's colorful verbiage would have had me doubled over in laughter, but not today. The hurt that shone in his eyes stirred the guilt I'd been feeling since I'd reflected on my immature response to William on Saturday night. I was certain that by the time I'd finished ruminating over our current conversation I'd be equally as disappointed in myself. But that's the thing about fears and insecurities. The meanings of those words become contradictory when you allow them to take hold and their inflexible grip lures you into a false sense of control.

I can't lose you too, Sawyer.

Tears stung my eyes, but I refused to let them fall. "I don't know what you want me to say."

"The truth."

"Sawyer . . . I . . ." A shudder moved through me, and I couldn't translate my thoughts into words.

He held a hand up. "You know what, Quinn? Never mind."

"No, Sawyer—just give me a minute to collect my thoughts. This isn't how I thought today was going to go when I saw you waiting outside my door. I need a minute."

He shook his head. "You don't owe me an explanation, and besides, I think I already know the answer."

Do you really? Maybe part of the answer . . . but not the whole answer.

"No need to rehash what a manwhore I've been. But I'm going to prove to you that I'm a changed man. I've changed because of you, Quinn. Because I want to be with you. I want to be your boyfriend."

I stood frozen, staring at Sawyer with my blankest expression.

He'd used *the B word*.

The word that I'd believed for three years was so foreign to Sawyer that he may have believed it was actually fictitious.

"I'm gonna head out." There was a noticeable shift in his tone, and I knew it was due to my latest reaction or lack thereof. "So you can *think* about how badly you wanted me to kiss you five minutes ago and how much more fun it would be to do said kissing on a date with all of this." He waved his hands up and down his body as though I needed a tutorial on how to visualize what was beneath the expensive clothing. But his attempt to cast off his own emotional exposure as humor didn't make it past my Sawyer sensors.

I nodded, relaxing my posture. "Okay."

I forced my feet to carry me until I stood directly in front of him. I gazed up at his brilliant, blue eyes that stared back at me with a look of uncertainty wrapped in—love. Sawyer was radiating irrevocable love.

Had he always looked at me that way?

Yes, and you look at him that way too.

Emotions I had long concealed threatened my logical decision to think before acting.

Sawyer wrapped his hand around the nape of my neck and pressed a tender kiss to my forehead. "Give me one chance—that's all I'm asking for. Let me prove to the both of us that I can be the man you deserve."

SAWYER

Fuck me sideways.

Just a kiss.

Kennedy had nearly sent me into cardiac arrest with that one.

I jogged down the stairs of her apartment building to the first floor and stepped out into the afternoon sun. The girl had no idea the power she wielded over me. She thought I was creative and committed to getting what I wanted when it came to football? Wait until she realized that making her mine was paramount to everything else in my life now—including my second-favorite *f* word.

If only getting from point A to point B could be a linear process.

I'd never had to make such a conscious effort to keep fucking breathing. First, she'd balked at my proposition, which had every defensive instinct in my body itching to be released. Then she'd somehow managed to poke at my *rare and infrequent* insecurities all the while only making me want her more.

Must be love.

Or voodoo.

I had to get out of there before I lost the shaky grip I had on my composure. I didn't know what I wanted more: to bang her or bang my head against the wall.

Fuck that. I definitely wanted to bang Kennedy more. It wasn't even a question.

But now it was abundantly clear that if I ever wanted that reality, I had a lot of fucking work to do.

Kennedy's hesitation may have slowed my roll, but it was only temporary. I was already feeling the tingling sensation that accompanies a fourth-quarter comeback snaking its way through my body, and I was all in on making every play count going forward.

I'd wanted to press her for more answers. The competitor in me needed to know exactly what I was up against so I could ensure the win, but when she was on the verge of tears, I couldn't bring myself to make it all about me any longer.

I slid into the backseat of a city cab, making the decision to swing by the Cougars' clubhouse since I now had the afternoon free. Tomorrow, I'd join in with the strength and conditioning program. Training camp loomed in the not-so-distant future, and the sooner I could get to work at making nice with my new teammates and into the good graces of management, the better.

One way I could prove to Kennedy that I was worthy of her?

Being a man of my word.

I'd promised her just three nights ago that I'd be on my best behavior and make the most of my new contract, so that's what I intended to do.

Don't take too long to think, pretty girl. I'm coming for you.

My phone chimed, and I smiled to myself.

That didn't take long.

My smile faded when I glanced at the screen and realized it wasn't Kennedy.

NY Realtor Payton: The apartment next to Mr. Walsh's is ready for viewing. I could meet you there tonight at 8 p.m. Would that work for you?

Having your own place since you are in fact a grown-ass multimillionaire couldn't hurt your cause.

Me: See you then.

12

KENNEDY

"I need to understand your thought process, because you're making no sense whatsoever." Brooke reached from her spot beside me on the couch for the pizza box on the coffee table. Propping our dinner on her crisscrossed legs, she added, "But first, we need brain food."

The second the door clicked shut behind Sawyer, I'd texted, *Boy trouble. Bring greasy carbs STAT.*

I'd never been so happy that Andrew had decided to share Brooke with me. He'd introduced us shortly after he'd stuck his tongue up my nose. With her unapologetic personality, enviable self-confidence, and the ability to always put a smile on my face, she'd quickly become one of my favorite people.

"I changed my mind about the food—I'm too emotional to eat." I leaned forward, faceplanting in a throw pillow that smelled suspiciously like Sawyer.

I may or may not have burrowed my nose a little deeper.

"That's an urban legend. No one is ever *too emotional* to eat." Brooke cracked open the box, and the aroma of garlicky red sauce and fresh mozzarella made my stomach groan.

"Fine, one slice—then I need to figure out what to do about Sawyer. Every minute I spend obsessing over him is a minute I *should* be spending going through William's to-do list.

See? Even the *thought* of a relationship with Sawyer doesn't align with my life."

Brooke slapped a slice on a paper plate and shoved it at me with a frown. "What happened to love-and-light Kennedy? Can we get her back? I liked her better than you."

I crammed the pizza in my mouth and rolled my eyes.

"Don't pretend you don't appreciate my candor," Brooke said. "You know that's why you sent out the Bat-Signal for me and not Andrew. Drew would be all, *Buttercup . . . just let me distract you with my abs and sweet riffs.*"

I laughed and felt the immediate sense of levity it carried with it.

"Okay, Miss Candor. Please, help me understand why I cannot wrap my mind around Sawyer wanting to *date* me. Maybe if he'd just asked to be friends with benefits I wouldn't be freaking the fuck out. But *dating*? Sawyer does. Not. Date." I turned to Brooke, wide-eyed. "He even used the word *boyfriend*."

As well as kismet *and* endgame.

"Why did you just cringe?"

"What? When? I didn't cringe."

"Yes you did! You literally just cringed when you said *boyfriend*."

"I did not."

Brooke raised her clenched fists and shook them in the air. "Kennedy's spirit guides, if you're out there, I implore you to help a girl out!"

Was I really being that impossible?

Yes.

Brooke set the pizza box back on the coffee table and shifted on the couch cushion to face me. "Why are you so surprised that now that you live in the same city he's willing to play by your rules?"

"My rules? I don't follow."

She flicked me on the forehead.

"Kennedy! You're like a purity-ring-wearing Jonas Brother with a vagina for fuck's sake!"

I crossed my arms and cocked an eyebrow. *How dare she?*

Brooke mimicked my body language. "Really? Oh, do tell me all about your one-night stands and scandalous hookups. How many guys have you bagged since Hunter? It's been three years . . ." Brooke lifted her hands and began counting on her fingers. When she reached ten, she scoffed in mock horror. "Gosh, with your sex drive, it's gotta be double digits by now. What. A. Slut."

What. A. Dry. Spell.

That was more like it.

I tossed the throw pillow I'd been manhandling at her face. "There is no need to be sarcastic. I'm a relationship girl! And since I haven't been in a *relationship*, I haven't had sex in . . . a somewhat long time. What's wrong with that?"

Brooke grabbed my shoulders and gave me a hard, slow shake. "Nothing is wrong with you! Don't you see? That's the point! You made the rules, Kenn. You've been drilling it in that poor, hot, hot . . . *so fucking hot* man's head that you wouldn't settle for anything less than a relationship and now he's ready to tighten his morals so he can get in your pants." Her face wrinkled in contemplation. "I'm guessing there's some *feelings* in there somewhere too." She grinned and winked at me.

Could that really be it? Was it that . . . *simple*? Had timing, location, and maturity—or *tighter morals*—been the trifecta Sawyer and I needed in order to explore a relationship beyond friendship?

Friendship.

Our friendship. Sawyer's and mine—it was unlike anything I'd ever experienced before.

He was a grounding force in my life. He was my home.

I knew he felt the same way, even before today. We'd created that sense of security together—through friendship. To disrupt the flow of our connection felt like too big a risk when the end result was so ambiguous.

"I won't have time for dating now that I have an agent." I wasn't sure who I was trying to convince, but based on the look on Brooke's face, I'd failed.

"Excuses."

Welp.

"Sawyer's football season is about to start. He'll be so busy *he* won't have time to date . . . and then there's the fact he'll be traveling so much . . ." My head teetered back and forth from shoulder to shoulder while I scrutinized the ceiling. "And then there's jersey chasers . . . and we all know my fragility when it comes to men and monogamy . . ."

Brooke yanked my ponytail.

"Ouch!"

"Lame. So fucking lame, Kennedy."

I sighed.

"Maybe you're right."

She was right.

Brooke shrugged and batted her lashes. "Of course I'm right."

All-knowing Brooke was indeed right, but she didn't have the rest of the answers I so desperately needed before I could put my heart on the line. Those answers required me going straight to the man himself. The stack of papers from William sitting on my desk would need to collect dust for just a little bit longer. I had Declan's address, and he'd already given my name to security so I could get inside.

"I need to talk to Sawyer."

A triumphant smile spread across Brooke's porcelain face

before she wrapped her arms around me and squeezed. "*And she's back, people!*"

SAWYER

"What's Whitmore's deal?"

Declan's face twisted in confusion. "Not sure I follow," he replied, handing me a cold beer. After I'd given Declan a play-by-play account of my afternoon with Kennedy, I'd moved on to my visit at the clubhouse.

"I've never had any interactions with the guy, never even met him in person, and today he acted like it wasn't worth the oxygen to talk to me. He barely accepted my handshake—which I think he only did because Jordan walked over and I was standing there with my hand out."

Declan shrugged. "Might have something to do with him getting a shitty one-year deal and you getting the biggest tight end contract in league history. He's not dumb—he knows his stats are about to get slashed with you joining the team."

That, I understood. Contracts and stats could make or break a friendship between professional athletes faster than a hot chick.

"He's a good dude, though. He might be a little butt-hurt for a while, but he'll get over it."

I took a gulp of beer, welcoming the chill. It was hot as fuck outside. "Hope so. Because I have zero interest in competing against my own teammate."

"A little friendly competition between position players is necessary, though . . ."

I chuckled and set my beer on the counter. "I'm just gonna do what Coach tells me to do. I'm just gonna do my job."

"What about Sterling? Did you see him today?"

I shook my head. "Nope. Wasn't there." I glanced at my watch. "I've gotta jump in the shower. Keep an eye out for the Realtor chick, will you?"

"Payton. Her name is Payton."

I met Declan's eyes. There wasn't a hint of humor. "Got it, dude."

I drew a shoulder back to change the angle of my reflection in Declan's bathroom mirror.

What was I thinking? Andrew's abs got nothin' on these babies.

"Jackson!" Declan's voice boomed, followed by the pounding of his fist on the door. "Stop checking yourself out and get your ass out here—Payton's waiting."

Wearing nothing but a towel tucked around my waist, I opened the door and followed in Declan's footsteps until we reached the kitchen. The Realtor stood there dressed like she was ready for a night out on the town. Her eyes made a quick trip up and down my body, and for a moment, I wondered if my Realtor was hoping I'd be interested in more than the apartment next door. The original version of myself would have been salivating at the idea of what the raven-haired chick in stilettos had in mind, but Sawyer 2.0 was a changed man.

"You seem a tad overdressed for an apartment showing." I didn't hide the judgment in my tone, and Declan shot me a warning glare that said, "Not cool, bro."

I couldn't care less what Declan or Payton thought of my manners. I'd decided my girl and my career both required that I hand in my playboy card. If there was even a whiff of something that could be perceived as scandalous, I was ready to drench it in bleach.

Payton offered a tight smile. "And you're underdressed, Mr. Jackson. Could you put on some clothes, please? Although, I should warn you that the apartment's central air unit is being serviced next week, so don't overdress. Also, I'm meeting my husband for dinner. So, if you don't mind, I'd like to get going. It's fifteen past the hour as it is." Her smile broadened, reminding me a hell of a lot like Kennedy whenever she made me check my occasional dickheadedness at the door.

Okay. I deserved that.

With a stiff nod, I retreated to the guest room.

Approximately four minutes and twenty-six seconds later, we stood outside the next-door apartment and Payton was slipping off her heels.

"The floors were just done," she explained. "But feel free to keep your slides on."

"Got it . . . and by the way, sorry for how I reacted back there. I'm not usually such a dick."

Payton smiled to herself as she stood back up and then unlocked the apartment. "No worries, Mr. Jackson. I'm sure you have your fair share of ladies throwing themselves at you and I don't blame you for being skeptical." She turned the knob and paused, looking over her shoulder at me. "And for the record, I don't normally get this glammed up before meeting clients either. Even if they are rich sports stars like yourself."

We shared an amicable chuckle and then entered the apartment.

For the next thirty minutes, we went room by room, Payton pointing out the features of each as we went along. Not only was Payton professional, but she was also sharp and quick to answer any questions I had. The thermostat read eighty-four, and by the time we'd finished, her once-silky tresses were in one of Kennedy's messy piles on top of her head, and my T-shirt clung to my sweat-soaked body.

We stood in the center of the open-concept living space as I did one last full rotation, taking it all in. Payton's thought-provoking comments from minutes ago echoed in my mind.

"The walk-in closets in the master bedroom are quite spacious."

Kennedy does have a lot of shoes.

"The former owner used this room as her art studio. You could expand the home gym by knocking down this wall."

Better yet—I could turn it into a music studio.

"Not sure if you're planning to have children, but this would make an excellent child's bedroom."

I blinked and spun around to face Payton. "Kids."

"Pardon?"

"A few minutes ago—you mentioned kids. You said that room over there." I jutted my thumb over my shoulder. "You said it would make a good kid's room."

Maybe it was the intense expression on my face, but something about the shift in my demeanor made Payton lift her chin. "I apologize—I didn't mean to insinuate—"

I waved my hands dismissively. "No, here's the thing . . ."

What's the thing?

My hands settled on my hips as my eyes searched the floor for the *thing*. My heart grew restless, and I found my hand rubbing my chest for the hundredth time in the last few days. I raised my head. "I want kids, Payton. I want lots and lots of kids. A roster full of little Kennedy and Sawyer clones." I swallowed hard as Payton's compassionate smile looked back at me. "Of course I hope they all take after their mother—maybe just a little bit of me mixed in, you know—for the muscles and the speed."

Payton chuckled, but quickly sobered up when she saw how serious I remained. "Ah. Oh. Okay. I see. And Kennedy? She's your . . . girlfriend?"

A nervous smile played at my lips. "Well, not quite. Not yet, anyway. She hasn't agreed."

Payton nodded, sympathy now written all over her face. "Okay."

After I'd stepped on my own dick in front of Payton for the second time in less than an hour, we decided to stand in the air-conditioned hallway to finish up our meeting. Payton stood fanning herself with one hand while her strappy shoes dangled off the fingers of the other. I couldn't wait for her to leave so I could peel my shirt off and take another shower.

"There's not a lot of interest in the apartment right now, so I think it's fine if you take a couple days to consider it. Let me know if you have any questions or want to see it again and I'll make myself available."

In the distance, the chime of the elevator sounded.

"Thanks, Payton. I'll do that. And hey, thanks again for—"

"Sawyer Jackson! You are unbelievable!"

Kennedy's angry voice ricocheted off the walls, and I turned just in time to see her ponytail whip around and her scrumptious ass march away from me. By the time she finished assaulting the elevator button, I realized the conclusion she'd probably arrived at.

"Quinn!"

But I was too late. The elevator door closed, and she disappeared.

"Oh my." Payton blew threw her lips. "No wonder Kennedy doesn't want to be your girlfriend."

"*What?*" I demanded.

Payton shook her head. "I'm just saying—women's intuition—but five minutes ago you made it sound like you were in love with *Kennedy* and now here's *Quinn*, who clearly thinks she had some ownership of you . . ."

I groaned and massaged my eyes with my knuckles.

"They're the same person. Her name is Kennedy Quinn, I call her Quinn."

Payton gasped. "Oh!"

Oh fuck! was more like it.

I dropped my hands in time to see her cringe.

"Then this"—she waved her hand back and forth between us—"probably didn't look too good."

"Nope."

"Sorry," she whispered, but I didn't have time to stand there and discuss my shortcomings with my Realtor. If I'd read Kennedy correctly, she'd already convinced herself that what she'd just walked in on was anything but innocent.

Fuck me.

With my heart racing and panic coursing through my body, I held my hands up, taking a backward step. "I've gotta go."

Payton looked at me like it was the smartest thing I'd said since we'd met. "Obviously! Go!"

"Later!" I called over my shoulder as I sprinted for the elevator.

13

KENNEDY

'd stepped out of the elevator and onto the ground floor when "Eye of the Tiger" called out from my purse.

Not a good time, William.

My mind spun with images of Sawyer and his hookup, and I considered sending my agent to voice mail, but thought better of it. The lobby was buzzing with human traffic, though, and the sidewalk certainly wouldn't be any quieter. I turned to the left and headed down a hallway just as I accepted his call.

"Hi, William," I greeted, trying to sound polished and not like I'd just suffered a mortal wound directly to left-center chest.

William's aristocratic tenor filled my ear. "Kennedy, glad to hear you're alive and well."

For the love.

Did he have someone spying on me?

A janitorial closet appeared on my right. The door was partially open, so I slipped inside. "Y-yes . . . um, why wouldn't I be?"

On instinct, I closed the door and leaned back against it. My hand searched the wall beside me unsuccessfully for a light switch.

"Paula Fleming is sitting across from me right now. She

said she didn't receive a call from you this afternoon, so I wanted to check in to make sure all was well." Both his words and the hint of displeasure in his voice had me sliding down the door and landing on my ass.

"I'm so sorry, William. Something unexpected came up and I forg—I made a mistake. I'm sorry. If she's still willing to work with me, I can talk to her whenever it's best for her."

"This afternoon was best for her," he drawled, leaving me at a loss for a reply. Finally, he added, "Tomorrow. Eleven a.m. Call her at the number I gave you. If you're timely, perhaps she'll consider accepting you as a vocal student. Have a good evening, Miss Quinn."

My phone hit the concrete floor, and I wrapped my arms around my knees, pulling them tightly against my chest. The tears I'd been fighting back made a break for it as sobs racked my body. How had this day managed to go so epically to shit?

My tears came harder as each reality became clearer. I'd let down William, and possibly ruined his impression of me and my work ethic. Paula Fleming—vocal coach to the stars—had agreed to train me at William's behest, and she may no longer want anything to do with a slacker like me. And Sawyer—*freaking Sawyer*—was the cause of my downward spiral into Loserville, population: Me. He'd also proven himself capable of breaking my heart before I'd even given him the opportunity to do so.

On the Uber ride to Declan's, I'd been high on the fantasy that if Sawyer could promise me that we'd always be friends, no matter what, and if he could vow to be faithful, then I'd accept his proposal for us to date. To do so would have required me to confront all my fears, but I'd been ready and willing to try because Sawyer had never let me down, and to assume he would this time based on his past with other women would have been unfair of me.

Or. So. I. Thought.

When I saw him standing in the hallway with that—that *beauty queen*—looking all disheveled, all the faith I'd conjured evanesced.

My reaction to how he'd chosen to spend his time while I was supposed to be "thinking" was visceral. Hurt was all that registered; anger was still a breakdown or two away.

How would we ever get past this? *Could* we even get past this?

My fingers swiped across my cheeks, and the back of my head rested against the door. I stared into the dark room. "I guess it's better to have found out now. What was I even thinking?"

I picked up my phone. No missed calls or texts.

Nice, Sawyer.

Not that I would have answered . . . but still.

I stowed my phone in my purse and inhaled deeply through my nose. My life was utter chaos at the moment, and the dark silence of the storage room was comforting. I chose to take advantage of it until I could no longer feel my butt. Only then did I get to my feet and wipe away any straggler tears.

Ready to face the real world again, I opened the door to see Brutus—I mean, Sawyer—sitting with his back against the wall opposite the closet, his legs splayed wide and bent, his elbows perched on his knees.

His dark hair stood askew as though he'd tried to tear it from the roots, and his skin was a shade lighter than its usual bronze glow.

He emanated defeat.

I stepped into the hallway and closed the closet door behind me.

He looked up. "Let me explain."

SAWYER

"How'd you know where I was?"

The rasp and strain in Kennedy's voice were worrisome, escalating the guilt I was already drowning in. But it was the tear-stained look of devastation that would haunt me for as long as I lived.

You did that, Jackson. That's on you.

"Would you believe me if I said I smelled coconuts? I'm like a bloodhound hot on a trail when it comes to you, Quinn." A lazy grin hesitated on my face, and a tremble inched its way down her body.

"Stop it, Sawyer."

If I had a white flag, I would have waved it. Christ, if I had a time machine, I'd have taken us back to the first night we'd met and had a do-over. I'd have grown the fuck up a hell of a lot faster than I did, and I wouldn't have let something as minuscule as distance keep us apart.

Hindsight is always 20/20. Amiright?

I swallowed, feeling the heat moving up my neck and face. "Okay. Well, here's the thing, Quinn . . . I'm a hell of a lot faster than you and it's New York City, so the likelihood of you catching a cab before I got there was slim. When I couldn't find you in the vicinity . . . I called in a favor with the security guard at the front desk."

Without releasing her watery gaze, I pointed to the security camera above us.

She shook her head in bafflement. "Of course you did. Whatever. I can't do this right now." She pivoted to leave but forgot I had the reflexes of a ninja. I was on my feet and had her delicate wrist in my grasp before she'd taken the first step of her escape.

"She's my Realtor."

Kennedy's face contorted into outrage. "You're such an ass!" she hissed.

Jesus fuck. She still didn't get it.

Track records speak their own language, dudebro.

And my girl was fluent in mine.

No longer complicit in letting failure to communicate botch my one chance with Kennedy, I dragged her back into the janitor closet, shut the door, and locked it for good measure.

"Sawyer! What are you doing?"

She squirmed in my arms as I pressed her to the door.

"We're not leaving this room until we get several things clear."

Maybe because it was the first time in fucking forever Kennedy didn't have a sassy comeback, or maybe she'd finally recognized my anguish, but either way, she stilled, and even in the darkness, I knew she'd agreed to a cease-fire—at least temporarily.

"I didn't touch her. She didn't touch me. She was showing me the place next to Declan's that just came available." When she didn't react, I took a half step back and rested my palms on the door, boxing her in. "The AC was out, so we were both sweating our fucking balls off. I think that's why it looked way fucking worse—I get why you came to the conclusion that you did, but I promise you, baby"—I dropped my forehead to hers—"nothing happened. Nothing is going to happen—with anyone—but you. When you're ready. I'll wait forever for you to believe this is real if that's what it takes, Quinn."

Kennedy's panted breaths turned into sobs, and then I had

her in my arms as her tears seared my heart. I'd rather gnaw off my right hand than make this girl cry.

"Everything is so messed up," she choked out.

She shifted slightly, and I loosened my arms to give her enough room to breathe. I wasn't ready to let her go just yet.

Even in the dark, my hands had super-Kennedy-awareness and found her face. "Do you want to go upstairs so we can talk in my room? The fumes in here are gonna make us high."

When she didn't laugh, I found the light switch and instantly regretted my decision.

The sheer number of tears I'd caused her was traumatizing.

I used the pads of my thumbs to wipe them away, and Kennedy avoided my gaze. "Baby? Upstairs?"

She shook her head. "No, I need to go home."

"Okay, let me just get my wallet and phone, and we'll head out."

Her cold chuckle was humorless, almost eerie, and dread lodged in my throat.

Kennedy's head tilted back. "I'm going home alone. I need time. I need space. I need . . ." She searched my face. "I don't know what I need."

"Do you not believe me?"

"I believe that nothing happened with your Realtor, but that alone doesn't solve all my problems."

She was either talking in code or this was one of those times I wasn't supposed to understand because I'm a guy.

"What problems?" I asked casually.

She cocked an eyebrow. "How much time do you have?"

Now it was my turn to hike my eyebrows to my hairline.

She drew in a shaky breath. "I missed an important call with an important person this afternoon because I was too caught up in all of . . ." She threw her arms up and then slapped her thighs.

I'd add that to the Shit Sawyer Fucked Up Today list.

"*And* . . . I don't think it's a good sign that I see you with another woman and I *immediately* assume you've just given her two orgasms!"

"*Only* two?" was on the tip of my tongue, but I knew better.

It didn't matter, though—Kennedy still gave me a scolding look that told me she'd read my mind.

"I need to go." Her broken record played with more assertion this time.

"Quinn."

"No, Sawyer."

Breathe.

"Have I ever lied to you?"

Her eyes snapped up to mine, and her lips parted. Reserved satisfaction ebbed.

"Have I?" I pressed.

Her top teeth sank into her bottom lip, and ever so slowly her head swayed side to side.

Pride and exultation urged me on. "I will never lie to you, Quinn. I will never cheat on you. I will never give you a reason to not trust me. None of the women from my past—*none of them*—ever had access to this." I took her hand into mine and placed it over my heart. "This is all yours. You own it."

Tears trickled down her cheeks, but even my entry-level boyfriend qualifications told me it was okay. Between our earlier conversation and now this one, I'd basically told Kennedy that I was crazy, madly in love with her ass and she didn't stand a chance of changing my mind that we were meant to be together and that this is what I wanted. I'd told Kennedy I loved her plenty of times, but the next time I used those three words, she'd know with certainty exactly how I meant them.

Her hand slipped from mine, and with a tiny voice, she replied, "I'm sorry, Sawyer. I can't."

14

SAWYER

Twenty-nine motherfucking days.

That's how long it'd been since Kennedy had spoken to me aside from a few texting sessions that almost always ended up in a GIF battle and never resulted in a diplomatic discussion of the status of the United States. I'd never gone this long without hearing her voice. She'd asked for time and space, and hell if I was going to deny her the only things she'd asked for, even if it did mean I had to settle for watching her Instagram Reels on repeat just to get my Kennedy fix.

"Get your head in the fucking game, Jackson," Sterling growled after I'd fucked up my footwork on a seam route.

I shot a wad of spit on the turf and then readjusted my mouth guard. "Run it again."

I didn't take Sterling's criticism personally. In fact, much to my wonder, he wasn't a total douche with his helmet on. Our chemistry on the field was Brady and Gronk caliber, and the news trickling out of training camp by the network and beat reporters had the already passionate fan base titillated.

On Sterling's next play call, I broke fast and toasted the double coverage to catch his perfect spiral in the end zone.

And that's how it's done, boys and girls.

The front of Declan's helmet collided with mine in celebration. "Fuck yeah!"

Coach blew his whistle, signaling the end of practice, and we headed for the locker room. I still had an afternoon full of offensive meetings, but showering first was a necessity if any of us planned to breathe without hacking up a lung during film study.

"You and Sterling are fucking money, dude." Declan's high praise was both accurate and welcomed.

"Yeah, he's not a total asshat."

Declan shook his head. "He hasn't brought up Kennedy, has he?"

"Nope. And if he has any non-football brain cells in that head of his, he'll keep it that way."

"Is she coming with you to the dinner tonight?"

The owner of the New York Cougars, Mr. Richard Ellison IV, was having the front office, coaching staff, and players over to his Long Island estate this evening for a preseason kick-off dinner. Our first preseason game against the Los Angeles Rams was in two days. We'd be on the team jet on our way to the Golden State in roughly twenty-four hours.

"She's still not talking to me," I gritted out, my heart twisting in my chest simultaneously.

Declan set his helmet in his locker. "Damn. It's been like a month. How long are you going to put up with that?"

Groaning as I lifted my shoulder pads over my head, I replied, "As long as I have to. She asked for time and space, so that's what she's gonna get."

"I don't know, man, doesn't sound like the right play call to me—*or* like the stubborn bastard that you are either."

He had a point.

"What else can I do? At least this, I can't fuck up."

"Sounds like it's time for a romantic grand gesture."

I rolled my eyes and chuckled. "Now *that*? That sounds like something I could definitely fuck up."

Maintaining my sanity while being distant from Kennedy was as challenging as doing the same when my mom had been going through chemo, but I knew I had to play the long game, which meant I needed to stay focused on what I could control.

Playing nice with Sterling—check.

Staying out of the media's crosshairs—check.

Keeping my seven-month celibacy streak alive—fucking *check*. As long as jerking off to thoughts of Kennedy didn't count, I was the fucking pope.

Declan was rambling on about male telegram strippers—something that did *not* sound like a romantic grand gesture if you asked me—when the slam of a locker door reverberated in my ears.

"When you ladies are done gossiping, we have a meeting."

I glanced to the side to catch Knox Whitmore's freshly showered figure as he turned to stalk off.

"Some of us had a longer practice than others," I shot back, knowing full well that the other tight end had been spending the majority of our recent practices on the stationary bike due to muscle cramps.

Whitmore spun around, his features twisting into a scowl. "What's that, Jackson? You got a problem with me?"

"Nah, man. Seems like you're the one who's got a problem with me. In fact, I think this is the longest conversation we've had." I offered him a "so fuck off" smirk and then closed my locker door with mock emphasis on the care I took to do so.

He chuckled sardonically. "Everything I have to say to you will come out on the field, Jackson."

The darker side of my personality engaged. "I guess our heart-to-heart will have to wait then, since I haven't been seeing too much of you on the field lately."

Whitmore lunged for me, striking like the snake he was turning out to be. Declan was just as fast, though. He jumped between us—rooting a hand on each of our chests. "Let's take it easy." He looked back and forth between us. "Both of you."

My shoulder blades eased down my back, and I gave Declan a chin jerk of acknowledgment. Whitmore shrugged him off and glowered at me.

"You're done, Jackson," he sneered.

The smartass comeback was on the tip of my tongue, but Declan's look of warning made me swallow my unspoken words. He was the only one outside of the Cougars organization and Trek who knew the fine-print details of my contract. Volatility in the aging NFL player wasn't a novelty, and I couldn't let Knox Whitmore and his self-loathing propel me into self-sabotage. He may have been a moody motherfucker, but at the end of the day, he was harmless.

***

KENNEDY

"What the hell happened to you?"

It was Andrew who found me slumped against the bathroom vanity nodding off but unwilling to leave the security that a nearby toilet had to offer.

"Whatever you do, don't eat the Chinese leftovers," I croaked.

"No shit. It's been in the fridge for two weeks."

I tossed my hands up. "Now you tell me."

Andrew knelt beside me and pressed the back of his hand to my clammy cheek. "Jesus, Buttercup, are you all right? Do you need to go to the emergency room?"

I shook my head. "No. But I do need to call my boss and tell her I can't come in tonight. I was going to cover half a shift for Tavon, but that's not happening."

Andrew stood, searching the bathroom surfaces, I assumed, for my phone. "No worries. I'm on it."

"I think I left it on my bed." I groaned as I made my way to my feet. The room spun, and I questioned the ability of my legs to keep me upright. I washed my face with cold water and brushed my teeth, and then Andrew was standing in the bathroom doorway with my phone in his hand.

"Valerie said not to worry about coming in. She said to plan on taking tomorrow off too, and if you need more time, just let her know."

"Thanks, man." I started to tug a brush through my snarled hair, but it required dexterity, so I aborted my mission.

Andrew's brows furrowed as his attention returned to my phone. "I'm trying to call Sawyer, but I can't find his number in your contacts."

"*What?* Why would you call *Sawyer*?" I hissed.

As soon as the words left my mouth, my knees gave out, and I stumbled against the tub. Andrew's arms came to the rescue just in time.

"That's why," he answered, guiding me to my feet again. "I'm Brooke's plus-one for a fundraising dinner with her dad, and you shouldn't be alone."

I shouldn't be alone with Sawyer was more like it. We'd been virtually incommunicado except for a few sporadic texts and GIF-offs. My Sawyer Jackson detox had me crying myself to sleep almost nightly, and I wasn't sure how exposure to him might impede my healing process.

Don't fool yourself, sister. You haven't healed shit.

"I haven't talked to him in twenty. Nine. Days."

Andrew's mouth formed into a sloped grin. "You're stage-whispering again."

I rolled my eyes, and a wave of nausea and dizziness sent

143

me into the side of the tub for a second time. "Fine. He's under *M.*"

"*M*?" Andrew muttered and began scrolling again. Then his face lit up, and he laughed. "That's fucking awesome."

"Don't ask," I muttered.

I shuffled past Andrew and went directly back to my bed. In a few minutes, he strolled into my bedroom with a bottle of water and my phone.

"Your hottest friend is on his way." He smirked as he leaned down and kissed my forehead. "I guess now I know how I rate."

"Aw, Drew. Don't worry, you can be My Sexiest Friend if you want," I cajoled, too weak and consumed with thoughts of seeing Sawyer again to tease him any more than that.

"Damn straight, Buttercup." He winked at me, then added, "Hey, not sure what time we'll be back, but Sawyer said he'll plan to stay the night."

Sweet mother of dragons . . . this is not happening.

"He has an away game in LA on Thursday, which means the team will fly out tomorrow. He needs to get his rest."

Just because we weren't talking didn't mean I still didn't know the man's schedule as well as my own.

Andrew cocked an intrigued eyebrow at me, but remained silent.

I blushed under his gaze. "I don't need a babysitter."

"Kennedy, be nice. The guy sounded really worried about you. I know I don't know all the details of what went down with you two—man problems are Brooke's specialty—but it's apparent that he cares a fuck lot about you."

Well, now I felt like a tool.

Sawyer did care about me. He'd even gone against every fiber in his nature to give me the time and space I'd requested. Classic Sawyer wouldn't have let me leave him in that janitor closet, and he wouldn't have chosen to respect my wishes rather than believing his powers of persuasion superseded my own self-awareness.

And you miss him.

Good grief, I missed him so freaking much. Some days, it felt almost impossible to breathe if I didn't hear from Sawyer. And that's exactly when he'd send me a simple text to check in or a GIF that made me laugh out loud. It was as though the connection we shared was celestial and defied the laws of time and space.

"Thank you for calling him."

Andrew's expression softened, and a knowing warmth filled the atmosphere. "I'll leave the door unlocked if we leave before he gets here. He shouldn't be too far behind us. Get some rest, Buttercup."

That sounded like the exact opposite of what I was about to get.

15

KENNEDY

The scent of leather and spice filled my nostrils.

"You're smiling . . . that's a good sign."

I'm smiling?

Sawyer's husky tone sent delicious shivers up my spine, and my eyes fluttered open just as he laid his head on the pillow next to mine, bringing us face to face. "I brought a fuck-ton of stuff. Brooke texted me a list. I didn't even know that ginger tea was a thing."

I licked my dry, chapped lips. "Look at you being all domestic, Tight End."

"Anything for you, Chuckles." His hand came up to push my hair back and tuck it behind my ear before it settled on the nape of my neck.

My eyes burned with potential tears. Sawyer's gaze locked on mine, and Father Time hit pause.

We both swallowed hard.

I'd gone longer than twenty-nine days without seeing Sawyer before, but this separation had been different. The knowledge that he was an Uber ride away at any given time had toyed with my psyche for the past month. Resisting him had been a self-induced prison sentence, and as my own warden, I needed to set myself and my emotions free.

Sawyer cleared his throat. "What do you want first? Tea? Ginger ale? Saltines? Popsicles?"

"I don't need anything right now."

Just you, I added in my head.

Sawyer's hand lingered, and he stroked my cheek with his thumb. He looked well rested, his hair was still damp from a recent shower, and he was freshly shaven. Training camp during the summer months had deepened his skin tone, and the purple bedsheets made his blue eyes shimmer in contrast. I'd noticed he was dressed in a button-down, and were those slacks he was wearing and not joggers?

Finally, I whispered, "Why are you dressed so fancy?"

A sly grin spread across his face. "It's been a while. I thought I should remind you of how irresistible I can be."

"I'd roll my eyes if I didn't think it would make me hurl."

He chuckled warmly, and the consolation of our familiar banter made my heart bolt into my throat. Being with Sawyer felt natural. It felt right.

"I was on my way to a team dinner when Andrew called."

I blinked. "You bailed on your team dinner for me?"

Sawyer's forehead creased, and he looked offended. "Fuck my team dinner. Christ, Quinn. You need me—period."

The stinging in my eyes returned, and I snuggled into his chest.

"Sawyer." It came out like a breath.

His Adam's apple moved along the top of my head, and his muscular arms embraced me.

"Can we never go this long without talking again, please?" I asked.

A chuckle reverberated through his chest. "You make the rules, baby."

That's what Brooke said.

I tilted my head back so I could stare at his chin. "I'm going to do so much talking now that you're gonna end up giving me a word limit."

"Impossible."

"Sounds like a challenge," I teased.

"Oh, is it now? All right, I'll play. Game on, Quinn."

I curled myself back into his chest, and the pounding of his heart was like a soothing metronome for my own. "I'm serious," I said just above a whisper. "This past month has been brutal without you in my life."

A shudder rumbled through his body, and Sawyer held me tighter.

"Same, baby. Same."

Everything my heart and mind had been weighing since our last encounter begged to be shared. I drew in a fortifying inhale and reminded myself that this was Sawyer—I could do this.

"Being apart isn't an option," I stated.

"Agreed."

"But if I take the . . . *package deal*—what happens if we break up?"

There was a pause, and then Sawyer replied, "I can understand what you're saying, but I don't think it's an either-or situation. I can't imagine a life without you in it. So if we . . . break up—which I'll tell you right now I am highly against—we'll do whatever it takes to stay friends."

"Easier said than done."

"So is making it in the NFL, but I managed to pull it off. Don't forget who you're dealing with here, Quinn. I'm a relentless fucker when I put my mind to something. I'm a goddamn honey badger."

"Well, yes, but . . ." My train of thought sputtered out on the track.

Sawyer gently rolled me onto my back and propped

himself up on his side. His gaze fell to my face, and he dragged the tip of his index finger down the bridge of my nose. "Use your words, baby. I think you have a challenge to win."

Everything about Sawyer's demeanor told me he was taking this seriously, but the flirtatious remark helped put me at ease. His hand fell away and settled on my opposite hip. The tiny circles his thumb traced above the waistband of my sleeping shorts lulled me into an even deeper state of relaxation.

"Do you want to know what the hardest part of not talking to you was?"

His grip flexed against me. "Mmm . . ."

"That every time something shitty or amazing happened, you were the one I wanted to tell—and yet, I couldn't."

"You could have told me."

"Semantics. You know what I mean."

He smiled and brushed a kiss against my forehead. "I do—you're right. And I know what you're saying because I felt exactly the same way."

"You did?"

"Yeah. I've been dying to tell you all about training camp and to ask you how everything is going with that French guy."

"You mean William." And I wanted to know how everything was going with Hunter, but that would have to wait.

"Yeah. Whatever."

I chuckled at Sawyer's jealousy—because let's call it what it was—and played with one of the open buttonholes on his shirt. "William has been kicking my ass."

He cocked an eyebrow. "That better be metaphorical. I don't want any part of his body touching your ass."

I giggled, and Sawyer's grin grew bigger.

"Oh, trust me. I think on William's likeability scale of one to ten, I average about a four point six on a good day."

He shook his head. "I don't believe it."

"Believe it, baby," I teased, but then I saw how Sawyer's eyes darkened at my use of the endearment. My breathing faltered, and my mind switched gears.

"You have to be monogamous," I blurted out.

Sawyer sobered immediately. "Okay—so we're doing this?"

"Is that a yes?"

"That's a *fuck* yes." Sawyer smiled so big I thought his face might split in two.

"And you have to promise that if we break up, we will still be best friends even if it's awkward as heck and you have to see me with other men." I put on my most demure expression, and Sawyer put on his most displeased.

"I am not entertained."

"Don't be mean to a sick girl."

"Sick, my ass—cruel is more like it. But you've got yourself a deal, Quinn."

I poked him in the chest. "I mean it."

He wrapped my finger in his and brought it to his lips. "So do I—Scout's honor."

"You were never a Boy Scout, Sawyer Jackson."

He shook his head dismissively and ran his teeth along my finger. "Mhmm."

"And no sex."

Sawyer choked on something—air, saliva, possibly his ego. "*And* she's getting crueler by the minute."

"You are going to prove to me that you can keep that thing in your pants and be a loyal boyfriend because once we have sex, all bets are off. I won't be able to tame my feelings for you."

Like you can now?

A wolfish grin erupted on Sawyer's face. "If waiting for the right moment with you was an Olympic event, I'd have won the fucking gold, silver, *and* bronze by now."

He got the eye roll that time.

"Also, I'm a busy woman. I have a job, gigs, classes, and an agent who is determined to mold me into something he can market—and he's *very* demanding. So between our rivaling schedules, date nights might be few and far between."

"I'll take what I can get. But I could eliminate one of those things right now."

I knew exactly what he was referring to, and I didn't want Sawyer's money. "Nope."

He sighed and slid down next to me, dropping his forehead against mine. "You'll change your mind eventually. Because when I agree to marry you, what's mine will become yours."

I laughed so hard my sour stomach threatened to revolt. "So now I'm going to ask you to marry me?"

"You do realize I'm never going to let you forget that you referred to me as a *package deal*, right?"

"I'm counting on it, Tight End."

We both released a sigh at the same time, and then Sawyer nuzzled his nose against mine. "How do you feel about our inaugural kiss being when you have food poisoning?"

"I think I'd prefer for you to just hold me for tonight. Let's save our first kiss for our first date."

"You got it, baby. You're my play caller now."

16

SAWYER

Sawyer Jackson: Boyfriend.

The title certainly had a ring to it.

It had only been forty-eight hours since Kennedy agreed to be mine, but I already had a ring of a different kind on my mind.

Slow your roll, bro. You've been in another state for thirty of those hours.

"Can I take a *selfie* with you?" the jersey chaser slurred in my right ear before I'd had the chance to block her from trying to maul me.

After our first preseason game, the team wanted to celebrate our win, and since our flight wasn't until the next morning, the majority vote had landed us at Club Lux in Downtown LA.

"He doesn't selfie well—how about you take one with me, sweetheart?" Declan gave me the *you're-welcome* look over the top of the chick's head, and I raised my chin in gratitude.

Being my hotel roommate made Declan my solo audience while I'd recounted my night of taking care of my sick *girlfriend,* and he'd promised to be my anti-wingman and self-proclaimed cockblocker or pussy protector. Whatever the kids called it these days.

Why? Because I, Sawyer Jackson, had a girlfriend.

Girlfriend.

Fuck. I was a boyfriend, and I had a girlfriend.

Shit was getting real.

My phone lit up, reminding me I still hadn't opened my *girlfriend's* last text.

My Girl: Sunday night?

She'd already gushed over our team win even though I'd only played five snaps and the ball had not been thrown in my direction. It was the preseason after all, and starters played a limited amount during the preseason to avoid injury. Knox Whitmore, on the other hand? The poor bastard had played all. Four. Quarters. He'd only rested as much as I'd played, which didn't bode well for him making the 53-man roster on final cut day.

Now, my girl and I were trying to come up with a plan for date *numero uno*. Friday was out because she had to work at the diner until close. Saturday, she had lessons and classes all day and then another late shift. She'd promised Brooke she'd have a girls' day with her on Sunday and help her find a dress for an upcoming audition. That's how far we'd made it through our schedules before I'd been so rudely interrupted by the very thing that I was trying to avoid: potential disasters in stilettos.

Me: My teammate is having his b-day party at Chalet, but I can check out early and we can get a late dinner?

Even the three dots bouncing around on my screen made my heart rate quicken. Everything about Kennedy catapulted my body's reactions into overdrive.

My Girl: Any chance you'd want me to join you at the b-day party?

Holy fuck.

Me: You're serious???? ALL THE FUCKS YES.

My Girl: K. Xx

A presence hovered over my shoulder, but the scent was masculine, so I didn't put up my hackles. "What's her name, Jackson? Number Four or Number Forty-Four."

Where the fuck are my hackles when I need them?

I closed my phone and tucked it in my pocket as I stood up from the barstool I'd been occupying. "Sixty-nine if you really must know," I drawled in reply to Whitmore's weak attempt to taunt me. I clapped him on the shoulder. "Maybe you should ditch the club in lieu of an ice bath, buddy. Heard the SoFi turf is hard on the ol' joints."

I let his curses pelt against my back without retaliation as I walked off. I still needed to reply to Kennedy, but there was someone I needed to speak to first.

I found Hunter Sterling standing with the second- and third-string quarterbacks, Rollins and Becker, respectively. After warm-ups, Sterling never took another step on the field tonight. Maybe in one of the next two preseason games he'd play a few series, but Coach wasn't about to let his QB1 take a beating for meaningless wins.

"Can I have a word?" I asked as soon as I was in front of the trio, my eyes locked on Sterling's. He gave me a nod, and after a round of fist bumps between the four of us, he joined me in a quieter corner of the private room the team had snagged.

A lot of good that did keeping the jersey chasers away.

Players desperate for easy pussy always found a way to skate the team rules.

"What's up, Jackson?" he asked in a cool and casual tone like we'd been friends forever.

Hunter had filled out significantly since he'd been drafted. He looked like a certifiable G.I. Joe now. At Seth and Abby's wedding, I'd probably had forty-plus pounds of muscle on him, but I no longer had quite that sizeable of an advantage—not that I'd be fighting my starting QB. The thought had never crossed my mind.

Uh-huh.

With Trek and Kennedy's warnings ringing in my ears, I reminded myself that for the past month Sterling had been nothing but professional with me both on and off the field when our paths crossed. I hadn't had the chance to tell Kennedy that yet, but I would.

"Listen, Kennedy and I are together, and she's coming with me to Lake's party. Are you and your woman going to be there?"

The muscles in his jaw flexed, but his expression otherwise remained neutral. "Yeah. We'll be there."

"Can I have your word that there will be no bullshit? I fucking mean it. *None.*"

Sterling gave a solemn nod. "You have my word."

His answer was fast, but my skepticism was faster. I raised an eyebrow. "Care to put that in writing and sign in blood?"

He chuckled and held out his hand. "How about we shake on it instead."

After a brief hesitation, I took his hand, gripping it tighter than necessary, and never released eye contact. "She's my fucking everything. If you or your woman fuck with her, you'll see a side of me that will make you wish you hadn't. Feel me?"

I waited for him to nod in agreement before I let go of his hand.

Sterling ran a hand through his hair and gave off a vibe that he had something to say.

"Just spit it the fuck out, man."

He dropped his hand and shoved it in his pocket with a sigh. "You'll get no shit from me or from Melody, but maybe think about chilling the fuck out." He looked around the room at the curious stares that had drifted our way. Then he put a hand on my shoulder and dipped his head slightly and lowered his voice. "Your contract details were leaked." He paused, but my mind was already filling the silence.

Who the fuck knows about my contract, and how the fuck do they know?

"Just watch your back—they may be your teammates, but some are willing to play a little dirty if it makes them look better. Hear what I'm saying, man?"

The words coming out of his mouth were not what I'd anticipated, but I'd heard, all right—loud and fucking clear.

"Yeah, I hear you."

He removed his hand and gave me space. "I'm glad you're on the team, Jackson. I think we're gonna have a hell of a season. And for what it's worth, I'm glad you're with Kennedy too. I know you don't want to hear my apologies, and she's made it clear she doesn't want to hear them either, but I am sorry."

I nodded, but what he was saying hadn't entirely registered. I needed to get ahold of Trek, and if Sterling's evaluation of our teammates was correct, I needed to stay alert. Shit just got even more complicated, and here I thought my next challenge was going to be breaking the news to Kennedy that her cheating ex and his mistress would be crashing our first date.

17

KENNEDY

Date night had *finally* arrived.

My day-date with Brooke had run late, and I'd had to convince Sawyer that even if we met at the club instead of him picking me up, it still counted as our first date. We'd debated the distinctions of a first date like a couple of hardcore law students trying to impress their professor. He'd only conceded after I'd pointed out that our first kiss was still on the table no matter how my ass ended up in SoHo.

I made my way through the congested first floor of Chalet toward the stairwell that would take me to the VIP section. Eyes prowled over me as I tried to navigate the grinding bodies with discretion, keeping my gaze turned downward as much as possible. I'd worn a deep violet slip dress that grazed my thighs and mile-high silver heels that I'd picked out on my shopping trip with Brooke. I had no idea what my date would be wearing, but he could pull off anything.

My date.

Fiddlefucksticks.

Sawyer and I were hanging out tonight. As. A. Couple.

Cue the choir because this felt like a holy moment.

When Sawyer was in Cali, I'd had the chance to adjust to our new *status quo*. A lot of journaling and high-pitched screeching while dancing in my underwear had occurred. Based on the perpetual smile on my face all week, Brooke was certain that love-and-light Kennedy was back from beyond the grave that she'd dug herself just over a month ago. Even William had commented on me not looking quite so pallid, and this was following a stint with food poisoning, so that right there's gotta tell you something.

There was a bouncer standing guard at the bottom of the stairs, but Sawyer told me it wouldn't be a problem; I was on the list.

"You're not on the list. The team said no party girls tonight. Sorry, honey."

I forced a smile and swallowed all the curse words I'd learned from Sawyer. "Just a second—let me call my boyfriend. He'll come down and fix this."

Boyfriend. Yeah, I played that card.

I was plucking my phone from my clutch when the bouncer asked, "Who's your boyfriend?"

"Sawyer Jackson."

He made some sort of guttural noise that sounded a whole lot like "Poor broad."

I blinked. "Excuse me?" I asked, my eyes narrowing. My feet already ached in the shoes I already regretted purchasing, and I was fresh out of patience for douchebags.

His shoulders shook as a crude laugh rumbled from him. "Just curious, sweet cheeks . . . does he know he's your boyfriend?"

Just when I thought this exchange couldn't get any more humiliating, I heard a familiar voice behind me ask, "Is there a problem here?"

My phone slipped from my fingers, crashing to the floor.

I hadn't heard that voice in years. It was deeper than before, yet still carried the same resonating tone that used to make my heart trip over itself. Sawyer had explained that Hunter and Melody would be here, but I'd kinda hoped the first time they saw me, I'd be composed and oozing self-confidence with Sawyer at my side. Instead, I was being denied entry and on the verge of tears.

A large body moved beside me, crouched down, and then stood back up.

"The screen's cracked, but it's still on," Hunter said as he held my phone out to me, not meeting my eyes.

"Hunter." It was more a realization than a greeting.

Amber eyes that I used to get lost in looked back at me, and my throat clenched in emotional retaliation.

Don't puke, scream, or smile at him.

"Hey, Kennedy."

It had been over three years since I'd been this close to Hunter. He no longer looked like the polished pretty boy who'd taken my virginity and promised me the world in college. Nor did he look like the arrogant asshole who'd cheated on me the night before our friends' wedding.

Hunter was all man now. Ruggedly handsome, with thicker, longer hair that curled around his shirt collar, and a disobedient piece fell across his forehead in a flirty way. He licked his lips, and my gaze dropped to his mouth. I knew the ridges of that Cupid's bow like I knew the back of my hand, but it no longer gave me the same giddy feelings it once did. Now I only thought about all the shady places it had touched since it'd been on me.

"Kennedy Quinn," he said loud and clear to the bouncer. "Add it to the list. She'll be on every list we ever have at this club."

I turned my head just in time to see the bouncer look back and forth between us. His right eye twitched. "So, she's with you?"

Hunter adjusted his watch with his other hand, a nervous

habit he'd had since I'd known him. "She's Sawyer Jackson's girlfriend," he replied earnestly.

Silently, the bouncer opened the velvet rope, and Hunter held his arm out. "After you."

I tried to thank him, but the words wouldn't come, so I nodded instead.

I gradually ascended the stairs, keenly aware of my proximity to Hunter and the fact that Melody was either wearing an invisibility cloak or wasn't with him.

"Have a good evening, Kennedy," he said as we both took the last step and moved into the VIP room.

I watched him walk away and toward a group of men and women off to the left. He was greeted with handshakes and shoulder slaps. He wasn't only their friend and teammate, he was their leader.

The moment wasn't lost on me; it felt almost mythical.

We'd spent our first Valentine's Day together visiting New York City and catching a show. How many times had I lain in Hunter's arms as we'd dreamed of a future together with him in the NFL and me on Broadway, living in the city we'd both fallen in love with?

Too many to count—that's how many.

I'd moved on to blatantly staring when Sawyer approached from the other side, startling me by wrapping his arms around my waist and lifting me in the air.

"I've missed you," he murmured into my neck and then kissed my temple. "You look gorgeous, baby."

I rested my head against Sawyer's chest as he lowered me to my feet. Sure enough, he was dressed in dark designer jeans and a button-down shirt, and he looked ready for a cover shoot.

A heartbeat in Sawyer's arms, and everything about my interaction with Hunter was long forgotten and replaced by the consummate amount of love I felt for Sawyer.

It had been a while since we'd said our *love yous*. Maybe the last time had been when we'd said goodbye at JFK Airport after Paris, and Sawyer had been about to race to his connecting flight to Miami.

I knew the next time we said it, it would have an all-new meaning, and with each passing day, I felt more ready for it.

"I missed you too," I confessed, holding onto him as tightly as possible. Then I tilted my head back so I could see his handsome face. "William was a total bear yesterday and the diner was a madhouse—all I wanted to do was eat pizza with you and watch those stupid cat videos you love so much."

Sawyer brushed my hair back and tucked it behind my ear. He searched my face and ran his thumb over my lips. "Do you want to go home? We can leave right now if you want to."

"Home?" I cocked my head. "You're homeless, remember?"

He chuckled. "Smartass." He kissed my forehead, then added, "I've already told the Realtor I want the penthouse in Declan's building when it comes available in January."

The mention of his flawless Realtor made my insides curdle, but I reminded them that Sawyer had made me promises and he had never lied to me.

"Penthouse?"

He grinned. "Yup. Might need the extra space someday. Plus, I hear chicks dig penthouses and there's this one chick that I'm trying really, really, *really* fucking hard to impress."

I shook my head in the sassy way that always got him riled up. "Don't think buying a grossly overpriced apartment in Heaven's neighborhood is the key to getting me on my back."

Sawyer's jaw ticked, his eyes gleamed with straight-up naughtiness, and I braced for his scandalous comment. "Oh baby," he purred, looking like he was ready to devour me right then and there, "I don't need you on your back."

Boom. Called it.

"There are support groups for people like you," I chided, patting his chest, and he laughed.

And just like that, after a month apart, we'd slipped right back into Sawyer and Kennedy's world where the potential for sex and feelings was our new reality.

Two hours and several shots later, the birthday boy was insisting all he wanted for his thirtieth birthday was for everyone to sing karaoke.

Jonny Lake sat across the table from where I sat sandwiched between Sawyer and Declan, and he had three beautiful women—all of whom Sawyer had whispered to me were jersey chasers—crawling all over him.

I thought there were no party girls allowed.

No one, not even Jonny, it seemed, knew their names.

The sheer travesty of it all.

Over fifty people were in attendance for Jonny's party, and much to my surprise, most were game to set their pride aside to serenade their friend on his birthday. The sound of good-natured jeering, pitchy ballads, and screechy rock lyrics filled the VIP lounge while the drinks kept flowing. It wasn't long before the mic was handed to me.

I shook my head and waved it away. "No, that's okay. You can give it to the next person."

Declan and Sawyer both turned to face me at the same time, giving me equally shocked expressions.

I held my hands up. "Calm down, boys. I'm good."

"It's okay if you can't sing, sweetie. Neither can I. Did you hear me sing 'Genie in a Bottle'? I wasn't that good," Blonde Number One said as she adjusted her perfectly enhanced breasts.

I opened my mouth, unsure of what I was going to say, but it didn't matter because Sawyer was on his feet and picking up the mic.

I looked up at him, my jaw becoming unhinged.

Sawyer tapped my chin to close my mouth and tsked. "You're not the only one who can sing, Quinn."

"I've heard you sing in the shower, man . . . you sure you want to do this?" Declan asked, putting my exact thoughts into words. "Not the romantic grand gesture I was thinking of."

I pressed my lips together and pulled the invisible zipper across the seal.

"You're welcome," Sawyer said.

He leaned down to press a kiss to the top of my head before walking away, leaving Declan and me bent over our table in hysterics.

"You do realize he can't sing, right?" Declan asked.

I nodded, wiping away tears as I continued to rein in my laughter. "Oh, I *know*."

I'd never seen Sawyer sing in public, but he did, in fact, sing in the shower, and occasionally, he'd crash my vocal practice, trying to make whatever I was singing into a duet. It always resulted in me giggling and crying simultaneously—just like I was doing right now.

The music started, and Declan and I composed ourselves just as my sexy-as-sin, vocally challenged football-star boyfriend began singing "All In" by Lifehouse.

My hands went to my heart, and my smile was so big my cheeks hurt, but I was no longer laughing.

"He's crazy about you," Declan said low enough that only I could hear.

"He's definitely crazy," I replied, not taking my eyes off the man of my dreams as he continued to sing so off-key I'd be cringing if it were coming from anyone but him.

When the song ended, everyone was on their feet, and a few wolf whistles rang out.

I was still clapping and watching Sawyer high-five everyone along his path back to me when I locked eyes with Hunter. My smile faltered, but then Hunter gave me his own warm smile, and I pulled mine back into place and looked away quickly. Then Sawyer was in front of me, beaming, and I was throwing myself into his awaiting arms.

"What did you think?" he asked. All I could do was pepper his face with kisses, but I avoided his lips. That would have to wait. There was no way I was letting all these people see our first kiss. "I know I'm no Andrew, but you gotta admit, that was badass, Quinn."

I shook my head teasingly, and my eyes narrowed. "So very badass, Tight End."

He waggled his eyebrows at me. "Can we go back to your place now so we can dry hump like teenagers?"

"I'm pretty sure you were doing a lot more than dry humping as a teenager, stud."

His cocky grin threatened my no-sex rule. "Fine—let's go have fake sex Southern-Baptist-teenager style."

I laughed and dropped my head to his chest. "You're incorrigible."

"Yes, but are you madly in love with me yet?"

My head fell back, and I stared into his dreamy expression, all the feelings lighting up my insides. "Not yet, I'm working on it," I lied, the teasing grin never leaving my face.

His hands slid down my back and over my butt until he was squeezing it and pressing me to him. His chin dipped and his voice grew gravelly. "Work faster, because I'm already there."

I batted my lashes. "I'm trying, but I keep getting interrupted by your ego."

Sawyer opened his mouth as though his next comeback

was a breath away, but he closed it and shook his head at me instead. I understood the sentiment. Everything about being together felt authentic and bona fide.

I was more than ready to leave, but the three drinks I'd consumed required something else. "Let me use the restroom first, and then we can go." I kissed him on the cheek, then grabbed my clutch before heading toward the back of the VIP lounge.

I'd just turned the corner into the alcove where the restrooms were when I nearly ran directly into someone coming the other direction.

"Oh, gosh! I'm so sorry!"

The mountain of a man with tired gray eyes and a crew cut offered me a small smile. "Are you Sawyer's girlfriend?"

"I-I am," I replied, a sense of unease tugging at my core. But then his smile widened, and he held out his hand in a kind gesture.

"It's nice to meet you. I'm Sawyer's teammate, Knox—Knox Whitmore."

I took his hand and smiled back. "Kennedy Quinn. It's really nice to meet you too, Knox."

The corners of his eyes creased, and his head tilted slightly to the side. He still hadn't released my hand. "Kennedy Quinn . . . that sounds familiar. Have we met before?"

"Nope!" I squeaked and pulled my hand hard enough that he let me go.

Pondering eyes penetrated mine. "Huh."

"What the fuck, Whitmore!" Sawyer growled, and I suddenly saw his entire football career flash before me.

Not on my watch.

"Sawyer," I said with forced calmness as I stepped into him and wrapped my arms around his waist, giving Knox my back. Sawyer's blue orbs darkened, and his jaw was so tight, it appeared sharp enough to cut stone.

"Everything is fine—Knox and I were just introducing ourselves. I almost ran him over because I wasn't paying attention to where I was going." I begged with my eyes for him to believe me, and let it go.

Fortunately, Sawyer and I had the ability to communicate without words.

Hearing my silent plea, he leaned down, pressing his lips to my forehead without taking his eyes off Knox.

"You stay the fuck away from my girl."

Sawyer had some explaining to do when we got home. He'd never reacted to me shaking another man's hand like this before.

This new behavior better not come with the boyfriend upgrade.

I never saw Knox's reaction, but as he passed us, he paused at Sawyer's side to look down at me. "Like I said, it was nice to meet you, Kennedy. Enjoy the rest of your evening."

Peeking over Sawyer's flexed bicep, I smiled weakly. "You too, Knox."

The moment Knox was gone, Sawyer spun me in place and pushed me through the ladies' room door. He barked at two girls I recognized as Jonny's "dates" to leave, and then he lifted me, setting me down on the bathroom counter. He had a hand resting on either side of me as he leaned in.

His eyes searched me with rabid fervor, and I think I saw his bottom lip tremble.

"Did he hurt you?"

"No, Sawyer. Don't be ridiculous."

"I'm not, Quinn. There's something not right with that guy. He's had it out for me since day one and now that he knows—"

"Knows what?"

Sawyer shook his head and avoided my eyes. "Nothing."

He's lying to me right now.

And I didn't know what to do with that thought. So I pressed, "Tell me."

Sawyer cradled my face in his hands and stepped forward to stand between my legs. "Just that now that he knows you're my girlfriend, I'm worried he might be a dick to you too."

Uh-huh. Likely story, friend.

But I was done hanging out with Sawyer in a ladies' room at a bar—talk about bad omens—so it would have to wait.

"I'd like to go home now."

———————

Back at my place, I told Sawyer he could stay the night, but we needed to keep it old school and keep our clothes on while we slept. He chuckled and tossed me on the bed after I'd slipped into my Miami Mavericks pajamas. On the ride home, he'd all but convinced me that he hadn't lied to me by omission. A sliver of doubt remained, but I was too ecstatic over the idea that Sawyer and I were spending our first night as an official couple together to let it ruin the mood—something I hoped wouldn't come back to bite me later on.

"I need to get you new pj's," he pointed out just before he shoved me to my side of the bed rather unromantically.

"No way, man. These bad boys are my favorites."

Sawyer growled like an animal. He shackled my wrists in his grip and raised them over my head. Then he lay on me, careful not to crush me into the first-floor apartment beneath us. "You better be talking about the pj's and not about you having a lady-boner for my old teammates."

I giggled and secretly hoped it would always be this way between us. My heart was fueled by the Sawyer-isms that made me laugh harder than anything else ever could.

"Jealous much?" I teased.

He lifted his chin and furrowed his brow in a playful scowl. "Yeah, what of it? A little jealousy is healthy between couples."

My eyes grew wide. "Oh, really! And did you learn this in boyfriend school?"

"You're fucking right I did. By the way, I not only aced the class—they asked me to teach it next semester."

Tears streamed from the corners of my eyes into my hair, and I choked on my laughter. "Well in that case, keep up the good work."

Only after my giggles had subsided and Sawyer had rolled onto his back, taking me with him, did the overwhelming need to consummate our new relationship with a kiss strike.

He really is the whole package.

"Quinn." His voice was low and full of gravel.

"Sawyer."

The corners of his mouth curled upward in a suggestive manner. "I'm going to kiss you now, pretty girl. I'm going to make you forget about every kiss that came before this one. These are the last lips you're ever going to taste."

His dangerously sexy declaration had a coil tightening low in my belly, and I squirmed in his embrace. "Okay . . ."

A flicker of awe and euphoria flashed in Sawyer's eyes, and then his mouth was on mine. Three years of suppressed kisses, forbidden touches, unspoken words, and denied emotions came flooding out by way of our lips and tongues.

We kissed long and hard, as though each of us was trying to convince the other of how deeply our love flowed. We moaned into each other's mouths, urging each other on, until finally we broke apart, both coming up for air with grins on our faces.

A sigh of pleasure escaped through my lips. "That was . . ."

Sawyer was quick to fill the pause. "Exactly what I knew it'd be . . . perfect."

18

SAWYER

'd severely underestimated my desire to fuck her.

A month into dating Kennedy and I was expert level when it came to foreplay and heavy petting. I'd resolved to let her call the plays if that's what it took for her to believe in the sanctity of our new relationship, but that didn't mean I wasn't jonesing to slide into her wet heat and put us both out of our misery. There was no denying that Kennedy wanted me just as badly as I wanted her. My girl was eager when it came to expanding our fake sex repertoire.

Three hours ago, the Cougars and I had landed in Dallas for tomorrow night's season opener. New York and Dallas had scored the first Sunday Night Football matchup of the season, a coveted spot. I'd ditched Declan at a sports bar after we'd crushed a couple of rib eyes and was heading back to our shared hotel room. Last I saw the wideout, he was riding a mechanical bull with a group of chicks in tiny denim skirts doing their best Dallas Cowboys Cheerleaders impressions. Coach had set a mandatory early curfew, which meant I only had a couple hours to myself before my roomie would return.

"How's it goin', partner?" Trek's fake Southern accent made me chuckle.

I readjusted my pillow. "Dude, that was spot-on."

"It felt god-awful coming out of my mouth. Remind me to never do that again, mate."

I continued to chuckle. "You got it."

"In all seriousness, though, how are you feeling about tomorrow's game?"

I dragged a hand through my hair. "My body feels amazing." *Aside from my pining dick.*

"And your mind? You got that on straight too, correct?"

"Yeah, man. Everything's . . . good."

I hadn't convinced myself with that response, so it didn't surprise me when Trek drawled, "Talk to me, Jackson."

After Sterling had given me the heads-up that some of my teammates might not be willing to have their ticket to the Sawyer Jackson bandwagon punched, I'd sent Trek on a mission to find the source of the leak. I wanted to know which teammates had it out for me.

"Whitmore—I swear he's following me around with his phone out, waiting to catch me doing something."

Trek's irritation edged his tone. "That fucking bloke—if Collingsworth hadn't torn his quad, he wouldn't even be on the bloody team."

Knox Whitmore making the 53-man roster had felt like a nail being ever so slowly tapped into my coffin.

Though he lacked proof, Trek believed Steven Moran to be the rat and Whitmore to be the threat. Trek wasn't a fan of either, but he didn't believe they were in cahoots. His theory was that Moran might have enlightened Whitmore with the hope that the veteran would help keep me on the path of righteousness. But Whitmore had a personal motive for wanting to see me fuck up.

I sighed, accepting for the seven hundredth time that I was going to be teammates with the sketchy fucker for at least the remainder of this season. "I've got both the

Cougars' golden boy gig and the boyfriend gig on lock, so don't worry—I'm not going to give him the opportunity."

"You're sounding mighty confident for a chap just getting his dick wet for the first time."

No dick wetting going on here, mate.

I grinned smugly, even though he couldn't see me. "Turns out being a boyfriend—a fucking Grade A boyfriend, if I do say so myself—isn't so hard after all."

After Trek's appreciative laughter had waned, he asked, "How are things working out between the lovely Kennedy and her agent?"

My free hand clenched and unclenched on instinct. "Can you believe he had the fucking stones to tell her that she needed to change her hair color to blonde and that she could 'stand to shed a few pounds'?"

Fuck no and no fucking way, fuck no.

"Shall I have someone break his legs?"

I grunted in reply and half wished he wasn't joking.

"Well, I hope she told him to fuck off."

Trek's sentiments echoed verbatim what I'd said to Kennedy after she'd told me about William's comments.

"Nah, she only dug her heels in deeper. She hasn't had even one audition yet, which is fucked up, if you ask me. He claims he's still 'shaping her into a star.'"

At least she didn't cave to his whims.

Trek made a disgruntled sound. "Remind your charming girl that I can help her find a proper agent."

I would, but my charming girl's stubbornness to see things through rivaled my own at times, and fuck if I didn't love her tenacity.

KENNEDY

It was the first time a Saturday night gig has been canceled at the eleventh hour, and Sawyer was fifteen hundred miles away in Dallas.

Thanks, universe. Not.

For the past month, our schedules had clashed like a drunk Scott Disick and the Kardashians. Sawyer got an A-plus-plus for effort though. My devoted boyfriend would flip Manhattan on its back if it hastened his route to reach me every time we both had a free moment.

Me: Gig canceled. Call me when you can. xx

I'd just picked up the romance novel I'd given myself permission to enjoy on my rare night off when the unmistakable sound of an incoming FaceTime call had my heart break-dancing in my chest. Sawyer's sexy smirk graced the screen, and my thighs intuitively squeezed together.

Sorry, broody book boyfriend, you've got nothing on my real man.

If Sawyer and I were in the same zip code tonight, my dry spell would have been a thing of the past. He'd surpassed every expectation I'd set for him, and I'd never felt more loved and cherished in a relationship—*any* relationship. Both my heart and body wanted everything Sawyer Jackson had to give. Lingering fears inspired by my past still chilled in the dark corners of my mind, but every day that Sawyer showed up in our relationship, the less I engaged them.

"Hey, baby," he greeted in that gravelly voice that always turned my nipples into steel.

"Hey, yourself, Tight End," I purred and chewed on my bottom lip.

Sawyer's eyes narrowed, and his chin tilted down.

"Whatcha doing over there looking like a sexy librarian?" I giggled and went to lift my black-framed reading glasses from their perch on my nose to the top of my head, but Sawyer stopped me. "Keep 'em on." His lazy delivery only made my breaths come faster.

"I'm reading . . ."

"Mhmm. I see that."

It wasn't often that I had time to read for pleasure—no pun intended—these days, but Sawyer knew that romance novels had been my jam pre-William Abreu. Since we'd begun dating, he'd also discovered that I'd relied on those books to help me survive the drought. I'd confessed this to him one night, and as only Sawyer could, he'd seen it as a challenge. He'd proceeded to give me the best orgasm of my life with his mouth—*over my pants*. Talk about erotic AF.

"Baby, prop me up on your other pillow."

My lower belly ached from his commanding tone. "Huh? Why?"

The naughty glint in his eyes didn't prepare me for what came out of his mouth next. "Because you're going to need two hands to touch those fine tits and that sweet pussy just the way I tell you to."

My throat narrowed, and I gulped. "Jesus, Sawyer! Too vulgar!"

His deliciously evil chuckle made said sweet pussy drip with my arousal.

"Hush, pretty girl. Now make sure I can see you, and then lay back and close your eyes. Just listen to my voice—trust me to make this good for you."

If I trusted Sawyer with anything, it was that he could make me come with the sound of his voice. My hands were a luxury option.

With trembling fingers, I followed Sawyer's instructions,

giving him the best angle I could manage with a pillow for a camera stand and lay back, brushing my loose bangs from my flushed face but keeping my naughty librarian glasses in place. As I settled into the down bedding, I pressed my lids closed with a ragged breath and then raised my hands a second time. Gripping the hem of Sawyer's OSU sweatshirt, I started to lift upward.

"Uh, uh, uh," Sawyer chided. "Did I tell you to take off my sweatshirt, Quinn?"

Hearing my original nickname flamed the longing for Sawyer that already burned in my heart. Unsure if a verbal reply was expected—being a phone sex virgin and all—I shook my head. His breathy laughter filled my bedroom, and a slight moan slipped through my lips.

Definitely going to come by his voice.

"My baby is needy tonight . . . Are you wearing one of those lacy bras right now, beautiful?"

I shook my head a second time.

"Use your words, baby."

"N-n-no . . ."

"Are you wearing something else or are those perky tits rubbing against my alma mater?"

I could hear his satisfaction before I'd even given him confirmation. "No bra . . ." I breathed.

"Fuck," he groaned—but I don't think it was directed at me. "Keep my sweatshirt on, baby . . . and pinch those hard nipples that I can't wait to lick and suck. I bet they taste like coconuts and strawberries."

My hips nearly shot off the bed the moment I obeyed, and I thought I heard rustling bedsheets that weren't my own. The thought of Sawyer masturbating while he guided me through my own self-pleasure was almost too much to bear.

"Can I open my eyes?" I begged.

In all our innovative pseudo-sex, I hadn't yet touched or even spied Sawyer's penis, but I'd ground against his hardness enough times to speculate nonstop about the grand mystery I couldn't wait to unveil.

"Eyes closed, Quinn."

Boo.

"Pull the sheet down so I can see what else you've got on . . . better not be anything with a Mavericks logo or I'm going to spank your traitor ass when I get home."

My throbbing clit cursed me for not having Mavericks stamped all over my body.

I lowered the bedsheet seductively and knew the moment he realized that his sweatshirt was the only stitch of clothing on my body.

"There's no panties under my sweatshirt either, is there, baby?"

"No . . ."

"You naughty little minx," he practically slurred. Sawyer was drunk on lust, and I was the only thing he was sipping. "Drag two fingers through those slick pussy lips, baby."

Maybe as a feminist I should have been offended by my boyfriend's derogatory nickname for my lady parts, but after hearing him croon that word with more affection than most men said I love you, I was ready to terminate my membership if asked.

I wasn't sure I'd ever been so embarrassingly wet, and for a moment I was glad Sawyer wasn't there to hear the sounds coming from between my legs.

"Are you wet, baby?"

"Yes."

"How wet?"

"Enough wet, Sawyer . . . Everything is—it's . . . throbbing."

"Fuck, baby," he gritted out. "Rub your clit with your fingertips . . . ease that throb."

His voice was a slow, smooth tongue over my sensitive nerves, and the moment I complied, my thighs quivered, and then I was moaning Sawyer's name.

"Sawyer . . . I'm—I'm . . ." I panted, but my orgasm robbed me of my freedom of speech.

A strangled sound from Sawyer had me wanting to open my eyes, but the aftereffects of my ecstasy left me spent, and all I could do was sigh and roll my head his direction.

"Fucking hell, that was the hottest thing I've ever seen. I'm gonna eat you right up when I get home."

A smile spread across my face, and my eyes fluttered open. Sawyer came into focus, and with the little remaining strength I had left, I reached for my phone. "Did you come?" I asked as I brought his virtual image just inches from my face.

"Nope."

I jerked upright. "What?"

"That was all about you, pretty girl."

My eyes narrowed. "But I heard . . ."

Sawyer's brows lifted. "What you heard were the sounds of your boyfriend's self-inflicted torture. I've only come from your greedy little pussy rubbing herself all over me for the past month."

Immune to Sawyer's graphic description of our simulated lovemaking, I fell back into my pillow with a sigh. "Noble, but unnecessary."

"What can I say? I'm obsessed with what you got going on between those thighs and it's all I want."

I considered his words for a moment and then turned on the sexy pout that I knew drove Sawyer crazy. "Then I guess you have no interest in what I've got going on between these lips, right?"

He growled, and even on the tiny screen I saw his gaze darken as his voice lowered. "You are so getting spanked, Kennedy Quinn."

"I'm counting on it, Sawyer Jackson."

19

SAWYER

The atmosphere was thick with sexual pheromones as the crowd fed off Kennedy's sultry voice.

Readjusting my cap, I made my way to the front of Foreplay, a nightclub in Times Square, as a few sets of eyes followed me with recognition. We'd won our first game last night—on the coveted Sunday Night Football platform, no less—and Cougars fans had embraced their newest tight end with unbridled enthusiasm.

Eventually, I found a spot where I could watch Kennedy—hopefully undisturbed—who was standing in with the band, Eclipse, for a friend who had a sick pet fish.

No, that was not a joke.

Musicians are a funky bunch.

I shoved my hands in my pockets and leaned back against the wall, trying to look as nondescript as possible. Regardless of whether I ended up surrounded by curious strangers or not, I wasn't going anywhere.

With the help of a few text message exchanges, Andrew and I had become buds, even after he'd gone and changed his name to My Sexiest Friend in Kennedy's phone, and he'd given me the heads-up that the guys in the band wanted in Kennedy's pants.

If I recall, his exact words were: "The drummer said he

wants to taste her honey, and the bassist offered to massage her vocal cords with his dick."

Never gonna fucking happen.

After our flight had landed, we had mandatory team meetings, and then I'd gone in search of my girl, so I could protect her from some horny rock stars who had a death wish.

Kennedy looked stunning. Her steel-gray jeans looked like they'd been painted on, leaving nothing to the imagination. The lacy camisole she wore showed way too much skin, and the straps of her bra had no shame.

Couldn't she sing just as well in long sleeves? A parka, maybe?

Who the fuck says parka?

Grandmas.

And don't get me started on the way she flipped her hair from one side to the other with a level of provocativeness that had my blood rushing below my belt. As she worked the mic stand, I longed to run my fingers through those messy mocha locks as I devoured her face.

Soon, bro.

Kennedy belted out a gritty rendition of "Smells Like Teen Spirit," and the way every guy on the stage—not just the goddamn drummer and bassist—looked at her, I was certain that we were a brotherhood of physical discomfort.

Fuck musicians.

I was contemplating a comparative analysis of football players—the real men who risked their bodies for the greater good—and the weak men who played instruments when Kennedy's voice rang out a good night to New York, and then she was leaving the stage.

Drummer boy was right there with his stupid sticks in one hand and groping Kennedy with the other.

Okay, maybe that was a bit dramatic—but he did have a loose arm draped across her shoulders.

Using my God-given ability as a top blocking tight end, I pushed through the few people who stood between us until the firm hand of a defensive lineman posing as a bouncer smacked against my chest.

"Where do you think you're going, *amigo*?" the guy with the face tattoo asked as he looked down his crooked nose at me.

Yes, he looked *down* at me. The bouncer was none other than Hagrid himself. I'd have bet his flying motorcycle was parked outside too.

"I'm Kennedy's boyfriend," I said with urgency. "The singer—just ask her."

With moderate reluctance, the Hagrid lookalike glanced over his shoulder. "Hey, Kenn, this guy with you?" he asked, keeping one eye glued on me.

He didn't seem to recognize me. Maybe if I made it clear who I was, he'd do me a solid and remove the drummer from Kennedy's body before I did something that resulted in me submitting my résumé to West Springfield High.

"Sawyer!" Kennedy ran to me and threw her arms around my neck with so much force I had to take a step back.

I looked over her head at the bouncer and lifted my shoulders as if to say, "I tried to tell you, man."

Hagrid smirked and gave me a nod of approval.

Then, the gorgeous woman in my arms had my undivided attention.

"You're here," she gushed, looking at me with the eyes I could never get enough of.

She held my shirt in her little fists and pressed herself against me, the curves of our bodies meshing in a perfect fit.

This was authentic Kennedy, the love of my fucking life.

I held her head back enough so I could look at her

breathtaking face. "Hey, you. You were incredible. What does a guy have to do to get a private concert?"

She giggled, and those puffy lips that I'd never seen painted red before drew me in, a beacon for my cock. "Anything for you, Tight End."

"Anything?"

She squinted her eyes playfully. "Prob-ah-bal-ly . . . *may*-be."

"Can we see Brooke sing another time and get the fuck out of here so I can have you all to myself?"

I'd already committed over text to staying for one of Brooke's sets with the same band if I'd made it in time, but after seeing my girl so very fuckable, I'd had a change of heart.

She leaned up and nipped at my chin. "Yeah, we can do that."

I grinned. "Really?"

"Really. See? You get rewarded if you *behave.* And Saturday night, you behaved *exceptionally.*"

Holy pussycat.

If this is how she reacted to a little FaceTime nookie, she'd be a certifiable nympho by the time I was done with her.

Kennedy gave a sassy head shake and thoughts of her coming all over her fingers at my command made me weak in the knees. "Now, give me a minute to say goodbye to the guys and get my stuff, and then we can get out of here."

She made to leave, but I held on to her, lowering my voice. "What are the chances of you letting me go with you to say goodbye to the guys?" I asked, not hiding my sheepish expression.

Hey, at least you asked and didn't demand.

Kennedy nodded in the direction the rest of the band had gone. "Yeah, yeah, handsome—you can come with," she teased, slipping her hand into mine before leading me toward the back with an extra sway in her hips.

You're staking your claim.

In the words of Walter White: You're goddamn right.

In the cab, Kennedy rested her head against me as she recapped her night, high on the adrenaline of performing. I listened as though she were giving me instructions on how to disarm a live bomb, not wanting to miss one detail. In that time, I also took it upon myself to finally run my fingers through her hair. Then I buried my face against her crown and inhaled her coconut shampoo.

I love you.

Kennedy glanced up at me, and her expression softened with a sense of knowing. "I missed you so much." Her fingertips trailed my jawline. "I always thought I missed you before— but now . . ."

Her lids were heavy, but she wasn't drunk. Her lips parted the way they did when she was sleeping, and her breath smelled like cinnamon. Taking advantage of her loss for words, I moved in for a kiss. I swirled my tongue against hers in lazy strokes, and she melted into me. I pulled back just slightly and found her eyes again. "I know, baby . . . Me too."

She nodded once and rested her head under my chin, and I swear I heard angels singing.

"Are you sure you want to do this?" I nuzzled her head, stealing another inhale at the same time I brushed her neck with my knuckles.

"Yes!" she whisper-yelled. "But why a *hotel*?"

She made it sound like I'd told her to get in the kitchen and bake me a chicken pot pie.

I shoved my fingers in her hair and brought my mouth to her ear. I didn't care if the cab driver heard us, but I wasn't sure Kennedy would be as brazen. "Because, baby, I'm gonna do things to you that are gonna make you scream my name all night long, and I don't want Andrew and Brooke to be jealous."

I studied her for a reaction.

Those emerald pools of light widened, and I wanted to rip my own heart out of my chest and offer it to her on bended knee, right then and there.

"O-oh . . . okay."

That was all she said—in the sweetest, most Kennedy tone she could have possibly used.

Her bottom lip jutted out, and I turned into a puddle of emotions.

"Quinn. I have waited three goddamn, motherfucking years for this. Once I start fucking you, I won't be able to stop. I'm gonna want to make love to you for the rest of the night, and probably all day tomorrow too."

She pulled her lips into her teeth to hold back her laugh. "Well, which is it? Are we fucking or making love?"

"If I have my way, baby, we'll be doing a whole lot of both."

Her face flushed, and I prayed it was from arousal and not because she was embarrassed. Because Jesus fucking Christ, she was sexy as hell. With those pink cheeks and pillowy lips, she had my cock screaming for his right to be set free.

She sighed and dragged her leg across my lap, her thigh placed right the fuck on top of my erection.

Maybe my little nympho-in-the-making wasn't quite so shy anymore.

My hand slipped under her top. A shiver ran through her body as my thumb teased at her lace bra. I found her hard nipple and rolled it between my fingertips.

"Sawyer . . ." she moaned into my collarbone, her fingers

weaving into the hair that just barely curled at the base of my neck.

"Come here, baby."

I lifted Kennedy onto my lap, and her arms came around my neck. One of my hands gripped her left ass cheek to balance her while the other massaged her perfect tit.

Taking my life in my own hands, I dipped my head, making eye contact and keeping it as I went lower. Then I took the thin camisole and bra into my mouth.

I sucked. Hard.

I bit down even harder.

Our eye-lock never wavered.

Kennedy hissed and sank her top teeth into her bottom lip. I was done for.

For all I knew, Jesus Christ himself could have been driving the cab, and I would have flipped him off if he so much as cleared his throat right now.

"Sawyer . . ." she repeated, sounding like she was in pain. Sweet, delicious, pussy-throbbing, nipple-aching pain.

My cock empathized.

My mouth released her and was instantly at her neck. "Yeah, baby?" I breathed into her ear as we panted against each other.

"I need . . . I need . . ."

Why the fuck is it taking so long to get to the hotel? My baby has needs, dammit!

Because you picked a hotel in east bumfuck.

Right—someplace without paparazzi lurking. Long Island would do.

And then Kennedy Quinn used her dainty little fingers to move my hand to that magical place that lived between her legs. The feel of her damp heat through those tight-as-sin jeans had me seeking oxygen.

"Fuck, Quinn," I groaned, and then I bit her.

Her head fell back and rolled to the side as she moaned through plump, scarlet lips.

I ran my tongue up her neck and over the spot my teeth had just faintly marked. Then, as though God had heard my prayers and had taken pity on my depraved soul, we arrived at our destination.

20

KENNEDY

Hello, Jesus? It's Kennedy. Here's the wheel. Consider it yours. You're welcome.

My skin hummed with the anticipation of Sawyer's touch, and my panties had been drenched since I'd inhaled my first breath of him at the bar.

He checked us in, and then told me to wait for him while he disappeared into the convenience store attached to the lobby. With my hands shoved in the back pockets of my jeans, I used the square floor tiles to walk a deliberate pattern, trying to stay present.

Does he need snacks?

When Sawyer returned, he was carrying a small plastic bag; I gave him a suspicious look.

"Logistics," was all he said. When I looked at him as though he'd spoken in Mandarin, he added, "Of the latex variety."

"Ohh!" I blushed.

He smiled and kissed my temple as he guided me to the elevator.

"Have I told you tonight how fucking adorable you are?" His teeth teased at my ear, and I wondered if anyone had ever orgasmed by having their ears touched.

I'd have to ask Siri.

"Adorable? Could you go with something a little more

186

age-appropriate since you *are* about to start giving out orgasms like Girl Scout Cookies." I glanced up and flashed him a coy grin.

Sawyer released a carnal sound, and as soon as the elevator door closed behind us, he had me up against the shiny steel wall with both hands on either side of my head. "Can we please not talk about Girl Scouts and their cookies when I'm about to do lots of dirty things to you. It's just weird, baby."

"Depends—how dirty are we talking?"

The corner of his mouth hooked into a crooked grin. "*Exceptionally* dirty. So dirty you're going to be praying to God by the time I'm done wringing every drop of pleasure from this hot little body." And then, as though his words alone weren't enough to make me whimper, he leaned down and applied the same potency to his kiss.

Every time Sawyer kissed me, it felt like he wanted to memorize every detail about my mouth from the inside out. My jaw relaxed as I let him govern our kiss with reckless abandon, and then my hand dropped to cup his hardening length that nudged at my stomach.

"Fuuuck, Quinn." His teeth latched onto my bottom lip so hard the sting of tears burned my eyes, but all I could do was moan and beg for more.

When he took a half step back, my tongue lingered over the swollen area. A hint of liquid pennies tasted on the tip.

"I'd rather not jizz in my pants tonight if I don't have to," he teased.

The chime of the elevator depositing us at our floor interrupted me before I could fire back a witty reply. Sawyer threaded our fingers together, and on my first step, my legs felt as useful as a jelly doughnut. I hadn't even had sex yet.

I stepped into what could only be described as a gross

display of wealth and shook my head in disapproval. "Why did you get the penthouse suite, you silly man?"

The plastic bag in his hand hit the floor, and then Sawyer spun around to face me. Being a mega-fit athlete, he moved with a prowess I didn't possess. His grip sank into my butt cheeks, and then he had me in his embrace with my legs curled around his waist in the span of a heartbeat.

"Humor me, Quinn. It's been a long three goddamn, motherfucking years, and I want everything to be right."

His stare alone had me on the edge of bliss, but it was the sovereign tone that had my heart on notice.

I need this man like I need my next breath.

"It already is right, Sawyer. Because it's us."

The salty flavor of my silent tears tickled my tongue. Sawyer backed me up against the wall and trapped me in place with his body. One hand came to my throat, and with a strong thumb he raised my chin so he could inspect my face. "What's wrong?"

I squeezed my lids shut and licked my lips with a sigh. Sawyer leaned in and kissed away every tear that littered my face.

His tenderness made me smile, and my eyes opened. "It's nothing. I'm being ridiculous. I'm just having all the feels right now."

He pressed his forehead against mine, and I felt his lips curve upward.

"I feel it too," he whispered.

I hadn't made him wait long—but in the time he did wait, his thoughtful actions had corroborated all his sweet words. I already loved Sawyer beyond measure or logic, and once we crossed this line, I knew that if I lost him, I'd never recover. My heart silently pleaded for confirmation that he appreciated the magnitude of this moment as much as I did.

"Sawyer."

"Quinn."

I swallowed my trepidation. "Make love to me."

He pulled his head back enough that I could see his eyes. "Quinn." His hot breath came out rough and shallow. "You know everything will change, right? There's no going back from this."

He understands.

But I didn't say that out loud. Instead, I nodded.

Sawyer cocked his head and lifted his chin. "You've gotta give me more, baby. Because I want you more than anything, and I need to know that you know how serious I am. I want *you*, Kennedy Quinn. I want *all* of you. And I want you for fucking ever."

This man.

The reply was stuck somewhere between my heart and my vocal cords.

"Use your words, beautiful. You're killing me here."

I blinked myself into awareness, no longer caught in the haze of my emotions. I held Sawyer's perceptive stare. "Fuck me, Sawyer."

With gentle precision, he guided my legs back under me until my feet were solidly on the floor. He dipped his head, planting a trail of sensual kisses from my ear, down my neck, and along my collarbone. My moan was a plea, and the back of my head rolled across the wall to give him better access to my exposed skin.

Sawyer's fingers fumbled with the button of my jeans, and I felt his body trembling. His raw and uncensored reaction was validating in some way. Sawyer always told me that I held all the power in our relationship, but I didn't believe that. And the more I'd considered it, I realized I didn't need that either. Our love had been forged in the most sacred friendship. A friendship where acceptance, honesty, and loyalty were always delivered, and support was unconditional. It took equal parts of both of us to create such a union, and the same was true now.

Sawyer's hungry lips and expert tongue explored their way across the tops of my breasts. His eager licking and sucking were bound to leave marks. He managed to ease my jeans over my hips and shimmied them down my thighs. When his mouth found my right breast, he paused to bite the nipple, just as he'd done in the cab. My back arched, feeding him more of my aching nub.

"Fuck, Sawyer . . . please get to my skin . . . I need your mouth on me . . ."

His controlled groan felt like a call for patience, and I may have shed a few tears in frustration.

My fingers threaded into his hair just as he dropped to his knees.

"How the fuck did you get these things on?" he gritted through his teeth.

He tugged on my pants until he'd accomplished his task of getting me halfway naked. Then, with sensual fingers and erotic purpose, he navigated his way back up my legs. His expression was one of unrelenting thirst, and I was his oasis. He stroked my calves so seductively that I felt insane with salacious need and battled against the sense of emptiness that I felt between my thighs.

Sawyer tapped just above the inside of my knee. "Open up for me, baby."

Five freaking words and I was verifiably a stroke away from sobbing and begging.

My hands still lost in his hair, I watched Sawyer's devilish mouth seal over my center—lace panties and all. The pressure in his grip increased. He let out a sound of masculine satisfaction that vibrated through my entire body, and my knees really did give way this time. If it weren't for Sawyer holding me to the wall, I would have crumpled in a helpless heap of yearning.

He hooked his fingers in the strings of my thong and then my panties were gone and the cold air on my wetness sent me into another series of sensations. I needed Sawyer's warm mouth to cover me before I hoisted the white flag, reached down, and took matters into my own hand.

Fortifying myself, I opened my eyes and looked down to find him staring longingly at my pathetic pussy.

"*Sawyer,*" I hissed.

"Quinn."

The tightening coil that sat low in my belly contracted.

"Don't *Quinn* me."

"Do you know how long I've wanted to taste you, beautiful girl?"

"Let me guess. Three goddamn, motherfucking years?" I replied, my desperation palpable to anything with a pulse.

That panty-dropping grin spread across his face, but it was a ludicrous waste of energy because my panties were already in shreds on the floor.

"God, I love you, Quinn."

In the next beat, several things happened in rapid succession. Sawyer's tongue swept upward through my folds, and my head fell back to the wall. We moaned in unison, my legs trembled, and Sawyer began to feast.

The tip of his tongue danced around the engorged bundle of nerves, and my head thrashed side to side. My hands left his hair to slap against the wall to help steady my stance.

"Baby?" Sawyer's curious voice cut through my delirium, and I looked down.

Did he really just stop to ask me a fucking question?

"What?" I snarled.

"Look at me. Watch. I want you to know it's me that's making you feel this good."

"Jesus Christ, Sawyer! Just—"

Then he was ravaging me and thrusting a finger inside. In the next breath, he added a second finger and took my pulsating clit between his teeth. Then the curling of his fingertips on my front wall had me screaming his name at the same time his cool, confident voice said, "Come for me, baby."

My body was still free-falling from the pinnacle of ecstasy when he lifted me again, wrapping my legs around his now-bare waist. While on his knees, Sawyer had somehow managed to give me the best orgasm of my life while losing his own jeans and rolling on a condom.

He was a man of many, many talents.

The dick that I'd yet to lay eyes on nudged at my entrance that was soaked in the magical cocktail of my orgasm and Sawyer's saliva.

Fingers that smelled like me dragged my damp bangs out of my eyes. "No going back."

"I don't want to go back."

"This one is gonna be hard and fast, but I promise, the next round, we'll play."

What we just did didn't fall under the category of play?

"That's a promise I'm gonna hold you to," I breathed. "Now just fuck me already, Tight End."

In one fluid stroke, Sawyer was inside me, and sweet mother of motherfucking dragons and all things that were holy, his dick was huge.

I gasped, and Sawyer stilled. "You okay, baby?"

"Uh-huh. Just give me a sec," I choked out.

Sawyer peppered kisses all over my face. I could feel his smile.

"Is this an appropriate time to tell you how fucking tight and perfect your pussy is?"

My forehead dropped to his shoulder, now slick from our combined sweat. I giggled. At least I was breathing. "Okay, I'm good. You can move that monster dick of yours now."

Sawyer's hips rocked into me, pumping in and out with a gentle rhythm. Each calculated thrust was an equal contributor to my next orgasm, which was building at a shocking speed.

"Did you really just call my dick a monster?"

The humor in his tone was so *Sawyer* that I fell a little deeper in love with him right then and there.

"I-I'm going to come again . . . come with me . . . ar-are you there?" My second climax was a mere thrust or voice command from Sawyer away, and my words came out as a desperate cry.

"Yeah, baby . . . I'm going with you." Two strokes later and Sawyer's head fell back, the tendons in his neck strung tight. "Fuuuck!" he roared.

The undeniable nirvana that our intimacy had provided him licked over my glistening flesh and then the walls of my pussy clamped around him as my second orgasm exploded from somewhere deep within.

I buried my face in the nook of Sawyer's neck and clung to him like a newborn koala bear unable to fend for herself.

"Was it worth the wait?" I whispered into his heated skin.

A shudder moved through Sawyer's body, and he spun us around. His broad shoulders leaned against the wall as he held me in an iron-clad embrace. His nose nudged at my ear, his breathing heavy and uneven.

"It was definitely worth the wait." There was a tremor in his voice. He pressed a kiss to my head and then dipped lower to place one on the pulse of my neck. "You know I would have waited forever for you, right?"

"I would have waited for you too."

It was an unspoken understanding that we weren't talking about sex.

Just when I thought his hold on me—both physical and metaphorical—couldn't get any tighter—it did. "I don't want to let you go, Quinn."

"Then don't let me go, Sawyer."

21

SAWYER

Eight hours and six orgasms later—but who's counting?— Kennedy sat across from me on the bed as she chowed on a slice of pizza.

Rocking her birthday suit, marked by our lovemaking, and with knots in her hair and pizza sauce on her face, she'd never been more beautiful to me.

I thanked the football gods for making our next game the Monday Night Game of the Week, which meant I didn't have to report to the clubhouse until tomorrow. I'd only allowed her to come—that was orgasm *numero cinco*—after she'd promised to call out at the diner today like the good little heathen I was helping her become. And since William didn't own a minute of my minx's Tuesday, that meant I had her all. To. My. Fucking. Self.

We hadn't slept yet and needed to rectify that soon, but first, we needed food because fucking for eight hours burns a lot of fucking calories. Every time I'd thought we were done and we'd start to doze off, one of us would suddenly have the urge to touch the other, and then it had been game on once again.

Kennedy had taken "next round, we'll play" to heart and had held me to my word.

Though what she called payback, I called the most epic, nut-busting, toe-curling, leave-me-seeing-spots blow job of my life. I'd discovered that Kennedy's slightly too-big mouth was useful for more than just unhinging her jaw to hit skyscraper notes. My monster, as she now referred to it, loved that talented orifice. I'd always known her neck was created from pure silk, but I'd never realized the inner lining was made of velvet.

Guess I should have seen that coming, considering everything about my girl was goddamn perfect.

After I fed her and we'd slept, I intended to make good on my promise to make love to her. Not that everything we'd done so far hadn't been done out of love—but I wanted to show her that our sex could be hot whether it was hard and dirty or slow and steamy.

"Baby," I coaxed.

I reached over and wiped sauce from the corner of her mouth before sucking it off my thumb.

"We need more condoms." I cocked my head. "Or *do we* need more condoms?"

"Why? You tired of me already? The sex was that bad, huh?" She raised her eyebrows before taking another ginormous, unladylike bite of pizza.

"Hardly. No, what I'm asking is can we go bare because if my opinion matters, I don't want there to be anything between us—figuratively or literally." I lifted her foot and pressed my lips against the arch.

She was still chewing, and her eyes were wide and questioning, so I released her foot and continued, "I know you're on the pill. I've seen you take it."

The way she gulped told me she'd swallowed before she finished chewing—because whatever she had to say, she wanted to say right now.

Fuck, was she gifted at swallowing.

Oh, the memories.

"I'd really rather not have this discussion right now," she said very matter-of-factly.

"Huh?"

"Well, you're in bed with me right now, and I'd really prefer not to discuss your—you know..." She held her hands out as though that was supposed to tell me what she was thinking.

"No, Quinn, I don't know." I could be patient. She was going to use her words.

Kennedy sighed. "Sawyer, I don't want to offend you but—well, come on. Don't make me say it."

With the patience of a fucking saint, I moved the large pizza box between us to the other side of the bed. Kennedy rolled her eyes and dropped her chin to her chest.

"Sawyer..." she drawled.

I leaned across the space between us and lifted her chin, forcing her to look at me. She was so not impressed with the conversation, but we were going to have it anyway, and I may as well be the one to start it.

I cleared my throat and made sure I had her full attention. "I had a clean bill of health in July when I had my physical."

"Okay," she deadpanned.

"*Okay*? That's it? So that means we can forego the condoms?"

She folded her arms across her chest. "You're telling me you haven't had sex since July?" Her eyes narrowed. "If my calendar is correct, it's September."

Brat.

"Yes! That's exactly what I'm telling you! Besides, if I had fucked someone else since my physical... and *I haven't*... I would have worn a condom."

Silence.

Did she not believe me?

With the reflexes of the highly trained professional I was, I hauled her gorgeous ass onto my lap. The look in her eyes told me she had no idea why we were still having this talk, but she was about to find out.

I tucked her hair behind her ear as I gathered my words. What I had to say was important to me—and I hoped it would be to her too.

"Not only have I not had sex with anyone since July, I haven't had sex—of *any kind*—since before you came to the Super Bowl with me."

I'd been wanting Kennedy since before we'd ever spoken a word to each other. It had been lust at first sight quickly followed by crushing on someone I couldn't have. As our friendship grew, so did my feelings. After the Super Bowl, her return flight to New York hadn't even left the runway before I was on the phone to Trek, telling him to turn down the mega deal offer from Miami and to do whatever it took to sign me with the Cougars. It didn't matter if they wanted to pay me in Monopoly money or if I'd be second string to Knox Whitmore, I'd just needed to be in New York. I'd needed to be with Kennedy.

There was a long pause, during which nothing about her expression changed. Then, her eyes dropped as though the weight of my words was finally registering. But rather than throw her arms around me and tell me how proud she was—okay, that's a little messed up; she didn't need to be *proud*—she threw her head back and laughed.

She actually laughed, and I think a part of my heart broke in my chest.

Kennedy's giggles subsided, and she righted her head. When she saw there wasn't a trace of humor on my face, she looked guilty as hell. I didn't want her to feel bad—because come on, she had every right to think my being celibate that long was a joke.

Fuck, there were times when I'd thought it was a joke.

Her fingertips pressed to my cheek, and I couldn't help it, I kissed her palm.

"Sawyer . . . you're serious . . ."

"Yeah, Quinn, I am."

"Well . . . why? Was something"—she looked down at our laps and did her version of sign language again—"broken or something? Was Monster sick?"

My head rolled to the side, and she got the "Really?" look from me.

"Okay—apparently not. Forget I said that."

The feelings in my chest threatened to revolt if I didn't just say what I needed to, so I let it all out, fallout be damned.

"Since we met, I've fucked a lot less than I did before we met. A *lot* less."

She cringed, and I forced myself to smile.

"Don't be confused, baby. Not mortal man numbers."

That, of course, made her give me the stink eye, but the little brat totally deserved it.

I gave her a jostle and pulled her to my chest, resting my chin on her head. "Being totally serious, Quinn. Since we met, a part of me knew it was always going to be you. Someday I had to figure my shit out, right? I just hoped that by the time I did, I wouldn't have to fight some guy to the death in order to have you."

She sighed into my arms, and her soft lips moved up to run along my jaw, and my semihard cock was now a beast ready for action.

"You know I love you, right?" she murmured in her sensual voice against my stubble.

My heart stuttered, and I drew in a rectifying breath. "Are you being an imp right now?"

She shook her head. "No, Sawyer." Her lips rested on my cheek. "I love you."

My eyes fell shut as the emotions lodged in my chest suddenly pole-jumped into my throat. I released the inhale I'd been holding. "I love you too, Quinn. I love you so fucking much."

Kennedy was the only woman I'd ever loved this way, and I knew she'd be the only one I'd ever love this way.

My fingertips skimmed across her lips, and then I kissed her deeply and with a passionate obsession I didn't know I was capable of.

When we finally broke apart, I asked, "So, we good then, you little brat? We can stop using condoms and you can stop pitying my poor, underused cock—unless, of course, you want to help him feel better and, in that case, please, give me all the pity. I can take it, baby."

She sighed and feigned annoyance. "Such a romantic." Then she sobered. "Yes. Agreed—condoms are no longer necessary, Tight End."

We were so fucking made for each other.

Fuck food and sleep, I'd show her romantic.

22

KENNEDY

Bathing was never my thing.

Wait, let me rephrase that. *Taking baths* was never my thing.

Showers? Those I did on the daily, but there was something about soaking in unfiltered, stagnant, body-debris-laden water I found unappealing.

That was until Sawyer prepared a bubble bath in a Jacuzzi. He even turned on the battery-operated candles like a pro-boyfriend should.

After I'd complained that my body felt like it'd been run over by a truck because we'd been banging like a couple of porn stars on crack, Sawyer decided to go romantic on me.

Who did he think he was fooling? He just wanted another excuse to do wicked things to my body.

He cradled me between his legs with my back against him, his hardness bumping every so often against my backside.

My head rolled back to rest on Sawyer's wet chest, and a moan escaped me as my eyes closed. "I don't think I can come again." The words flowed from my mouth, but Sawyer pinched my nipple and called my bluff.

"That's not a winning attitude, baby. I'd expect better from you."

He added his thumb to the mix, working my clit while he fucked me with two fingers.

My climax was still peaking when he whispered in my ear. "Little liar."

I reached back and patted his cheek. "Overachiever."

"There's a reason why these babies are insured for millions of dollars." He held up his hands, and I was too drunk on endorphins to ask if he was serious.

When I came down from my high, I remembered we were sitting prey for all the dead skin cells floating around us, and I stood up rather quickly. I stumbled, and he grabbed my hips to steady me.

"Hang on, Princess Ariel. First day on your human legs?"

I giggled, and Sawyer stood up behind me before giving me a sharp spank on the ass. Too bad I couldn't tell him how much I liked it because if I did, he'd take it as a call to attention and I'd be over his knee.

The man was committed to his craft.

And though he didn't come right out and say it, I was fairly certain he was hopeful that a bevy of orgasms would act like a mind eraser and he'd make me forget about any and all sex I'd had BS—Before Sawyer.

My inner Magic 8 Ball prediction: "It is decidedly so."

Dried off, we snuggled into the obscene comfort of our hotel room bed, and Sawyer held me in his arms.

"I have to leave by six to swing by Declan's before practice tomorrow morning." His tone was lazy as he rested his head against mine. His fingers drew circles on my neck and shoulder, and every once in a while, he'd stroke my cheek or kiss my forehead.

"What's on your agenda tomorrow?" he asked.

"I'm meeting with William at one, and then I work at four." I closed my eyes. His soft caress was like a lullaby.

"Stay as long as you want tomorrow, sleep in, order room service, take another bath if you're feeling adventurous. I'll leave word downstairs to add another day and to not bother you. Don't worry about checking out, I'll take care of it later."

Sweet as it may have been, that got my attention.

I crawled on top of him, folding my hands on his chest and resting my chin on top so I could look him in right in those baby blues.

A sexy smirk blessed his handsome face. "I thought your vagina was on the PUP list?"

I knew that PUP stood for Physically Unable to Perform in the NFL.

"It is. We're *talking* right now."

The expression on his face told me he could tell I was serious, and in return, he was amused.

Damn him.

"You're scowling, baby."

"Well, I need you to know that just because you're my boyfriend now doesn't mean I'm going to let you spend your money on me. Same rules apply as before. Don't think a handful of orgasms promotes you to sugar daddy."

Sawyer's eyebrows shot to his hairline. "A *handful*." He said handful like it was a personal foul against him. "Sure, baby. Go ahead—minimize my accomplishments if you must."

Knowing I could drag this out all day if I really wanted to cause him emotional distress, I coyly replied, "No, you're right . . ." I tapped my chin and studied the headboard over his shoulder. "I think you gave me a hat trick."

Sawyer's eyes thinned. "Baby, there will be no use of hockey metaphors if you ever want that pretty pussy to get licked again."

I batted my lashes. "Fine—and there will be no sugar-daddying if you ever want your cock to get sucked again."

Two can play this game.

Sawyer audibly gulped, and then his head fell back on his pillow. "Really? This?"

I shoved my finger in his nostril. "I mean it, Sawyer Jackson—nothing changes."

His head snapped up. "Oh, baby. *Everything* has changed."

Suddenly, I was on my back and Sawyer's chest was sprawled across me.

"Quinn, I have a shit ton of money and I never spend it. Christ, I don't even own a car or a house. You're going to let me spoil you. You have to give me this."

Controlled rage rippled through me, and I knew my face matched the red duvet that covered our nakedness. I wiggled underneath him to get free, but he just laughed and kept me pinned. "Sawyer! I'm serious! Donate your money to charity or something!"

"I do. Next?"

"Buy your mother another house."

"Why would I do that? I already bought her one—isn't one enough? You're the one who doesn't like frivolous spending. Next?"

Did I just growl like a rabid dog?

"Pay for Maddie's college," I grunted.

"Did that, um, like four years ago. Be more creative but keep squirming—Monster likes it. Next."

My body exhausted, I gave up and went limp beneath him.

Sawyer continued to grin at me. I knew he thought he'd won—but he was dead wrong. We'd revisit this discussion when I had more energy.

"You done, tiger?" he asked, his eyebrows raised.

"Stop talking and kiss me."

"Now that's the kind of creativity I can work with, baby." He kissed me slow and deep, claiming and sensual.

Suddenly, Sawyer was pulling us apart, and the worried look in his eyes made my insides freeze.

"What?" I practically yelped.

"Sorry. Didn't mean to scare you. I just thought of something I wanted to tell you."

His expression relaxed, and I could breathe again.

Jesus, Sawyer could be dramatic at times.

I slid down into my spot alongside him where we could talk comfortably. "Do tell," I urged. "Inquiring minds want to know what's going on up there." I tapped my index finger on his forehead.

Sawyer wrapped his hand around mine and nibbled on my finger.

"You really do like eating me, don't you?"

As soon as the words were out of my mouth, I realized my faux pas and felt my cheeks catch fire.

Sawyer chuckled and tapped my nose. "My foul-mouthed little vixen. God, I really did corrupt you all those years ago, didn't I?"

"I was talking about how you like to put your teeth on me." I poked him in the chest.

"Yeah, baby. Sure, that's what you were talking about. But now that you mention it, it's true—I always want to eat you right up. You okay with that?" His words were laced with lust, and then he dragged his teeth ever so lightly down my neck.

"Totes okay. . . " I sighed, then playfully yanked on his messy tresses. "But didn't you have something earth-shattering to tell me?"

Sawyer's head snapped up from where he'd been nuzzling my breasts. "Fuck. Yes. You're too distracting, woman." He sat up and ran his hand through his hair. His expression told me that whatever he was about to say had been on his mind until our sexcapades had taken precedent.

"Dude, so listen to this." I adored how he could so easily slip into best-friend mode. "You know how I told you Melody was supposed to be at Lake's party, but then she wasn't?"

"Mhmm."

"Turns out, when Sterling told her you'd be there and that she had to be civil and shit—she lost a fucking screw and went off on him. He broke up with her right then and there."

"Well, that seems like an overreaction," I mused.

The absence of emotions I felt over this news—or even the mention of Hunter or Melody—was comforting.

That's your past; your present is far more exciting.

"Yeah, when Declan first told me, I was surprised, but the more I thought about it, I started to think that maybe I'm not the only one who's done some growing up."

"Oh really?" I drawled.

Sawyer groped my boob to capture my entire attention. It was his way of saying, *I'm being serious.*

"I'll never forgive him for how he hurt you, but maybe he really is sorry. Maybe he even regrets fucking up what he had with you."

The shift in Sawyer's tone from contemplative to skeptical made me look up. A darkness had washed over his expression as he stared out into space. I knew Sawyer well enough to know that his thoughts had taken a hard left into jealous territory, and that would not help him keep his nose clean.

I snapped my fingers in his line of sight. "Head in the game, Tight End. Who cares about what Hunter may or may not regret?" When he didn't respond, and it seemed like his thoughts lingered where they didn't need to be, I tried a different tactic. "Hey, what about that guy Knox? You haven't mentioned him since Lake's party—have you been getting along with him?"

As an NFL fan, I really should have known more about Sawyer's teammate, but the guy had never been on my radar.

Snapping out of his self-induced Hunter dilemma, Sawyer offered me a fleeting smile. "Everything's fine with Whitmore, baby. He's just a grump. Nothing to worry about."

He pressed a sweet kiss to my temple, and when he pulled back, I watched the finer muscles tick in Sawyer's jaw. They always told me the true story even when he was rattling off placating bullshit to make me feel better.

His blasé attitude seemed like a far cry from how he'd reacted when Knox shook my hand. I found it hard to believe that Sawyer had just up and changed his position on the man so quickly without sharing with me the story of how it had all gone down.

These were the kinds of details that best-friend Sawyer would have told me without prompting. Boyfriend Sawyer needed to take a page out of his former-best-friend playbook before his omissions made me sour.

"You're not keeping things from me, right?" I asked.

He studied me a moment, his expression softening before he dropped a kiss to my forehead. "It's just football stuff, baby—not a big deal."

23

SAWYER

The Wednesday edition of the *New York Post* slapped against the boardroom table, and I leaned back in my chair and crossed my arms. It had been just two hours since I'd left Kennedy in our hotel room, and I could still taste her.

"Everyone can fuck off. I've done nothing wrong," I said with absolute certainty.

Trek shifted in his chair beside me and shot me a side-eyed glance that either said, "Let me do the bloody talking," or "Shut the fuck up, mate."

I wasn't quite sure; we hadn't gotten much of a chance to talk before Steven Moran had bulldozed his way into the clubhouse boardroom, waving his newspaper in the air like a smoking gun.

"Steven." Trek cleared his throat. "I think what my client is trying to say is that he has not broken any contractual obligations, and that it is far from his control what the tabloids choose to publish or how they may spin something as innocent as him and his *date* enjoying an evening out."

"Date?" Moran sneered, his knuckles boring into the table as he leaned forward.

If his purplish face were any indication, the director of player personnel had anger issues and hypertension to go right along with them.

"This city boasts over a million single women—not that marital status would matter to someone like you." His beady eyes zeroed in on me. My brows raised, my interest in whatever shit he was going to spew next piqued. "And you have to screw the only one who holds the power to fuck over this team?"

I looked down at my clasped hands and heaved a patience-gathering sigh. If I gave a damn about what the windbag thought of me, I'd have made it crystal clear that I wasn't screwing Kennedy, that we were in love and in it for the long haul—but he wasn't worth the energy.

Still, he wasn't about to get away with talking about the love of my life like she was some Yoko Ono jersey chaser.

"You may be my"—I waved my hand around and then made air quotes with my fingers—"boss, in some capacity—for argument's sake only—but I won't sit here and let you speak about my girlfriend that way. So either be respectful, or I'm walking out of here."

"Girlfriend?" he gritted through clenched teeth.

Dude was going to have an aneurism at this rate.

"Yes, sir," I drawled. "Kennedy Quinn is my girlfriend, and as Mr. Evans already stated, my contract doesn't say who I can and cannot date. I assure you that Ms. Quinn and I prefer to keep our relationship private, and will not be doing anything to antagonize the media. Got it?" Without waiting for a reply, I stood up. "Good. Now, if you'll excuse me, I need to get to the weight room."

Moran's beefy hand motioned for me to sit back down. Glancing over at Trek, I could see the only man in this room whose opinion mattered to me hadn't budged, so I reluctantly reclaimed my seat.

"This is not a joking matter, Jackson. If your taste in women has any ill effect on this team—if Hunter Sterling is in any way—"

Bingo.

"Ah—there it is. That's what's really got you all hot and bothered, isn't it?"

"Sawyer," Trek warned, but he was too late. Moran had made the mistake of dragging Sterling into what was supposed to be a lecture about putting the team first, not a lecture about the hazards of dating a teammate's ex.

Moran shook a threatening finger at me. "Don't test me, Jackson."

I rested my steepled fingers under my chin. "Don't disrespect my girlfriend again, *sir*."

Moran snatched the newspaper off the table and stormed out of the room, slamming the door behind him.

Trek's sigh reverberated off the walls.

I spun in my chair to face him. "Well, that was fun."

"Charming, mate." The Brit was holding back a small smile, I could tell. "Being with Kennedy looks good on you," he added.

"Yup."

I couldn't resist smiling like I'd just won the Super Bowl and I'd be going to Disney World tomorrow. In reality, I'd never achieved such a victory, but considering how I felt about my current relationship status with the most incredible woman in the world, I couldn't imagine a better feeling.

"Good. You two belong together. Anyone who's ever spent more than five bloody minutes with the two of you at the same time can see that. You turn into a lovestruck puppy whenever she's around."

The sincerity in Trek's voice was a cheap shot to my manhood. I didn't need him getting all sentimental on me. After making love to Kennedy for hours on end and spending my morning daydreaming about a future with her that involved diamond rings and green-eyed babies with toothy grins and big hands, I was already feeling emasculated enough.

"So, we're cool then?" I asked.

Trek stood up, taking his black leather suitcase with him. "We were never not cool, Sawyer. I've got your back when it comes to your girl, but you've got to keep up your end of the deal—stay out of trouble."

"Duly noted. I had no clue there was a pap in the hotel lobby Monday night."

Trek brushed the invisible lint from the sleeves of his Armani suit coat. "I don't care about that. I'm talking about your teammates and anyone else who might see this as an opportunity to fuck with you."

I rubbed my temples, a headache taking instant hold. "Yeah, I know."

Trek didn't have to spell it out for me. By now, most of the team knew that Kennedy and I were together, and there hadn't been a negative word breathed in my direction. But by making it public, the gossip article had upped the ante.

"Did Kennedy give any thought to me helping her find a different agent?"

I wish.

I shook my head and twirled a pen through my fingers like a baton. "She's stickin' with the douche she's got now. Told you, man, she turns into a hellkitten when I suggest she move on from that prick. Apparently, he's assured her that there is a 'big audition' in her near future. Says he's working on something, but won't tell her what it is just yet. I still think he's a sketchy fuck."

Trek paused with his hand on the doorknob. "Don't forget, Jackson, even douchey Broadway agents fall under the category of people you cannot fuck with."

I gave him a salute. "Aye-aye, Captain."

KENNEDY

"Explain to me again why you're turning down yet another Chicago audition, Ms. Quinn?"

William only called me *Ms. Quinn* when he was displeased with me. If I told him the real reason—*because this is where my boyfriend lives*—I'd never hear the word *Kennedy* out of his mouth again.

Still digesting my "heads-up" call from Sawyer that prematurely ended just as my Uber dropped me off at William's office, I didn't know if I had the wherewithal for this conversation right now.

Damn you, Alexander Hamilton. Wasn't winning a revolution enough? Did you really need to start a tabloid too?

William drummed his fingers on the cover of the *New York Post*, but my agent hadn't mentioned that the woman on the cover with New York's most famous tight end looked mighty familiar. The paparazzi may not have figured out my name yet, but if anyone who knew me cared to stare at the image long enough, they'd know it was this girl.

"Uh." I swallowed hard and twisted my fingers together on my lap. Eight hours ago, I'd been in a state of sated bliss in Sawyer's arms in our Long Island hotel room. Now, I was one challenging question away from a breakdown.

"Because I'd like to stay in Manhattan, sir."

When he called me *Ms. Quinn*, I called him *sir*. It was an unspoken rule that I'd long ago added to my very long list of both spoken and unspoken rules set by William.

"I see." He lifted the tabloid, flicking his wrists so the paper snapped with a crisp *crack*.

He spoke to me as he stared at the photo of Sawyer kissing

my temple. I'd only caught a brief glimpse of the image on my phone as I rode the elevator to William's fourth-floor office, but I knew there was an illustrated bright red circle around the plastic bag in Sawyer's hand. The question on New Yorkers' minds on this fine Wednesday afternoon: Who's the mystery woman Sawyer Jackson banged.

"Ms. Quinn," he began, after an uncomfortable silence, setting the paper back down on his desk, "Chicago's *Hamilton* is nothing to sniff at. I'd think if you were serious about your career, you'd be willing to relocate for such a part."

Damn you two times, Alexander Hamilton. You keep fucking up my day, dude.

"I understand . . . sir. And I am grateful for the opportunity, but I'm sorry, at this time I have to decline. Please . . . I'd like to stay in Manhattan. Broadway, Off-Broadway—I don't care—just please, I need to stay here."

I need to stay with him.

William chuckled without humor. "Very well, then. You'll need to increase your vocal lessons to four times per week, dance to five"—he glanced up—"you need the extra fitness anyway, so that should help. And you'll need to enroll in an eight-week intensive acting clinic being hosted at NYU. I'll see to it that you get priority entry."

My mind spun as I tried to compute how his orders would fit into my already overpacked schedule. Not that all of William's prior recommendations hadn't been effective. Indeed, they had been. My range and vocal endurance had reached unnatural levels by any standards, and I was able to hang with the best dancers in my classes. But I was also living paycheck to paycheck, mentally and physically depleted, and my one restorative resource—my already limited time with Sawyer—was about to take another cut.

"Yes, sir."

"Fine. That's all. My assistant will email you the details and we'll meet again in two weeks. She'll send you the date and time as well." He motioned to the door. "You can show yourself out, Ms. Quinn. Have a good day."

I rose to my feet and hitched my bag onto my shoulder. "Thank you, sir."

As I turned to leave, William's voice gave me pause. "Oh, one more thing, Ms. Quinn."

I drew in a fortifying breath before turning back around, my fake smile already in place. "Yes?"

"I'd much rather see your photo and read about you in a *Playbill*."

There it was.

"Yes, sir."

24

SAWYER

Where's Kennedy?"

I dropped my gym bag by Declan's kitchen island as Brooke looked up from the chopping board. "Happy Thanksgiving to you too."

I reached for a piece of carrot, but Brooke raised her knife and flashed me a scowl, so I had a change of heart. "Happy Thanksgiving. Where's Kennedy?"

"Buttercup almost fell asleep making pie crust, so we sent her back to bed," Andrew answered, turning away from whatever he was doing at the stove. "Your girl is burning the candle at both ends, bro."

My jaw clenched. "Tell me the fuck about it."

The front door opened and closed, and I knew Declan had arrived. I'd ditched him in the lobby when we ran into Payton. If my roommate weren't such a stand-up guy, I'd be convinced he was trying to get in those married-as-fuck pants of hers.

"Why are the two of you avoiding your families today?" I asked.

"I'm not drunk enough to answer that question," Brooke answered flatly.

Accepting her reasoning, I shifted my gaze to Andrew, who was taking the top off a beer.

"Moral support."

I nodded in understanding. Kennedy hadn't given any details, but when she asked if we could have a Friendsgiving, Declan had offered up his place immediately. Jordan and Sarah were supposed to be stopping by at some point this afternoon too.

"What about you guys? Why didn't you fly your families in or why aren't you flying there?" Brooke had resumed her chopping with an alarming degree of force.

Whatever was going on with Brooke and her family must have been significant, but since she didn't offer more, I wasn't about to pry.

"My family is coming in two weeks when we have our bye week," Declan chimed in as he opened the fridge door and snagged a beer for himself. "Jackson? You want one?"

"Nah, I'm good," I replied, then turned back to Brooke. "The team flies to Miami tomorrow for a Saturday game. I'm going to spend a long weekend there with my mom, but my sister is in Paris."

Brooke paused her aggressive meal prep. "Is Kennedy going with you to Miami?"

At the mention of my girl's name, I started away from the kitchen and toward my bedroom. "Do you really think ol' Billy boy would give her the holiday weekend off?" I shot over my shoulder.

The murmurs of agreement behind me confirmed that I wasn't the only one who disliked Kennedy's agent.

Andrew had worded it perfectly—after our photo had appeared in the *New York Post*, Kennedy was thrust into an unrealistic frenzy of lessons and classes. When I asked her if this was William's way of punishing her for ending up in a tabloid, she'd sworn up and down that it wasn't, but that's where the conversation had ended. She'd accepted his orders like a good little soldier and powered on. But I was done just standing by and watching her work herself into the ground. I'd already planned to have a heart-to-heart with her about these things when I had more time during the bye week, but when I opened my bedroom door and saw my Sleeping Beauty passed out in a tiny ball, I knew I couldn't wait that long.

I crawled onto the bed and wrapped an arm around her, pulling her back to my chest. When I'd left for practice this morning, she was sprawled across the bed, snoring. I had no idea how long she'd been awake, but it was only one o'clock now.

I dropped a kiss on her shoulder, and she mumbled something unintelligible.

"Keep sleeping, baby. You're tired and you have no place to be today."

Kennedy shook her head. "I need to help cook . . ." She yawned and wiggled herself around until she'd tucked herself into my chest with her head beneath my chin. "I'm not supposed to nap until after I've eaten turkey." She yawned a second time.

"Inconceivable!" I mocked, quoting one of her favorite movies. She giggled, and my heart beat a little harder.

Kennedy drew her head back, a grin spreading across her angelic face. She felt smaller than usual in my arms. She had dark circles under her eyes. The longer I stared at her, the more her smile started to falter.

"Sawyer? What's wrong?"

I schooled my expression, realizing I'd been scrutinizing every detail that proved how overburdened my girl was, and it had alarmed her.

"Baby, we need to talk," I replied.

Kennedy ripped herself from my embrace with such force that I rolled onto my back.

"Why! What happened!" she asked, panic in every word. "Was it Hunter? That Knox guy? Were we in another tabloid?"

Holy fuck, she was wired.

"Quinn," I said as calmly as I could before reaching for her. "Nothing's happened." I chuckled nervously, but tried to soothe her with a grin. "Come here, you little wildling."

I pulled her back into my arms. Her heart was racing. I'd been worried about Kennedy and her schedule for months, but the way she was behaving right now sent waves of fear through my body.

Shoving down my own emotions, I continued, "I just want to talk about some things—that's all. Good things. I promise, baby."

The moment her body surrendered and she went limp in my arms, I took a deep breath of relief.

"Okay," she whispered, snuggling in closer again.

I pressed a kiss to the crown of her head.

Here goes nothing.

"I've been thinking—and I know how important everything that you are doing is to you—but . . ." Kennedy froze in my arms. "You can't do it all, Quinn. You're exhausted all the time, you tell me you're so busy you forget to eat or that you're too tired to eat—neither of which is okay, by the way—and I'm worried about you."

My sweatshirt didn't muffle her sniffles. I gave her a moment to process my introduction and then I lifted her chin. Her tired eyes were pools of tears.

"Quinn . . . please . . . let me help."

She gulped. She knew what I was suggesting, but I was willing to bet my lucky mouth guard that she didn't know everything I was about to say.

"Payton said I should be able to close on the penthouse right after the first of the year." Kennedy blinked back her tears, but she didn't speak, so I pressed on. "I think it would be best if you could just focus on your stuff with William—no more diner, no more gigs unless you really, *really* want to do one occasionally."

A rattled breath slipped out. "What are you saying, Sawyer?"

She hasn't said no.

I held back the triumphant smile that was waiting to erupt. "Move in with me, Quinn. Let's live together."

"Because you want to make my life easier?"

I dragged my thumb across her lips. She was clearly dehydrated. I'd need to get her water after she'd conceded.

Professional Athlete 101.

"Yes, I want your life to be easier, and living together will eliminate your need to pay rent, which means you can quit your job and at least half of your gigs. But also, selfishly, I want more time with you. I don't want you fading away in front of me for another minute, and fuck, Quinn, I just want your shit everywhere around me."

That last part made her giggle. She coughed on her tears, and I rubbed her back, trying to tame the corners of my own mouth because I still hadn't gotten a commitment from her.

"Move in with me," I repeated.

Kennedy bit her bottom lip, and I hauled her up my body until I could brush my nose against hers. "Say yes, Quinn."

"Do you promise that once I land a part that you'll let me help pay for things?"

I waggled my eyebrows at her and grabbed her ass.

"Not in sexual favors."

I frowned. "Well, that's disappointing."

"Be serious, Sawyer."

Right.

Relying on every serious cell in my body, I replied honestly,

"Yes, when you become a Broadway star you can help pay for things. *But* . . . starting now, I'm paying for your rent and whatever else you spend your money on so you can quit the diner— like, *yesterday*—and turn down any gigs that won't advance your career. Deal?"

Kennedy's sigh of relief wasn't lost on me, and it made my chest fill with my own sense of solace.

"Deal, future roomie."

"Oh, hell no." I flipped her onto her back. "There's no fucking way I'm being downgraded from boyfriend to roommate."

She laughed a true Kennedy laugh, and I realized I hadn't heard that sound in what felt like forever.

It was music to my ears.

25

SAWYER

The moment Kennedy walked into the ballroom on New Year's Eve, her presence sucked all the air from my lungs, leaving me breathless and with a raging boner on sight.

The floor-length silver bandage dress had a slit clear up to her hip and a plunging neckline that screamed my baby was on fire tonight.

And well rested—as she should be.

She was the most gorgeous woman here—fuck that, in the goddamn universe. An ethereal being created just for me.

That's right, she was mine.

All mine.

My new reality had changed me. Things that were either out of my control or, at the end of the day, weren't really my fucking business—like what Knox Whitmore thought about me—rolled off my back like I was a duck and they were the water. I'd even let go of the budding jealousy I'd had over the possibility that Sterling had realized what a fucking mistake he'd made when Kennedy was his.

Her hair tumbled in soft waves over one shoulder, and the diamond teardrop earrings I'd given her for Christmas last week shimmered under the chandelier lighting. I slipped a finger into my collar so I could breathe properly.

Classic reaction to my goddess.

I'd been waiting with bated breath for my date to arrive. She'd have driven here with me if she hadn't had a mandatory dance class to attend first.

Declan whistled beside me. "You are one lucky fucker."

Fuck yeah, I am.

I handed him my glass of whiskey and he clinked the ice as I straightened my bow tie. Coach Daniels had given us a two-drink limit since we still had one regular-season game left to play in two days, but I'd given myself a pass for only one. Regardless of if we won our next game or not, we'd failed to secure the number-one seed in the AFC, which meant we had to play Wild Card Weekend. My body was in peak form, even after a brutal season, and I needed it to stay that way. The holidays weren't an excuse to deviate from my day-to-day wellness strategies. It was one of the many reasons why I'd broken every regular-season record for a tight end by week fifteen.

Besides, now I was so drunk on the siren who'd just entered the building that alcohol was the last thing I needed.

"Later, man."

I crossed the cherry herringbone floor in as composed a manner as my eager legs would carry me, drawn to my girl like Icarus to the sun. She was all-consuming, and I welcomed the burn.

"Quinn." I barely got her name out. Standing in the glow of her radiance had left me at a loss for proper words.

"Sawyer."

The corners of her scarlet lips turned into a nymphlike grin, and I didn't know what part of her body I wanted to dirty first.

"The last time you had lips that shade was the first time I fucked you." I lowered my mouth to her ear. "And I did so in every hole."

Her face turned nearly the same brilliant color as her lips. "Jesus, Sawyer—you really do say the sweetest things to me."

I chuckled and settled for looping my arms around her waist and holding her to me. "You are *breathtaking*, baby."

We began to sway to the band's rendition of "Baby, It's Cold Outside."

Her eyes fluttered closed, then opened on a sigh. "Now that's more like it, Tight End. Man, I really want you to kiss me so bad right now."

She pouted, and I nearly came in my pants.

"Well, I do always aim to please when it comes to you." I made a move to grant her wish, but her finger came to rest against my lips, bringing me to an abrupt halt.

"Sorry, handsome, but Mr. Ellison stopped me in the hallway and asked me to sing. Can't have you messing this up." She drew a circle in the air around her face.

"Really?" I deadpanned.

I took her hand and spun her away from me, and a cascade of glossy waves fanned over her naked shoulders. She curled back into my embrace, her back against my chest.

Looking up over her shoulder, she replied, "For reals, yo."

Fuck me. And fuck the team owner.

She was so getting spanked tonight for saying yes.

I kissed her temple, my hardening length pressing impatiently against her lower back, and then swayed us gently from side to side. "And when are you going to be singing this song? Because I'd really like to hold my girlfriend and kiss her while she's looking so very fuckable right now."

I nibbled on her ear; last I knew, she didn't put makeup there, so it was fair game.

"Soon," she replied with an airy sigh. "I ran into Knox and finally met his wife, Amanda."

Hearing my nemesis's name on her tongue flicked at my irritation, but I was able to temper it. "Uh-huh."

"Amanda is really sweet," she continued. "I like her. I think we could be friends."

Kennedy had been welcomed into the WAGS (wives and girlfriends) group with open arms after our relationship became public. Since she quit her job and almost all gigging over a month ago, she'd even begun helping Jordan's wife with their children's literacy foundation.

"Sounds good, Quinn, but don't even think about us going on any double dates."

She giggled softly, and I skimmed my lips over her neck, teasing at her pulse with the tip of my tongue. For a while, Kennedy would drop not-so-subtle hints that she was curious about my relationship with Whitmore. The truth was, discussing Whitmore brought up thoughts about my contract and the addendum I hoped she'd never learn about. Not only did my sweet girl have enough to juggle, but the addendum was a reminder of the man I used to be, not the man that I'd become.

Kennedy was in love with the current me, reflecting on the old me wouldn't help in moving our relationship forward.

And fuck, did I want to move it forward.

I'd wanted to put diamonds on her finger, not her ears last week.

Soon. Patience.

She ran a fingertip along the edge of my jaw, and my cock made a move for it behind my zipper.

Kennedy lifted her chin and arched an eyebrow. "Easy there, Monster."

"Monster and I are not in an easygoing mood tonight."

Her lips parted, and a restless breath slipped from her mouth.

A moan died in the back of my throat. "Baby . . ." I growled in warning.

But before I could finish my depraved thought, the owner of the New York Cougars, Mr. Richard Ellison IV himself, joined us.

"Sawyer—it's good to see you tonight, young man. You're having a fine season." He patted me on the back. "And thank you for your willingness to share your lovely date with the rest of us. I've heard all the buzz, and now I want to hear her for myself." He was talking to me but winked at Kennedy, and I wondered which would be considered the worse offense—punching the team owner or punching a nearly eighty-year-old man.

Kennedy stepped out of my embrace, and in a bold move, Richard Ellison hooked his arm with hers.

Deck him anyway.

Okay, so maybe I hadn't quite turned into Buddha himself—but I was pretty fucking close.

Kennedy studied my face, and then pulled out of his arm enough to lean up and kiss my cheek. "Behave yourself—it's just one song. I'll be right back."

I slipped my hand under her hair so I could hold her neck while I whispered in her ear. "I'm going to spank you so hard, you won't be able to sit down for days without thinking about me."

Her tits rose and fell in a heavy sigh, and the two emeralds looking back at me pooled with wanton desire. "Don't make promises unless you intend to keep them, Tight End."

Declan was right. I was one lucky fucker indeed.

Kennedy sang Idina Menzel's version of "Silent Night," and the entire ballroom stood motionless, mesmerized by her grace and voice. The sound of her voice raised goose bumps across my flesh. If I had shed a tear, I would have worn it as a badge of honor. I was the man she'd chosen to love, honor, and protect her. When she hit the longest run, I had to press a hand to my chest to keep my heart from liberating itself from my ribcage.

The classic holiday song ended, followed by an explosive standing ovation, leaving me overwhelmed with pride and awe.

Kennedy Quinn was a fucking star.

With my playoff berth waiting in the not-so-distant future, and Kennedy's *Frozen* audition on the same fucking day—because the NFL and the Broadway gods liked to fuck with me—we'd planned to make our escape shortly after the clock struck midnight and we'd kissed each other senseless. That still gave me over an hour to dance with my girl before taking her back to her place and ringing in the New Year in private.

We'd barely made it through the front door of her apartment before Kennedy covered my face in warm, sweet kisses and she was shrugging out of her coat until it hit the floor.

One of her legs came up to hook on my hip as she pressed herself against me almost desperately. My cock begged to be given permission to do as nature intended, seeking his home right between Kennedy's thighs. In one uninhibited move, I slithered her dress to her waist and sank my fingers into her ass. I lifted her, and her legs enveloped me.

"Make love to me, Sawyer." Her request was part cry as her body became languid in my arms and her kisses wetter.

When the salty taste hit my tongue, her sob drove the message home. My baby needed me. Our love was the stuff of songs and poetry, and it always carried over into our sex.

We shed what we could of our clothes between the front door and her bedroom. Brooke and Andrew were both away for the holiday, and we had the place to ourselves. In a matter of days, we'd be moving in together.

When I lowered my half-naked girl to the bed, she refused to let me go. I rolled across the down comforter with our limbs entangled. Her fingers found my belt, and she grunted in frustration as she tried to unsheathe my lower half. I smiled against her swollen lips, and for the first time since we'd walked through the door, she pulled back, and I drank in her beauty.

I brushed back the hair that clung to her damp cheeks and cupped her jaw. "I love you, Quinn. I love you more than I've ever loved anything. There is nothing I wouldn't do for you, wouldn't give you . . . you know that, right?"

Without hesitating, she nodded. "I do."

I kissed her nose. "Good—because in return, I want everything."

"You can have it all, Sawyer. It's all yours."

My heart pounded against my sternum. "What's everything to you, baby?"

Say it. I need to know. I need to hear you say it.

Her wide smile had me sliding my slacks and boxer briefs over my hips before the words fell from her lips.

"All of it. You. Me. Us. Forever." Her thighs fell open, and I tugged her panties to the side to allow me access. She gasped. "Marriage . . . I-I want to marry you."

A single thrust. Her wet warmth welcomed me, and her eyes closed.

"Babies." When I thrust a second time, her ankles hooked at my lower back. I held her wrists over her head with one hand while my free hand worked over her tits. "I want your babies, Sawyer . . ."

Her admission made me drive into her like I was trying to touch her soul with my cock. She begged me for harder and more as we climbed to the summit of paradise together. The soundtrack of her soaked pussy and our primal vociferations echoed off the walls.

Her delicate tightness spasmed around me, milking every drop of my seed as our mouths collided. After I'd kissed away the last of her energy, I rolled to my back, taking her with me.

"You're mine, Quinn. All mine."

"Always, Sawyer."

26

KENNEDY

We'd been living together in the penthouse for less than forty-eight hours when the energy shifted between us.

"Are you sure everything's okay?" I asked for the second time in less than a minute as Sawyer stood up from where he'd been sitting at the dining room table.

He closed the laptop abruptly and offered me a forced smile.

"Yes, Quinn, everything is fine."

I swallowed and tightened my ponytail. My hands felt like they needed something to do. "Were you talking to someone?" I tried to sound casual.

He paused at my side. I thought he was going to answer me, but instead he wrapped an arm around my waist and kissed me with an aggression I wasn't used to first thing in the morning. When he broke away, he released me so quickly I stumbled slightly, but he didn't seem to notice.

"My mom," he called over his shoulder as he strolled off in his low-slung pajama pants.

I stared after him for a few beats while I talked down the crazy girlfriend thoughts racing through my head. Was it his mom who had him cursing at his text messages as he'd read them beside me in bed? Was I already infringing on his personal space? Did he already regret asking me to move in? Since

Thanksgiving, I'd quit my job at the diner and other gigs almost immediately, and we'd never been closer. After we'd christened every single room on move-in day, I was convinced living with Sawyer would be domestic bliss.

Until this morning.

I hurried to catch up with him. Between the palatial size of the penthouse and Sawyer's long legs I had ground to cover. I finally reached him in the master bedroom as he was tugging on a pair of joggers.

"Is your mom okay?"

"Everything. Is. Fine. Quinn."

The bite in his words made my throat spasm. I turned my head to avoid his gaze should he look my way when I noticed the time on the bedside clock.

"You're late," I said, tiptoeing to a loveseat next to one of the windows.

Sawyer had never been late for practice that I'd ever known of. Punctuality was one of his strongest attributes. Coaches always loved that about him. His first playoff game was this upcoming weekend. Every practice this week mattered more than the last.

As I sat down with my legs folded under me, he pulled open a drawer from the new dresser that had been delivered yesterday.

"Fucking A." He slammed the drawer, looked around the room, and then stormed out. "Quinn! Do you know where the fuck they put my shirts! The box they were in is no longer in the bedroom!" His voice bellowed from the depths of the penthouse.

I sprinted for guest bedroom number one. I'd found some of my own clothes in there last night after I'd returned from dance class.

"Over here!"

Sawyer careened around the door and went directly for the box where he knew his shirts would be.

"Thanks, baby."

"No problem."

He yanked a shirt over his head and went to exit before pulling up short just before he crossed the threshold into the hallway. He spun around and stalked toward me. He circled his arms around me, lifting me to his chest before delivering another punishing kiss.

"I'm late. I gotta run. I love you."

Being this close, I saw the worry—no, scratch that—the *panic* in Sawyer's eyes.

This look had nothing to do with being late and everything to do with whatever happened between the time he'd woken up this morning and now.

I brought my fingertips to his jaw. His eyes closed, and his chest deflated on an exhale.

I knew he wouldn't answer me truthfully if I repeated my question, so instead, I said, "I love you too."

He opened his eyes; an expression of temporary peace had replaced the agitation that had been there moments ago. "You must have a long day today. Check in with me when you can."

I shook my head at the same time guilt crept its way up my throat. "I don't have anything until my dance class tonight. I'm free all day. I'm having lunch with Sarah to go over the donations list for the silent auction."

Sawyer nodded and set me back on my feet. "Good. I'll see you tonight after your class. I've got a full day at the clubhouse." He pressed a kiss to my forehead and then he was gone, and I was all alone in Sawyer's multimillion-dollar penthouse.

Who did I think I was having lunch with an NFL wife and talking about her charity when I should be working—or at the very least, doing something to prepare for my audition this weekend?

Pulling my shoulders back, I marched to the master bedroom en suite. I'd run vocal scales in the hot shower until my skin pruned while I tried my best to forget about Sawyer's unusual behavior this morning.

When I got home that night from dance class, Sawyer was studying film in bed with the laptop. I heard the unmistakable sharp whistle blows of an NFL referee echoing down the hallway as I approached the master bedroom. We were going to need more furniture if this place was ever going to stop sounding like the MoMA.

"Hey, Black Swan." He grinned as he set the computer to the side. He crooked a finger at me, and my heart pitter-pattered in my chest.

My Sawyer is back.

I crawled onto his lap. "Am I Natalie Portman or Mila Kunis in your dreams?"

He scoffed. "Neither—you're Kennedy Fucking Quinn."

I giggled and nuzzled my way into the crook of his neck.

"I'm sorry, baby." Sawyer's voice was low and soft. One of his hands stroked up and down my spine while the other wedged itself between my legs just above my knees.

"For what?" I asked, but I already had my suspicions.

"For how I acted this morning. I'm on edge because of the game on Sunday, and I took it out on you. I'm sorry. It won't happen again."

"That's a lie," I deadpanned.

I felt Sawyer gulp, and his body tensed. "No it's not. I'm just stressed about the game, that's all. It's my first playoff game as a Cougar—it's natural, I'm bound to be fucking stressed, Quinn."

Well, now you just sound defensive.

I tilted my head back and narrowed my eyes. "Dude, I was kinda kidding. I wasn't talking about your stress; I was talking about the fact that you said you'd never take it out on me again. Sometimes taking out your stress on your partner happens. That too is *natural.* If we're going to live together, Sawyer, it's going to happen from time to time. Let's just not make a habit of it—that's all."

I wasn't sure which of us I was trying to convince more.

He nodded, seeming to catch on to what I was saying.

I slid off his lap, linking our fingers as I did. "I need to shower; will you wash my hair?" I purred, trying to reset the dynamics of our night.

He tugged me back so he could land a peck on my lips.

"Sorry, baby. I've got tape to watch. I'll be here waiting for you when you get out, though."

I walked to the en suite with my heart feeling like a lead ball in my chest. I wasn't sure what had happened since Sawyer and I had fallen asleep in each other's arms last night, but whatever it was, it had the power to change the landscape of our relationship.

As I turned on the shower, I let my first tear fall.

27

SAWYER

On the day of the Wild Card game, the sky was dark and ominous. Threatening electricity crackled in the air, making the tiny hairs on the back of my neck stand up.

I stood in front of my locker, my forehead pressed to the cold metal, and shut my eyes. Metallica streamed through my AirPods on the highest setting as I tried to drown out the non-football-related thoughts determined to fuck with my game-day mindset.

Fucking cancer.

Four days ago, I'd found out that my mom's cancer had returned, and two days ago I'd Skyped with my mom, Maddie, and my mom's oncologist. At least the latter Skype had happened when Kennedy was at a vocal lesson.

I'd felt like a serious dick lying to her all week, but I'd kept the disturbing news suppressed, not wanting to burden my sweet girl just before her big audition. I wanted to tell Kennedy about my mom, not just because she was my girlfriend, but because she was my best friend, and in the past, she'd been my rock when my mom went through treatment the first time. Choosing not to tell her felt risky. Every time I caught her staring at me with a worried expression taking over her face, I'd kiss her reassuringly and tell her that I was just nervous for the big game—that's all. I'd planned to tell her everything tonight.

In another week, the brave woman who'd given me life would begin her second stint with chemo and ultimately radiation. Maddie was flying directly to Miami this week to be with her, and just as soon as our playoff run ended, I'd be there too. I'd be at her side right now if I didn't have the most important game of my career to play. It was moments like these when I wondered what it would be like to have a normal job—with normal expectations.

That's not what your mom wants for you, and you know it.

I swallowed the acid that burned the back of my throat and tried to visualize today's game plan. When I'd realized my brain fog was due to carrying around this massive secret, I finally caved and broke down. I'd divulged everything to Trek as soon as he met me at the stadium this morning.

Soon, the team would take the field for pre-game warm-ups. That was also the time it became mandatory to turn off all cellular devices. The use of cell phones during an NFL game came with heavy consequences, which meant I wouldn't know how Kennedy's audition turned out until many hours from now.

I glanced at my phone and saw she still had another hour before the auditions were set to begin.

Me: Hey, baby. Gonna have to turn off my phone soon. I'll call as soon as I can. Go be your sexy little badass self and blow them away, Quinn. I fucking love you. Break a leg!

Three dots appeared.
Good, she still had her phone on.

My Girl: GO COUGARS! RAWR! I LOVE YOU! P. S. Please don't break any legs.

I chuckled for the first time today.
In the next beat, a shove from behind slammed me face-first into the partially open locker. An AirPod crashed to the

floor, reducing the sound of heavy metal by half and making me keenly aware of the monstrous growls resonating in my now-empty ear.

A searing pain shot across my forehead and down the bridge of my nose.

"WHAT THE FUCK! YOU FUCKING COCKSUCKER!" my QB1 roared behind me.

What the fuck was right.

Clambering against the locker, I forced myself to spin around, narrowly dodging Hunter Sterling's fist as it came flying at my head. The locker to my right crumpled like a tin can under his force.

Dazed from taking a locker to the face, I shook my head to clear my vision.

Sterling cocked his arm back a second time, prepared to launch another strike, when Declan broadsided him.

"How could you do this to her? You fucking piece-of-shit asshole! I knew you didn't deserve her!" Sterling spat.

There was only one her that he could be referring to—Kennedy.

"What the fuck are you talking about!" I barked, wiping at the trickle of blood from my eyebrow.

The lunatic had chosen an interesting time to make his jealousy issues known.

I looked up, catching an in-focus view of Sterling's expression for the first time. The man was on the verge of busting a blood vessel. Nostrils flaring and chest heaving, he appeared straight-up ready to commit first-degree murder, and I was his intended victim.

Declan struggled to hold back our quarterback, and finally two linemen joined in.

"What the fuck, Jackson!" Lake shouted over his shoulder at me as he wrapped Sterling in a bear hug.

How is this my fault?

Jesus fucking Christ. If someone didn't tell me what the fuck was going on, I was going to flip my shit.

Then, several things happened in rapid-fire succession. I remembered that for some reason, Sterling seemed to be talking about Kennedy, and Declan looked as if he'd be kicking my ass himself if he wasn't already busy holding off Sterling. I scanned the room to find the majority of my teammates looking at their phones with a variety of reactions written all over their faces—shock, confusion—something I couldn't quite read.

"Why'd you do it, Jackson? *How* could you do it?" The sound of Declan's voice laced with disgust and revulsion brought my attention back to the clusterfuck of my teammates in front of me.

"I have no idea what the fuck is going on right now! Anyone care to enlighten me, or would you rather just crucify me now for whatever it is you all think I did!"

"She trusted you! What do you even get out of doing this? She's never gonna forgive you, you fucking asshole!" Sterling fought against his human restraints trying to get to me, but I was no longer concerned with him. Words like *trusted* and *forgive* ricocheted inside my head.

Whatever was happening—or had happened—wasn't good.

The double doors dividing the main locker room from the treatment room pushed open, and a string of coaches stormed in. Coach Daniels led the pack, his expression set on pure rage.

"JACKSON! MY OFFICE. NOW!"

Thank fuck Trek was in the building.

If he hadn't been standing in front of the closed door while

I'd stormed around Coach Daniels's office, ready to tear the place down, I'd have probably required a tranquilizer dart to the leg.

"It's Whitmore. It has to be," I gritted out. Then I threw a chair across the room, sending it crashing into the wall.

The journeyman was a healthy scratch from today's game. I hadn't run into the fucker yet today, but Trek said he'd seen him milling around not long before World War III had broken out in the locker room.

Trek—the coolest fucking cucumber I ever knew—began to type on his phone. "On it, mate. I know a guy. I'll have him here in twenty. Daniels—have someone round up all the cell phones. I'll handle this, you lot got a playoff game to go win." His fingers stopped moving and he looked up from his screen. "We're going to figure this out, brother."

"I need to call Kennedy."

Coach Daniels, who'd been quiet for the last several minutes, cleared his throat. "Listen, Jackson. I believe that it wasn't you who sent the video, but Trek is right, we've got a game to play, son. I'm afraid if you call your girlfriend right now this is just going to continue to spiral."

My stomach sank, and I almost relented, but then I thought of my perfect girl waiting for her audition to begin. What if she got word of what had happened before I'd had the chance to tell her? It would have been Sterling's prophecy come true—*she'd never forgive me.*

I shook my head, decision made. "Sorry, Coach—this is one play call you don't get to make for me."

I snatched my phone off his desk, where it had been sitting ever since the three of us had pooled our limited technology skills and tried to figure out what the fuck had happened.

We'd come up short, though, and we still didn't know who, how, or why the video of Kennedy giving herself an orgasm at my command had been shared with my teammates and head coach. The one thing we did know was that it wasn't on social media yet, and based on Coach Daniels's quick but thorough investigation of the coaching staff and personnel, he and my teammates had been the only ones to receive it.

After Coach realized I was moving forward with my intent to call Kennedy, he informed me that after I was done, he wanted to talk with Sterling and me alone, and then the team as a whole. We had less than twenty minutes to get our asses on the field for warm-ups.

Coach and Trek cleared the room, and I slumped into a chair. The poison of defeat notched its way through my body. What the fuck was I going to say to her?

Kennedy's phone went right to voice mail.

I swallowed hard when her melodic voice floated into my ear, causing my chest to constrict and my lungs to ache.

A broken smile tugged instinctively at my lips. *Fuck, I love her.*

Beep.

I cleared the lump of shame in my throat. "Baby . . . hey, listen, sweetheart . . . it's me . . . I need you to do me favor, baby. *Please.* When you get done with your audition, you know, the one I just know you're going to crush . . ." My throat clenched, and my next breath was a wheeze. *I can't fucking do this.* "Baby—I need you to turn your phone off, okay? Listen—I know this sounds weird, but you've got to trust me, okay? Please . . . when you get done, turn off your phone. Go home. Watch the game. Order us a fuckton of takeout and then watch some *Real Housewives* or something that's gonna make you laugh, okay? I'll be home a couple hours after the game. Until I get there, baby . . . no phone, no computer—okay? Just trust me. I love you. I love you so fucking much, Quinn. I'll explain everything when I get home. Everything's going to be okay, I promise. I love you."

In an apparent suicide, my phone met the concrete floor.

I scrubbed my face with my hands and slowly got to my feet.

Trek stood with his hands in his pockets outside of Coach's office. He offered me a silent nod, and when I was close enough, he rested a hand on my shoulder. "Security will bring my guy back here when he arrives. I'll handle this. You go win this fucking game, mate. Get through the next eight hours and then go home to that peach of a girl and make it right. I'll take care of the rest."

Trek knew best; all I could do now was my job. My team needed me. I was failing Kennedy, and I was failing my mom. I was a playoff game loss away from failing the entire Cougars organization. Just maybe, I could salvage this one thing and then work like hell to fix everything else I'd already fucked up.

"Treat this like a matter of national security. I'm not fucking kidding."

Trek nodded, his jaw hard. I knew he wasn't taking this lightly.

"I want his ass in jail," I said.

"Understood. No one is getting away with fucking with Kennedy on my watch, mate."

28

KENNEDY

R ain pelted the floor-to-ceiling windows with a ferocity that matched the railing of my heart in my chest. In the eerie darkness of the penthouse, I wrapped myself tighter in a throw blanket and willed for myself another reality. A reality where I hadn't been betrayed by the man I'd given my heart to.

How could he do this?

The sound of Sawyer's approaching footsteps echoed through the empty space. Most of our belongings still lived in unpacked boxes, and we'd planned to let Maddie take over the decorating when she came to visit.

I'd tried to brace for our imminent confrontation but lacked the mental strength. I was depleted from the tumultuous day and evening I'd endured. Just opening my eyes was a feat. When I managed, the faint outline of Sawyer's silhouette filled my vision.

"Quinn . . ."

Tears I'd imagined I'd long run out of were instantly replenished, and they careened down my cheeks with abandon. He'd expertly packed all the genuine emotion of his pending apology and plea into that one word, fraying at the edges of my anger.

My broken sobs ripped from the back of my throat just as Sawyer clicked on the lamp. Our eyes met, and he dropped to his knees in front of me, resting his hands on the couch and only pausing for a beat before burying his face in my lap.

"I'm so sorry, baby . . ."

I had so many questions, but "Why?" was the only one to make its way out from the pits of my despair.

Sawyer lifted his head. His eyes matched the sorrow that consumed me, and my heart cracked just a little bit more. Unchecked grief appeared to have aged him since I'd kissed him goodbye this morning.

He shook his head slowly as though he couldn't believe the fallout of the day, a day that was supposed to have been spent making both of our dreams come true. Instead, Sawyer had had the worst game of his career, being the sole cause of two turnovers and ending the game without one contributory catch. But at least his career wasn't in shambles, and his team had won. One bad playoff game in the NFL could make you the punch line of some viral memes, but it wouldn't get you blackballed for life.

One disastrous Broadway audition, on the other hand, could do exactly that.

How I'd found it in me to not only watch Sawyer's game, but to also identify with his distress was something only the universe could explain.

It's because you still love him. Unconditionally.

"What do you know?" he asked, the desperate expression on his face telling me that he was already anticipating the worst.

"I talked to Sarah . . ."

Sawyer's hand went to cover mine, but I pulled back, tucking both of my hands under the blanket. He pressed his eyes closed at my brush off, and when he opened them again, he met my gaze and gave a single nod. "Okay . . . what did Sarah tell you?"

Sarah was eight months pregnant now. I should have

waited until after my audition to call her, but when I'd received her SOS text, I'd worried something was wrong with the baby and that she couldn't reach Chase.

"She told me that you sent Chase a video of me . . . she called it a *very private video* . . . and she thinks a lot of players received the same text." I sounded a lot more composed than I felt. Perhaps the numbness that had settled into my bones was good for something. "But that didn't make sense to me . . ." I lifted my gaze from where it had been burning a hole in the neighboring couch cushion and directed it at Sawyer. "Because you've never taken a video of me—at least not without my consent—right?"

My resurrected anger became more intact with each passing breath.

Sawyer winced at my words, and that's when I knew that my hypothesis was correct. As soon as Sarah said private video, my thoughts reeled, but when she mentioned an OSU sweatshirt, I'd had a guess at what video could be in circulation.

"Baby, I—"

I didn't need to hear Sawyer's apology wrapped up in excuses. Guilt was stamped across his face.

I got to my feet and shoved past him.

"How could you, Sawyer?" I spun around so that I could look him in the eye when he tried to explain the unforgivable.

Sawyer was on his feet now. He raked his hands through his hair and began to pace the room while I remained still, rooted in my concoction of disbelief and anguish.

"It wasn't me—I mean, yes—I'm the one who recorded our call, but I didn't send it to *anyone*. You know me better than that!"

"Do I?"

Sawyer stopped dead in his tracks, his eyes moving over

me as though he needed proof that those two simple words had indeed come from me. "Seriously, Quinn?"

"Yes! Seriously! *Sawyer.*"

He laughed without humor, his hands on his hips, and shook his head. "Well, just to be *extra fucking clear*—I would *never* do that."

The potency of his words and energy rocked me back on my heels, but my stoked fury fueled my impressive recovery. "Then who sent it from your phone? Who got the text? *Why do you even have that video?*"

Sawyer dragged a hand down his face. "I'll tell you everything. Just give me . . . a minute. I need a drink. It's been a fucking day."

Stunned that he felt it pertinent to pour himself two fingers of Jameson before he could answer my questions, I was quick on his heels as he retreated to the extravagant kitchen we'd yet to do anything but have sex in. Right now, our relationship felt as comforting and homey as Sawyer's new overindulgent pad.

This isn't my Sawyer.

"Tell me, Sawyer. *Why* did you record me?"

This—betrayal number one—I wanted and *deserved* an answer.

With an unsteady hand, he poured himself a generous serving.

Make that four fingers.

Sawyer swallowed half of his drink, and then cleared his throat with noticeable force. He turned to face me, leaning back against the kitchen counter. "I missed you. I miss you *a fucking lot* when I'm on the road. I'd intended just to record us talking so I had a video of you that wasn't you singing, so that when I needed to hear your voice, I could. I'd forgotten it was even recording—I didn't call you planning to have phone sex just so I could record you. You know me better—oh wait, that's right—you don't." Keeping his eyes locked on mine, he swallowed the last of his whiskey and then poured himself another round.

His line of defense was falling flat for me, and my seething raged on, but before I could shoot down every one of his weak excuses, he continued, "*And* it wasn't me who sent it. When I found out, I figured it was Whitmore, and Trek's guy confirmed it. He must have gotten ahold of my phone during a meeting—Coach always has us turn in our phones before meetings. Whitmore cloned mine . . . that's how he got the video . . ." His voice softened at the end, the touch of pettishness crawling to a halt.

Sawyer raised a hand, securing my chin between his thumb and index finger, and my eyes thinned at him, challenging him to say something that made him worthy of touching me right now.

"I'm sorry, Quinn. I'm so fucking sorry." He swallowed hard, his eyes welling with tears. "I promise, Trek has three different people working on it right now. It went to my teammates and Coach Daniels, but we know for certain now that it didn't go beyond that, and all copies of the video have been destroyed. Trek made everyone sign an NDA, and they all did it willingly. That's why I'm so fucking late. I wasn't going to leave until everything had been handled. The last thing is pressing charges, which I—*we*—will do once we know what to do next. Trek's working on it."

I believed him—I did. But it did little to alleviate the mayhem ransacking my mind and body. Sawyer's teammates and coach—men I would unavoidably have to look in the eye again—had seen me in the most intimate way, without my consent.

And my audition . . .

Surviving a sex video scandal—because let's be honest,

even though everything was covered, that's exactly what it was—was just phase one of reclaiming my self-worth and redeeming my reputation.

With a forceful swallow, I censored the commiserating tears, the compassionate reply that hovered on the tip of my tongue, and my need to curl into Sawyer's arms and beg my best friend to make it all better.

I stepped back, and Sawyer's hand fell away. "I'm grateful to Trek, but there are some things he simply cannot fix. There are some things that can't be undone."

SAWYER

Don't I fucking know it.

Like cancer for one.

Kennedy didn't appreciate my explanation and apology strategy; it was written all over her tear-stained face. And if that wasn't enough to convince me that I had a long night of groveling ahead of me, her body language drove the message home loud and clear.

"I'll call all my teammates and make them swear on their fucking lives right now with you on the line that they will never breathe a word about what they saw."

"Please, don't," she deadpanned, and I knew right then that Kennedy was close to sending me straight to Hell.

Can you blame her?

"Okay, let's pretend for a minute that life doesn't totally fucking suck right now . . . I need to hear something positive from you right now, baby . . . or I just might fucking lose it. Tell me, did you blow them away at your audition?"

Kennedy was murderous intent personified.

"You're fucking unbelievable!"

She threw her hands in the air and stormed from the kitchen, leaving me to backtrack through the last sixty seconds to see what the fuck I had said wrong. Deciding she must have thought I was making light of the situation—which had not been my objective—I went in search of her.

Kennedy was in the master bedroom, shoving her things into a suitcase with determined haste.

What. The. Fuck. Just happened?

I froze in the open doorway, my mind trying to process the sight before me, and my body unwilling to move and give Kennedy the opportunity to leave the room.

To leave our home.

To leave *me*.

As the scene unfolded, my shock and fear morphed into something that felt like disappointment and frustration.

How could she just leave? How was it so easy for her to just go?

"Quinn," I said as calmly as my inner turmoil would allow.

Seconds ticked by, and she didn't answer, only pausing her poorly thought-out packing job when she stubbed her toe on the en suite doorjamb. She hopped back to the bed on one foot and crammed her makeup bag inside the suitcase. Even if she had to do it on one leg, she was committed to getting as far away from me as possible right now.

"Quinn," I repeated. "Can you please talk to me? I'm sorry if—"

She slammed the top of the suitcase and then spun to face me, a feral look in her eyes as she stalked toward me. "There was no audition, Sawyer." She dropped that bit of knowledge on me with the freakishly calculated tone of a serial killer.

What?

She paused, most likely at my perplexed expression, and a ghost of a fake smile edged at the corners of her mouth. "Unless, of course, you count me walking out on stage after crying and puking my guts out in the restroom, only to forget my lines *and make a total ass of myself*!"

Reality struck.

Fuck. Kennedy had talked to Sarah before her audition. It was the only explanation. It must have happened in the span of time when I'd been with Coach Daniels and Trek. Kennedy folded her arms.

"Yeah, Sarah got to me before you did."

She didn't want another apology, that much I knew, which left me at a loss for words.

All the guilt from all the things that I'd been collecting over the past several days continued to mount the longer Kennedy stared at me with such contempt. The whiplash I felt in my head and heart was consistent with the back-and-forth onslaught of contradictory emotions that kept me teetering between my desire to prove to her how sorry I was and my need for her to give me just the tiniest of breaks. I feared I was reaching the end of my self-restraint and needed at least a temporary resolution—and fast. Perhaps that's what motivated me to say what would inevitably be my downfall.

"I'm sure that fucker—your agent or whatever—will know how to make this right."

She blinked. "William? William fired me as his client, Sawyer." Her stoic expression shed little light on how she felt about this development.

"Maybe that's for the best, that guy took how long to get you this audition? Four, five months, was it? You're probably better off without him." I knew I sounded like the asshole I'd allowed my guilt and defensiveness to reduce me to.

"That guy?" The shrill sound of Kennedy's loathing that was directed at me had returned with a vengeance. "*That guy* has offered me many, *many* auditions, Sawyer. Auditions that I *wanted* to say yes to, but I didn't!"

My exasperation shook loose like a rogue wave and my inhibition capsized. "Fuck, Kennedy! Why! *Why* did you say no if you wanted to say yes so badly?"

She snapped her head back as though she'd been slapped across the face. I searched myself and came up empty for an apology, allowing my unprecedented reaction to hang uncomfortably in the air between us.

Fresh tears sprinted down her cheeks. "Because of you . . . because I wanted to . . . be with you . . ." Her pained whisper and broken sobs made my heart seize. "They were in Chicago . . . and you . . . you're here."

I staggered to the bed and sat down, no longer having the capacity to stay upright.

Her words were a dagger to my insides, a knife twisted so efficiently that all I could do was pray for a timely exsanguination to put an end to my misery.

Kennedy resumed zipping up her suitcase, her sniffles the background noise of my self-destruction.

I only looked up from my trembling hands when she was in the doorway, looking over her shoulder at me. Her lips were parted as though she had something to say, but the words wouldn't come out.

"Where are you going?" I asked, my voice hoarse and unsteady.

"To stay with my friends."

I nodded in understanding. What else was there to say?

I wasn't the friend she wanted right now, and I didn't even know if I was still her boyfriend.

"You know . . ." she began, tilting her head slightly. Her eyes were softer now, no longer arresting me with torment, but her petite frame looked even smaller cloaked in the heartache I'd caused. "That's the first time you've ever called me Kennedy."

29

SAWYER

Trek yawned. "You're depressing me, mate."

This was Trek's latest attempt at goading me into discussing the situation with my girl. I shot him back a look that said, "I don't give a fuck, mate."

It had been exactly two weeks since Kennedy walked out of our penthouse—walked out of my life.

Was she still my girl?

I hoped the fuck so.

I just might die if she wasn't. The girl was my heartbeat, and every day without her smile lighting up my life felt like twenty-four hours of unimaginable torture. It's believed that the ancient Persians developed the most malevolent way to kill a man, but I'd bet my left testicle that a broken heart by way of Kennedy Quinn was far worse.

We stood on the field at Ingenuity Stadium dressed in nearly matching Armani suits, soaking up the final minutes of relative quietude before the chaos of the AFC Championship Game would begin. After our sloppy win on Wild Card Weekend, we'd turned it around to blow out Kansas City in the Divisional Round. Now, we were one win away from a Super Bowl match-up against either Tampa Bay or Green Bay. I personally hoped we'd play the former Bay. I hated those fuckers.

Earlier this morning, we'd received word that Whitmore

had been banned from the league, forcing him into early retirement. I was still awaiting feedback from my attorneys on whether or not we could press criminal charges. The fuckwit still had to pay for what he'd done to Kennedy, regardless of the league ramifications.

With the help of the team's spiritual advisor—yes, that's a real thing—my teammates had rallied around me, and they would rally around Kennedy too if she'd ever take me back.

Brooke refused to talk to me; she was Team Kennedy all the way. And while I knew through texts with Sarah and Andrew that Kennedy was "okay," until I heard that sentiment from Kennedy's lips and felt her physical form in my arms, I'd never believe it with any degree of certainty.

I'd had a lot of time over the past fourteen days with my last conversation with Kennedy on replay in my mind, and it didn't take me long to realize how, when under pressure, I'd reverted to the former immature, hot-headed version of myself.

To reclaim my integrity, I'd spent my days focused on football, followed by checking in with my mom and Maddie each night when I got home. After the day had stilled and before I'd lost my sanity craving my better half, I'd continued drafting a letter to Kennedy that expressed my deepest feelings and admitted my sincerest regrets. It'd taken me the entire two weeks—I'm not fucking Voltaire—but I'd managed to finalize it this morning before I headed to the stadium.

"It's been a fortnight since you've talked to her, perhaps it's time to man up and do something about it?"

I shook my head at my pushy agent. "Nah, man, last time I gave her time and space it worked, so that's what I'm doing now."

Trek raised a skeptical eyebrow. "Time and space," he drawled. "Sounds utterly fascinating."

The muscle in my jaw twitched. "I did write her a letter."

Trek's surprised expression was a drastic shift away from the sterile one he'd been laying on me for the past twenty minutes. "Well, that's a start. Bravo."

"I didn't say I gave it to her."

His head dropped to the side in clear annoyance. "Jackson, give me the fucking letter." He held his hand out, waiting for me to comply. When I didn't, he added, "If I know you like I think I do, it's in that fucking sack. Give. It. To. Me."

I sighed and bent over, unzipping my game-day bag.

Heat crept up my neck and singed my ears. "When are you going to give it to her?" I gritted out. I knew his intent the moment he demanded the damn thing.

"I'll pay the lovely Kennedy a visit soon. I'll offer her my services to help her find a proper agent, and I'll give her the letter at the same time."

I stood back up and handed over the letter, but I paused when Trek had it in his grasp. "Don't fucking lose it. I wrote it by hand, so it's the only copy I have."

A debonair grin spread across his face. "Leave it to me, mate. I'll make sure it reaches your darling girl at exactly the right moment."

KENNEDY

On the day of the AFC Championship, I was dressed in my Jackson jersey with the number eighty-eight painted on both of my cheeks in eye black.

"You need an exorcism," Brooke declared, plopping down on the cushion beside me, her overflowing bowl of hot popcorn spilling onto both our laps.

Since everything went down, she'd been living and

breathing my love language, watching every playoff game with me. She'd even gone so far as to allow me to leave it on the NFL Network whenever I was home. I thought it was sweet until I caught her ogling Hunter like the man-eater my sex-positive friend was known for being.

I shrugged with knowing acceptance. "He's a part of me. He always will be." Then I flashed her a goofy grin. "Do you want matching twelves on your cheeks?"

Said cheeks flushed, and I almost lost an eye to a dangerous piece of snack food she fired at me.

"Have you talked to him yet?" Andrew asked as he readjusted his sprawled position on the other end of the couch.

Brooke and I swiveled our heads his way in unison.

He chuckled and tsked. "I'm talking to Buttercup—keep it in your pants, Brookey."

Andrew's question essentially reiterated, I shook my head in reply, self-doubt charging through my veins.

"Kennedy, you know I love you, but, girl, don't you think your plan is a touch psychotic?"

Leave it to Brooke to be the blunt voice of reason.

"It has to be this way," I countered, picking mindlessly through the popcorn as though there was a most perfect piece to be found.

Andrew's sigh of disagreement resonated with my soul. "How many hours before the game starts? And why are we watching the NFC right now?"

Finally, questions I could answer with confidence. "About three hours until kickoff. And we need to know who the Cougars will be playing in the Super Bowl when they win today. Personally, I hope it's the Buccaneers. I hate those guys."

A smile edged across Andrew's face. "Is our little law of attraction specialist back in business?"

I grinned the biggest grin I had in weeks. "Yeah, I am."

In that moment, the only thing I desired was for Sawyer's dreams to come true. My emotions surrounding everything that had happened were still raw—but the further I moved away from that fateful day, the more I found myself drifting into a place of acceptance and forgiveness. Neither Sawyer nor I had communicated as effectively as we needed to when shit went down, and that was an integral flaw in our relationship design. But my heart longed for his love, my body ached for his touch, and I couldn't deny the fact that I was still inescapably in love with Sawyer Jackson.

The rest we could figure out together—right?

And that's exactly why I'd decided that after the Super Bowl—because they *were* going to win today—I'd ask Sawyer if we could talk. Until that time, I would suffer all by my lonesome. Well, except for Andrew and Brooke, who took turns being my shoulder to cry on whenever the mood struck. If I were being honest, my friends had a full-time job mopping up my tears.

Andrew and Brooke proceeded to discuss me as though I wasn't right there.

"I think Kennedy's decision makes absolutely no sense. What do you think, Drew?"

"Word" was his only reply, but it said enough.

I glanced up to find both of my friends staring at me, but Brooke was the one to speak. "What are you waiting for? If he wins this damn game that's two . . . more . . . weeks." She collapsed dramatically against Andrew's feet and threw an arm across her eyes.

Andrew and I sat there anticipating the encore.

Brooke popped back up, her smile bright. "That was a good death scene. Admit it." She tossed a piece of popcorn in her mouth and crunched down on it with a wink.

I was about to give her props when the intercom buzzed, and then Andrew was on his feet.

"Yo," Andrew answered.

"Trek Evans for Miss Kennedy Quinn."

I choked on a kernel.

Fuck me.

"Who is *Trek Evans*," Brooke purred.

I read right through her question straight to the part about his sexy accent and if he was single.

"Bedroom! Now!" I pointed at Andrew's bedroom, my eyes pinned on Brooke first and then shifting to Andrew. "Please. Tie her up if you must."

Andrew chuckled, taking a scowling Brooke by the wrist and leading her away. "My pleasure, Buttercup."

Not five minutes later, Trek Evans stood in the middle of my living room in a three-piece charcoal suit, eyeing me like I was the Eighth Wonder of the World in my Sawyer-Jackson's-personal-cheerleader uniform. Trek had always been polite and friendly toward me, even if his presence did make me feel like my eloquence was lacking.

"Bloody brilliant. I've got to snap your photo, love. I send this to Jackson, and he'll break every postseason record today."

What was the term I'd heard Trek use in the past? Sod off?

"Not happening, *wanker*."

A dubious smile broke out on his face.

"Sorry," I said, wrinkling my nose in embarrassment. "I just find your accent inspiring. I had to try it out."

"You and Jackson truly are kismet, aren't you?"

I blinked twice. "*What* did you say?"

"Kismet. Fate. Destiny. Lady Luck. All of those things. The two of you are the human incarnation of serendipity. It's uncanny, really."

I launched myself at Trek, wrapping my arms around his

center and resting my cheek against his chest. He was the same height as Sawyer, his body equally as hard yet leaner. He remained a rigid form in my embrace until I began sobbing incoherent words into his vest that I was certain cost more than my entire wardrobe.

"There, there . . ." He patted me awkwardly on the back, his unmalleable posture immune to my outburst.

I pulled back, lifting my chin to take in Trek's ridiculous flawlessness. The tiny beauty mark beneath his right eye added character to his otherwise immaculate face.

"Sawyer always says that."

An easy smile unfurled. "It's the truth, love. You are."

My heart needed to hear those words, and it whispered a silent reply of gratitude to my unlikely messenger.

"Why are you here?"

Trek's expression softened. "I brought you something." Slipping his hand inside his jacket, he promptly revealed a white envelope. My mind spun with the possibilities of what could be inside as he offered it to me.

"You've got mail, darling."

If two weeks ago I'd experienced the worst day of my life, then today was definitely the most bizarre.

"You sure it's not tacky that I'm wearing his jersey and have his number on my face?"

Sitting on the other side of the backseat in the black sedan, Trek waved a dismissive leather-gloved hand at me. "Nonsense. Jackson will be beside himself when he sees you. For a professional athlete, there's nothing that feeds the ego more than seeing his woman wearing his number. It's the closest thing to pissing on you and marking his territory."

Unwilling to visualize the vulgarity, my eyes drifted to the window, where I caught my first glimpses of Ingenuity Stadium. My heart rate quickened.

"You're going to be brilliant. And what a better *fuck you* to Whitmore than for you to stand up there in front of a packed house in your man's jersey without a trace of shame."

I turned my head to find Trek watching me, his expression kind and sincere. "Thanks, *mate*."

He chuckled and muttered something about Sawyer and me being cut from the same "bloody cloth."

I tried to focus on the task ahead of me, but my thoughts continued to drift to Sawyer's letter, which was safe and secure in my suitcase in the trunk of Trek's car. Now I understood Sawyer's strange mood all week, but his reason for not telling me weighed on my heart.

His mom, the kindest woman I'd ever met, was no longer in remission.

When I'd read in the letter that he didn't want to tell me until after my audition because he didn't want to worry me, my heart broke. I wanted to be there for my boyfriend when he struggled. I wanted to be the person he told everything to. Not the one he thought he needed to shield from the inevitable challenges that life will throw at him.

Because that's what life did—to all of us.

Sawyer's mom. His contract. Knox.

So. Many. Secrets.

You've kept secrets to protect him too.

"Gah!"

Trek didn't even flinch at my random outburst. He merely cocked an intrigued eyebrow. I cringed and then shrugged in return.

"You Americans with your silver-tongued language. I swear I'll never understand it. It's basically barbaric."

I sighed. "I'm just thinking about how many secrets we've been keeping from each other and how much I've sucked as a girlfriend."

"Christ, you're as dramatic as your boyfriend."

I turned to square off with Trek. "Did you know about his mom?" Trek nodded. "Obviously you knew about the addendum to his contract. Did you know about Knox giving him a hard time all season too?"

That may or may not have come out a little accusatory.

Trek rolled his head to the side and gave me a look that confirmed my assumptions: yes, definitely accusatory.

"Yes, love. And I was the first one he told, almost a year ago now, that he'd rather New York pay him in Monopoly money than take the astronomical offer from Miami. Trust me, my bank account is well aware of some of your boyfriend's decisions—especially those made in the name of love."

I sat stunned into silence. Sawyer had given up what sounded like the contract of a lifetime in Miami to be in New York with me. My hands went to my chest, my throat ached, and the threat of tears tingled behind my lids.

Don't fall apart now—you've got a job to do.

Trek's gaze raked over me from head to bloody toe.

"Blimey. He didn't put that last bit in the letter, did he?"

I gave a slight headshake just as the car parked outside the back entrance of the stadium.

"How about you pack that one away for later, Kennedy. You and Sawyer will have plenty of time to talk after this day is over."

After I'd only moderately recovered from Trek's bombshell, he ushered me through the back door security reserved only for players and personnel.

"You're sure Millie Braxton has strep throat, and her understudy isn't available? Seems kind of convenient and sketchy if you ask me." Possibilities on the tip of my tongue, I paused and met Trek's stare. "Sawyer didn't have her poisoned, did he?"

I was kind of, sort of kidding.

"I swear on my beloved granny's grave, nothing dodgy has taken place. I heard the rumor floating around the stadium this morning and what can I say . . ." He held open a door for me. "Just more kismet, love."

I rolled my eyes and shook my head playfully, a smile now permanently in place.

"Besides," he continued, "Mr. Richard Ellison IV is quite smitten with you. It was hardly worthy of a discussion. One mention of your name and he looked like the team was already on their way to the Super Bowl."

We stood in the visiting team's tunnel, which would lead us out to the field. The familiar sound of the stadium was amplified by the stakes of today's pivotal game. For the first time since Trek had strongly suggested that I sing the national anthem at the biggest game of Sawyer's career, jitters threatened the state of my equilibrium.

Trek stayed at my side as I was escorted to the stage by a security guard and a woman with a clipboard whose instructions came out so fast, I could barely keep up. She offered me an earpiece, and my fingers trembled as I crammed it into place. When I tried to convince her that I wasn't crazy, and yes, I only wanted the pianist to accompany me, she threw her hands up in the air and warned me not to "ruin the program."

"No pressure." Trek chuckled as Chatty Cathy walked away to reorganize the musicians in waiting.

My stomach churned, and a cold sweat broke out under Sawyer's OSU sweatshirt. I'd decided to wear it under his jersey. It was late January in New York—layers were necessary.

As though he could read my mind, Trek leaned down and

spoke close to my available ear. "Just look at number eighty-eight. Let the rest of it go, love. He's all you need."

I barely heard him over the deafening crowd. I smiled weakly and nodded. "Right—I've got this."

Instead of waiting for Trek's reply, I turned to the stage stairs. Flashbacks of my catastrophic *Frozen* audition plagued my thoughts, but remarkably my legs carried me forward.

At least you're not crying or puking.

Glass half-full.

After a few words with the pianist, I adjusted my mic and took a moment to scan the stands, immediately regretting that I had. Trek's words of wisdom echoed in my mind, and I shifted my gaze to the players on the home-team sideline.

I spotted Sawyer—*the man who'd given up so much to be with me*—through a sea of football players and staff. My heart fell into a healthy rhythm for the first time in two weeks.

I glanced over my shoulder at the pianist. He looked at me expectantly, and I nodded in return.

It was time to prove to myself and my boyfriend just how strong I was.

As Sawyer would say, I was Kennedy Fucking Quinn.

30

SAWYER

Game time.

Against Kansas City, I'd had triple digits in receiving yards and three touchdowns. I'd broken tackles and blown up my stats in the yards after catch category, meaning it was really fucking hard to take me down.

It seemed like lately the only thing capable of bringing me to my knees was my undying love for a woman I couldn't have.

Talk to her.

I wanted to. Fuck it all to Hell, there was nothing I wanted more—even more than a Super Bowl ring—than to talk to Kennedy, to hear her sweet voice, and to untangle the mess of where things had gone wrong. Maybe if Trek gave her my letter this week, I'd have the chance to make things right before the Super Bowl.

Because we were gonna win this motherfucking game.

And then I was going to focus on getting my girl back. To have Kennedy in the stands at the Super Bowl would ensure I'd walk away with a championship ring.

I set my navy and silver helmet down on the bench and joined my teammates on the sideline, where we locked arms for the singing of the national anthem. Hunter was on my right, grinning at me like a fool. I shook off his inappropriate cheerfulness. He needed to get his head in the game. I'll admit, I was glad we were on good terms again, but this was not the time for shits and giggles.

Approximately five minutes to kickoff.

Before I saw her, I heard her. I'd recognize that sweet sound anywhere.

Standing on a stage parked over the Cougars logo on the fifty-yard line and wearing my jersey, there she was—Kennedy Fucking Quinn.

My everything.

I liked to think of myself as a manly man. I said "fuck" like it was necessary, could hold my liquor, and was Kennedy's official spider assassin, but in that moment, I was a straight-up sappy motherfucker.

From eighty feet away, I could see the double eights on her cheeks and the way she gripped the mic with sheer confidence as she belted out America's song, and I may or may not have relied on Hunter and Declan to keep me on my feet— maybe—just a little bit.

As an elite football player, it was my job to read body language from halfway down the field, and all my senses told me that Kennedy was in her element. She looked like a mirage and sounded like nirvana.

My insides liquefied at the thought of touching her again, kissing that mouth.

If given the chance, I'd make sure she knew exactly how I felt about her every single time she was in my arms from this day forward, and I'd never let a lack of communication fuck up the best thing I'd ever had again.

Does she realize I am completely at her mercy?

The song ended, and I was pushed forward by two hands, each belonging to a separate body but unified by one common goal.

"Go get your girl, Jackson," Declan ordered, and I knew that Hunter shared the sentiment, even if he didn't voice it.

Without asking permission, I strode onto the field like it was my birthright, heading directly to the woman with the huge red smile on her face.

Kennedy moved to the front of the stage where I anticipated joining her, but then I watched in absolute fucking horror as she proceeded to jump off the front of the stage, landing on the turf like a baby deer on her new legs.

I broke into an all-out sprint, but it was too late. By the time I reached her, she was already on her knees in a fit of giggles.

"Baby," I managed through my own uncontained laughter.

I squatted in front of her, hooking my arms under hers and lifting her with me. I didn't stop when she got to her feet. I continued hoisting her up until her legs wrapped around my waist, resting on my hip pads, right where they belonged.

"I don't think you're supposed to be on your knees, Quinn."

She twined her arms around my neck and cocked a brow at me. "You never complain when I'm on my knees."

This girl.

"I love you," we said in unison. We both laughed, and then Kennedy's face sobered.

"Your mom . . ."

"You read my letter?"

"I did. I'm so sorry about your mom."

I swallowed hard. "She'll be okay, baby. We'll fly down and see her this week for a quick visit, and then after the Super Bowl, we'll spend a lot more time with her. She'll love it."

Kennedy nodded, but the look in her eye told me she had something else she needed to get out. "What is it, Quinn?"

"You . . . you turned down a better offer from the Mavericks to play for the Cougars."

That wasn't in my letter.

Trek. Dammit.

"Yeah, baby, I did." I skimmed the tip of my nose down the bridge of hers. "You're here." I parroted the words she'd said to me fourteen days ago. The way she melted in my arms told me she got the meaning.

Nuzzling my nose against hers, I added, "I've gotta hurry, but I love you and you were incredible."

I kissed her for not nearly long enough, but I'd rectify that just as soon as we won this game. I'd never let another day pass without kissing her like I was a dying man and she was my last breath.

As she slid down my body and to her feet, she asked, "Do you think the whole world just saw me face-plant?"

"Nah, it's commercial break right now. Only ninety thousand or so saw you." I winked at her, earning myself her throaty laugh that made Monster forget he was sheltered beneath a hard plastic dome with very little wiggle room.

"I gotta go this way," she explained, nodding her head toward the opposite side of the field. Only then did I look up to see Trek waiting about thirty yards away, wearing a shit-eating grin.

"You've got a lot of explaining to do, baby." I raised my brows in mock warning, then pressed my lips to hers one more time for good measure.

As I turned to head back to my team, her tiny hand slapped my ass.

"You've got a game to go win, Tight End."

"You got it, Quinn."

31

SAWYER

Kennedy and I were still making confetti angels on Ingenuity field when most of my teammates, coaches, and their respective families began filtering out of the stadium. The majority would end up at a post-game party hosted by the team owner, but Kennedy and I had already made the decision to spend the rest of the night with just each other.

"Thai or pizza?" I asked, threading my fingers through Kennedy's as we continued to lie on our backs side by side.

Her cheek pressed into the turf as her eyes found mine. "I'm gonna have to go with pizza right now, but can I reserve the right change my mind all the way up until the time when we actually order?"

I chuckled. "It wouldn't be a Sawyer and Quinn kind of night if I said no to that, now, would it?"

She shook her head. "It wouldn't be. You're right." Smoothing her features she added, "Traditions are important in a relationship."

I released her hand and rolled onto my side, propping my head up. I laced our fingers together again and raised our clasp so I could place a kiss on the inside of her wrist. "I can think of one tradition we should do away with tonight."

With a knowing look, she said, "Is it the Sawyer and Quinn

tradition of keeping secrets from one another even when it feels like the best option at the time?"

"Mmm. Smart cookie. That's the one."

She used her free hand to touch my cheek. "I'm sorry I didn't tell you about the auditions I was turning down. You might not have resented William so much if you'd known he really was coming through for me."

"Fuck. That. The guy told you to bleach your hair and go on a starvation diet."

She rolled her eyes. "Sawyer, that's not what he said, and you know it."

"Same fucking thing."

"Not even a little bit," she scolded. "You're getting off track. Let's talk about your secrets."

She had me there. My list of violations per omission was legendary, and not something I was proud of. I'd had two long weeks to reflect on all the times I'd turned left when I should have kept going straight in our relationship, and I'd shared as much with Kennedy in my letter.

"Did you think I couldn't handle your truth?" I recognized her vulnerability when she asked.

"Maybe a little bit, but not every time. When it came to the contract addendum—mostly I was embarrassed, and it happened just before I confessed that I wanted us to be together. I didn't think it would look too good on my boyfriend application."

She scooted a little closer and pressed a kiss to the center of my chest. I had to bite back my smile when she wrinkled her nose. I'm sure my jersey didn't taste or smell all that great.

"But with Whitmore, I didn't want to scare you or cause you stress while William was constantly up your ass. And when it came to my mom—yeah, I didn't want to freak you out before your big audition."

Kennedy drew in a breath, and then her brows knit together. "You know, I think some of your reactions and beliefs may have been more acceptable when we were *just friends*—because back then I think your sole objective was to keep me safe—emotionally, physically—at all costs." She lifted her chin, meeting my gaze, and her expression softened. "But now we're partners, Sawyer, which means we're together in all of this. No more shielding. No more protecting. We approach everything side by side going forward."

I dipped my head, pausing when our lips were just inches apart. "When are you finding time in your busy schedule to study psychology, Miss Quinn."

I felt her lips curve upward.

"No more secrets?"

I knew it wasn't a question.

"No more secrets, baby. I promise you. You get to see all my baggage going forward."

She twined her arms around my neck. "Good—because you get all mine too. We've already said that we want *everything* from each other, well this deep shit we're talking about, that's part of everything."

I leaned in the last couple of inches, but when our lips brushed Kennedy pulled back just slightly. "Did you really tell Trek almost a year ago that you wanted to come to New York?"

"I did."

"Is that when you knew you wanted to be with me?"

This close, I couldn't see her expression, but I could feel her emotion, and I could hear the faint quiver in her voice.

Only truth now, Jackson.

"That's when my head knew, but my heart, Quinn, my heart—it knew when you tucked your arm in mine right before we walked down the aisle at Seth and Abby's wedding."

Kennedy leaned up to seal her mouth against mine, taking

command of our kiss. When she eventually pulled apart, her eyes found mine. "Let's go home."

"Not yet."

Her eyes widened. "Why not?"

"I need to apologize first, not through a letter, but right here with you in my arms."

"Oh—okay."

"The video . . ."

"I know, Sawyer. It's okay. I know it's not your fault that Knox stole it from you."

My heart squeezed in my chest. She was honestly ready to give me an out, but I didn't deserve it.

"I never should have recorded you without your consent. It doesn't matter that I wasn't expecting us to get down and dirty when I called you, I still should have asked your permission. I was irresponsible, and because I was, I caused you so much hurt. I am so fucking sorry for what happened. All of it—the video, your audition, even William. And I am so fucking proud of you for what you did tonight on live national television."

Tears fell from her bottom lashes, and I kissed them away.

"I forgive you, Sawyer."

The vice grip I'd felt around my heart for the past two weeks finally slipped away.

———

"You look like you've been Magic Miked."

Say what?

"Oh, really?" I replied, climbing up Kennedy's body as she lay sprawled across our bed in nothing but my jersey. "Are you making that a verb, baby?"

"Well, if the shoe fits. Jesus, Sawyer, look at you. What

did you do for the two weeks we were apart, live in the weight room?"

Well, yeah. Accurate.

Kennedy's fingers threaded through my hair as I raised the jersey, giving me access to what I was craving: the two gorgeous nipples that had been neglected for weeks.

"Don't you need food and sleep?" She arched her back, feeding me more of the nub I was suckling on. "You must be exhausted. I'm exhausted from just watching you play."

On the drive to the pizza place, Kennedy had changed her mind, so we ended up bringing home Thai, but we hadn't even opened the bags before we were tearing at each other's clothes.

Priorities.

After round one in the living room, we'd moved to the bedroom for round two.

I grunted in response against her perfect tit. "Sleep, later. Fuck, now."

Laughter vibrated her body, and I smiled against her heated skin. Hooking my arm around her waist, I flipped onto my back, causing her to straddle me.

"On or off?" she asked, and I answered by lifting the jersey over her head and letting it fall on the bed behind her.

Ah. Now I have the perfect view.

My hands found her thighs, sliding up until they gripped her hips, my thumbs rubbing in a circular pattern.

"I love you," I said, holding her gaze I knew was drowsy with lust.

She leaned forward, both her soft hair and her hard nipples grazing over my chest and drawing a groan from me. "I love you too, but I want to talk about something."

More talking? Now?

"Fine, but stay where you are—everything is more fun when you're naked and on top of me."

"Sawyer."

"Quinn."

"I'm serious."

"Yes, baby, and so am I. Have you looked at your tits in the mirror lately?"

I knew I was walking the fine line that Kennedy liked to draw for me, the one that separated charming and obnoxious, but in nearly four years, I'd never gone so long without a dose of her, and I was a junkie in desperate need of a fix. Fucking, bantering—it didn't matter. As long as I was getting lost in her in some way, everything else bled away, and that was all that mattered.

Spying the adorable yet devious expression on her face, not unlike the spiteful kittens on YouTube always causing havoc in their owners' lives, I decided to stay mum and let her talk.

"*Well*," she purred. She tucked her hair behind one ear, flashing me a coy grin, and my cock wanted to pounce.

"Yes, Quinn," I gritted out through clenched teeth.

"I was *thinking*," she continued in her bedroom voice.

Involuntarily, my hips shot upward, my cock nudging at her ass. She tsked and wagged her index finger from side to side, slowly, sensually.

Evil.

My girlfriend was pure evil.

"I'm still talking," she said and bit back her smile.

"Use your words, baby, or I'm going to fuck them out of you."

Her head fell back, and she laughed so hard it was contagious. Then she righted herself and leveled me with her bright green eyes that had a way of undoing me.

"Marry me," she said. It wasn't a question; it was more like a sweet demand.

"What?" I was unable to tame the broad grin that threatened to split my face in two.

"Sawyer Jackson, will you marry me?"

I sat up, and her legs curled around my waist, bringing us as close as physically possible, absent my cock being buried deep in her wet heat.

"Are you really asking me to marry you, Quinn?"

"I am. And the longer you take to say yes, the longer you're gonna wait to spear me with your dick."

"Christ, baby, where'd you learn to talk so sweet?"

"My foul-mouthed boyfriend. He's a real charmer, I tell you."

"Sounds like it. You sure you want to marry a guy like that?"

"Sawyer."

"Quinn."

"Just answer—"

I cut her off with my lips. The kiss was tender and gentle, like the whimpers she fed my tongue, and it was hot as hell.

When we broke apart, her lips were swollen, her eyes glossed over with need.

I brushed her hair back and dropped my forehead to hers.

"I'll marry you if you agree to wear my ring, the one I bought four months ago."

She gasped, then whispered, "You *did*?"

I replaced my forehead with my lips. "I did."

"After you win the Super Bowl, can we go directly to Vegas?"

I pulled back, needing to witness her expression firsthand. "You want to get married in two weeks?"

"Damn straight."

A chuckle of raw joy floated up from the depths of my soul. "Then we will get married in two weeks."

She beamed her brightest smile, and my heart tripped over itself.

I'd have married her right then and there if I could have.

"Fuck. I love you, Quinn."

She laughed with a breathy sigh, and then she cocked her head to the side. "I love you too, Sawyer Jackson."

EPILOGUE

SAWYER

One Year Later

Super Bowl Sunday.

Most players considered themselves blessed if they were fortunate enough to make it to one Super Bowl during their career, and here I was, emotionally invested in my second championship game just one year later.

I grabbed the cup of hot tea I'd just prepared off the kitchen counter—sans sugar cubes—and padded across the penthouse to the master bedroom.

Steam seeped from below the closed door to the en suite, and the sound of my wife running scales made my heart flutter. I cracked open the door to catch a glimpse of her naked silhouette as she wrung out her hair. I'd timed it perfectly, knowing she was just about done with her vocal warm-up.

The water cut off, and the glass door opened, revealing the most gorgeous woman I'd ever laid eyes on—Kennedy Fucking Jackson.

My best friend.

My wife.

My everything.

"Mr. Jackson."

"Mrs. Jackson."

"You're staring," she accused.

"You're goddamn right I am."

I set the cup of tea on the vanity and leaned into the doorframe with my arms folded across my chest as I watched Kennedy towel herself off, wishing it wouldn't totally fuck with her mojo if I licked away the rivulets of water racing down her silky skin. But I knew the importance of my wife's preperformance ritual as well as I knew my own pregame routine, and I valued my life.

I glanced at my watch.

Besides, in roughly four hours, I'd have her naked and underneath me.

I'd survive. Right?

Dressed in a satin robe that barely grazed the bottom of her perky ass, Kennedy stood on her tiptoes and pressed a sweet kiss to my lips. I didn't bother unfolding my arms to touch her because if I did, I wouldn't be able to stop, and we'd be fucking.

"Don't get any ideas, handsome. I already told Abby we're staying for the whole game. We need to be there to support Seth in his first Super Bowl."

Fine—make it eight. In roughly eight hours, I'd be able to sink myself into my wife.

Maybe I wouldn't survive after all.

I moved into her, resting my hands on her hips and pulling her against me so she could feel how crazy she made me.

Like she doesn't get reminded multiple times per day.

"Want me to help warm up your throat?" I waggled my eyebrows, and rather than rolling her eyes at me, which is what I'd expected, Kennedy began to loosen the sash she'd just tied around her waist.

"All right—you win. You're just too irresistible, Tight End. But mouth and throat are off the table." She bit her bottom lip. "I'm sure there's something else we could do."

That was all I needed to hear.

I swept her off her feet in one smooth move and carried her bridal style into the bedroom. I lowered her to the bed and then stood over her for a moment to take her in for a second time.

Kennedy slipped off her robe and raised her arms above her head, bending one knee and arching her back.

"You have no idea what you do to me, Quinn," I growled as I stepped out of my joggers.

Fortunately, they were the only thing I wore, so in a half a second, my naked body was on hers and I was nestled between her shapely thighs.

She dragged a finger along the tattoo stamped on the inside of my left bicep, the one that read DFIU. I'd had it done in Vegas right after we'd won the Super Bowl, the same night I'd made Kennedy my wife.

I tilted my hips, grinding my hard cock against her. She was already wet and ready for me, but I'd drag it out as long as I could.

"*Sawyer*," she pleaded. "Just fuck me already."

"Baby. Baby." I tsked. "Patience."

I pushed against her again, and this time she giggled and went limp, surrendering to whatever game she knew I was about to play.

Our playbook was creative as fuck. Ingenious—if you asked me. It was as thick as the A Song of Ice and Fire series and The Lord of the Rings trilogy combined. Make that the box set—*The Hobbit* included.

"Do what you will, just don't make me late."

"Are we picking up Brooke?"

Kennedy shook her head. "Nope. She's not coming—family drama."

I thanked the old gods and the new for Brooke's fucked up family dynamics, and then a devilish smile spread across my face just before I dropped my head and brought my wife to ecstasy not just once, but twice.

Kennedy took the stage, and the crowd cheered so loud that if the dome had already been closed, it would have blown right off the stadium.

Ingenuity Stadium, home of the New York Cougars, was hosting this year's Super Bowl, and there was no one more desired than Kennedy Jackson, the hometown Broadway darling, to serenade the over ninety thousand people in attendance with the national anthem.

After last season's AFC Championship game, Kennedy's phone had blown up with offers for representation. Trek had helped her weed through the list of agents interested in my woman's limitless talent, and by spring, she had made her debut as Ella in the Broadway production of *Cinderella*.

She'd been born for the role.

Kennedy's dreams had come true, and every morning I got to wake up with her in my arms, so my dreams came true too.

She finished her vocal masterpiece under an explosion of fireworks and then made her way to the sidelines where I waited, a permanent smile on my face and a fullness in my heart that only Kennedy stood a chance at making possible.

"You were incredible, baby," I breathed into her ear as she clung to me. "Sexiest national anthem ever."

She giggled and chided me, but I silenced her with a kiss that was just a little bit dirty, undeterred by whoever was watching or how many cameras were pointed in our direction.

I placed my hand on her barely there bump. "You sure Baby Jackson doesn't want to go home now?"

She sighed as she threaded her fingers through mine and

tugged at me to follow our escort off the field. "Nice try, Tight End. Baby Jackson is just fine."

A man could try.

"It's not what you're thinking, Quinn."

She may have ditched the last name legally, but she'd always be my Quinn.

I knew what she *thought* I was thinking. She thought I wanted to go home to bone her. Sure, sexual fantasies involving my hot wife were on constant loop in my mind, but right now, all I wanted was to be curled up next to her on the couch, watching football with a beer and some nachos.

Yup—I'd embraced married life. In fact, I craved it.

I couldn't wait to try family life on for size. Considering I wanted enough babies with Kennedy to fill a team roster, I'd say my eagerness to become a dad rivaled my love of football.

But it was Kennedy I loved above all else.

Standing by the elevator that would take us to the suite level, Kennedy circled her arms around my waist and rested her chin on my chest.

"Hey," she whispered. "Let's get out of here."

My eyes widened. I couldn't contain my surprise or excitement. "Really?"

"I think couch, football, nachos, and a foot rub sounds like more fun."

Fuck, we were a match made in domestic heaven.

Four hours later, after we'd swung by my mom's apartment—the one next to Declan's—for a quick visit, we'd both gotten what we wanted and lay snuggled in each other's arms. It was the two-minute warning, and Seth's Knights were leading by six. When the broadcast returned from commercial break, the TV cameras were scanning the crowd as the announcers pointed out celebrities in the stands.

Kennedy was nodding off, drifting in and out of sleep as I

played with her hair, when the cameras landed on a couple in the throes of a hardcore make-out session.

"Baby?"

Kennedy stirred. "Mmm."

"Baby!"

"Jesus, Sawyer. Dramatic much?" she grumbled, rubbing the sleep from her eyes.

Her gaze followed my outstretched hand as the remote control pointed at the television. *As it pointed at the couple kissing on the screen.*

Words evaded me.

"Andrew?" Kennedy blinked, recognizing her former roommate turned global rock star.

Then she gasped.

Madison Fucking Jackson.

My baby sister.

THE END

ACKNOWLEDGMENTS

Thank you for reading Kismet! Sharing Sawyer and Kennedy's love story gave me the opportunity to combine two of my favorite things—football and Broadway—and I am so grateful to all the special people who helped make it possible.

To Caroline Acebo, you truly are a godsend! When I first contacted you, I was an eager writer bursting with fictional characters and story lines, backed with some rough manuscripts—and zero clue about how to get from point A to point B. Finding you was my Lady Luck! Thank you from the bottom of my heart for taking me on and sharing your gifts with me.

A heartfelt thank you to Stacey Blake for creating covers that inspire me to match their beauty and the feelings they engender with each chapter that I write. And to Liz Gilbeau for making everything just perfect. To a Virgo like me—you and your craft are priceless!

To my husband and son, you are the best hype-guys a girl could ask for, and I appreciate you so very much. I know how lucky I am. Husband, yes, you still have to read every book I ever write even though reading is not your "thing." Son, yes, you still have to wait until you are thirty-five to date, and maybe then I'll consider letting you read what I write with some pages ripped out. Maybe.

ABOUT THE AUTHOR

Reina Bell writes romance novels that promise to inspire all the feels. As a reader, she alternates between thrill-seeking romantic suspense, deeply emotional love stories, and palate-cleansing, sassy rom-coms. Her goal as an author is to offer the best of those worlds to readers—keeping it captivating, sexy, and with a soul-satisfying happily ever after each and every time. When she's not writing or helping animals (that's her other life), you can find her watching all things NFL, cooking like it's her job (maybe in her next life), and making lists. She resides in a quaint New England town with her husband, son, a whole lot of pets, and where the NFL Network is always the background noise. You can find Reina at www.AuthorReinaBell.com and on Instagram.